The Beast

CW00920008

About the author

David J H Smith was originally from Slough, Berkshire but is now living in Somerset.

He graduated from Thames Valley University with an Honours Degree in History & Geography before going on to study History at Post Graduate level at Westminster University.

David has worked in various jobs such as Immigration, Retail Manager, Facilities Officer and IT before becoming a writer and setting up 'Things From Dimension - X' which specialises in the sale of rare and collectable comic books.

Other Works
The Titanic's Mummy

Coming Soon

The George Roebuck Chronicles
(An ongoing series of Steampunk adventures)

The Dark Star Diamond
The Army of the Resurrected
The Anteros Murders
The Emmaus Grail
The Hellfire Club

The Beasts of Karlstad

By

David J H Smith

David Smith

FIRST EDITION

Paige Croft Publishing, Yeovil, Somerset

David J H Smith asserts the moral right to be identified as the author of this work

A catalogue record for this book is available from the British Library

Cover art 'The Karlstad Beast' by HuwJ

First Edition – 2016

Published by Paige Croft Publishing

ISBN – 978-0-9568305-2-4

Printed and bound in England by
CPI Antony Rowe Chippenham Wiltshire

CHAPTER 1

"Out of my way!" cried Professor Charles Montacute, as he cut a path through the crowd. "Any sign of her, Mr Mallory?"

"No," replied Richard Mallory, anxiously looking around, "I can't even see the racecourse itself and I know that's somewhere in front of us!"

"Damn and blast that girl!" growled the Professor, stopping. "When I get my hands on her, I'm going to put her across my knee and give her a good hiding, assuming of course that the police don't get to her first!"

"Well I just hope that she doesn't do something stupid." Mallory paused. "Well, more stupid than she has already."

Over the past few months Jazmine Montacute had been taking an ever active role in the woman's suffrage movement, which had been campaigning for women to gain the right to vote. As the behaviour of the Suffragettes had become ever more extreme, Jazmine had seemingly risen to the challenge. In February, part of the Chancellor of the Exchequer's house had been damaged in an explosion and this seemed to coincide with some dynamite, that Professor Montacute kept in his house 'for emergencies,' going missing, and the strange fact that Jazmine seemed to know far more details about the event than the police had given out. In the past week, Jazmine had been arrested twice for trying to chain herself to railings, and once on suspicion of setting fire to a mailbox. On both occasions she had managed, through a combination of charm, persuasion, tears, and promises, to be let off with just a small fine and a severe warning. However, it was a note that the Professor had found by accident that very day that caused him real concern. It was written to Jazmine by one of her fellow Suffragettes, which implied that they would go down in history that day by causing a 'major incident' at the finish line of the Epsom Derby. The Professor had tried to confront Jazmine about it, but she was nowhere to be found. In response he contacted his friend and colleague Richard Mallory, and the two had immediately headed over to Surrey to try and find her. After entering the racecourse the two started to make their way towards the finishing line, where not only was the Royal Box positioned, where the King and Queen would be present, but also a Pathĕ news film camera was located to capture the final moments of the race, and if Jazmine and her suffragette friends had their way, whatever stunt they had planned.

"Can you see any sign of her?" called the Professor.

Mallory, who was just behind him, shook his head before turning to the nearest man in desperation. "Excuse me Sir we are looking for a young girl…."

"Aren't we all!" came the reply, cutting Mallory short.

"Well this one is my daughter!" growled the Professor, turning, making the man instantly look uncomfortable because of his remark, "and she would chew you up and spit you out again before you knew what had happened. Now, she is short with dark hair, I believe that she is wearing a long blue dress."

The man shook his head. "Didn't see a girl in a blue dress, but I did see four young women together wearing red dresses. They looked a bit strange, almost nervous."

"Where?" asked the Professor.

The man pointed to his right. "They were going that way."

2

"Heading towards the start of the race?" queried Mallory. The man nodded, and then quickly moved away.

"Do you think they could be connected?" asked Mallory.

"I'm not sure," replied the Professor, "the note clearly said whatever was going to happen would be at the end of the racecourse, but still, four women together looking nervous? That does send out an alarm bell."

"That's hardly definitive proof is it?" replied Mallory.

"Indeed, but we are running out of time! The race is about to start." The Professor shook his head. "Blast it! Mr Mallory we are going to have to split up. I'll carry on as planned and head towards the finish line, while you move up to the start, and hope that between us we can find her."

"I'm not sure we will need to!" cried Mallory, excitedly pointing. "Look there! I think we may have found some other members of their party."

The Professor looked over to where Mallory had indicated. There was a group of five women, their large hats visible through the mass of bobbing heads.

Mallory and the Professor immediately started to push their way through to them. Surprisingly those in the throng allowed it, due in part to the fact that they were actually heading slightly away from the race track, and very soon the two men found themselves by the women who, on seeing them approach, started to move away.

However, it was clear that Jazmine was not one of their number.

"Oh no you don't!" cried the Professor, reaching forward and grabbing one of the women by the arm, making her turn.

"Hey, leave me alone!" she shrieked.

"Where is my daughter?"

3

"Leave me alone or I'll scream!"

"Oh, I don't think that would do you much good Miss."

This was true; despite the close proximity of others, no-one was paying them any attention. In fact people seemed to be moving away, not wanting to get themselves involved, and soon the Professor, Mallory and the woman found themselves in their own little space in the crowd.

"Now where is my daughter, Jazmine Montacute?"

The woman pulled her arm free, and then looked the old man up and down. "Oh, I presume that you are the mad old Professor, the father she keeps going on about."

"What the..? 'Old'? 'Mad'? How dare you, Miss!"

"Look," cut in Mallory, "we know you have something planned. All we want to do is make sure that Jazmine is not part of it."

"Part of it?" the woman laughed. "It's a bit late for that; she could not be more part of things if she tried! It was her idea to come to the Derby in the first place."

"To do what?" asked the Professor.

The woman smiled. "To make sure that this race goes down in history!"

"What do you have planned?"

"We are going to disrupt the race!"

Mallory and the Professor looked at each other worriedly.

"How?" they asked simultaneously.

"By running out onto the track with a banner!"

The Professor reached out and grabbed the woman by the arm again. "Oh no you're not!"

She threw her head back and laughed. "Oh you silly old man! I'm not going to be doing the running. My friends and I are here to ensure that when it happens, we cause as

4

much commotion as possible; the more of us that are arrested for this, the bigger the story and the bigger the impact on our cause!"

"Jazmine? Is she going to run out?" asked the Professor. The woman nodded.

"Where?"

She smiled. "Tattenham Corner, on this side of the track. As the horses run past the rail she is to wait for a suitable gap, then duck under it and step out in front of them."

"But she'll be killed!" cried Mallory.

The woman shook her head. "No, Jazmine is not stupid. It's dangerous yes, but sacrifice is not the object of this exercise."

From somewhere a roar of excitement went up; making them all look round.

"You're too late! I'm guessing that cry means that the horses are lining up!" the woman said with a gleeful grin.

Dropping the woman's arm the Professor, with Mallory not far behind, immediately moved away from the track until they reached the edge of the crowd, before they could run unhindered towards Tattenham Corner.

"Perhaps we should call the Stewards?" suggested Mallory, as he broke out into a run.

"No time!" retorted the Professor, running as fast as he could. "Besides, we cannot risk Jazmine being detained. We need her for our planned outing tonight. Without her the whole scheme falls apart like a pack of playing cards! Blast her! This is a bad situation by no mistake!"

Minutes seemed to pass and eventually they arrived in the vicinity of Tattenham Corner. It was Mallory who managed to spot Jazmine first. She was standing with two other women at the edge of the crowd.

5

Then from somewhere there were more cries and cheers, which could only mean one thing; the 1913 Epsom Derby was now underway.

CHAPTER 2

"Jazmine! Jazmine!" called out Mallory, as he made his way over to her.

"What are you doing here?" she said, clearly surprised to see him there.

"Take an educated guess," came the reply, not from Mallory but, from her Father. "We are here to take you home."

"Certainly," she replied, almost sweetly, "but let's just watch the race first shall we? Emily and Florence here are dying to see the race."

"Not a chance!" said the Professor sternly. "We bumped into some of your friends. We know what you have planned."

"You can't stop us you know!" said one of the women Jazmine was with.

"Of course they can't, Emily," replied Jazmine.

"I wouldn't be too sure of that if I were you," said the Professor gruffly.

"Oh really?" countered Jazmine, looking almost right through him. "So what are you going to do to stop us?"

"I'm not interested in stopping them; I am interested in stopping *you*. Aside from making sure you don't get yourself killed; have you forgotten our plans for tonight?"

Jazmine quickly shook her head and glanced awkwardly at her friends. "No, of course not."

"Then how exactly are you aiming to carry out this mad scheme of yours and still be available for our outing?" the Professor continued. "You would either be dead or in prison."

"I'm going to escape," replied Jazmine with a smile. "Suitable steps have been taken to ensure I do."

"Really?" asked her father. "And what hair brained scheme were you going to put into operation?"

Jazmine took hold of the top of her dress and pulled it down slightly; underneath could be seen a collar and tie beneath a brown jacket.

"Hey!" cried Mallory in annoyance. "That's my best suit!"

Jazmine smiled wickedly. "Yes, not the best of fits, I had to take it in a bit, but it will do. I simply step out of the dress and then disappear into the crowd unnoticed in the guise of a man."

"Very enterprising," said the Professor, with a grudging smile, acknowledging his daughter's ingenuity and cunning. "But you can't go through with this."

"Sorry Father, my mind is made up," said Jazmine firmly.

The Professor nodded. "I can see that. You are so like your dear departed Mother, she would have been so proud of you. She always said that she would have loved to be able to vote, but of course that never happened."

"Don't you dare try and use Mother against me you wily old fox!" cried Jazmine hotly.

The Professor looked genuinely surprised, and even a little hurt. "Jazmine, how could you? I never would try and drag her memory into an argument. She was a living saint. She had to put up with me and my adventures. She

7

even forgave me for my involvement in………" He broke off suddenly and looked to the ground, embarrassed and flustered.

"Involvement in what?" asked Jazmine.

"Nothing!"

"Father!"

Emily, Florence and even Mallory found themselves moving in closer, aware that some great secret was on the verge of being exposed.

"This is not the time or the place my dear!"

"Father!" hissed Jazmine.

The Professor paused. "Alright, truth be told it will be a relief to get it off my chest. Just before you were born I was involved with a gentleman who was part of a Tontine. The money at stake ran into the thousands. Of course the last one left alive in the group gets the money, but the man I was hired by did not want to leave the outcome to natural selection. So he gave me the names of his fellow competitors and I sought them out one by one. And, well, let's just say that for every name that was crossed off the Tontine list, I was well rewarded."

The small group let out a gasp.

"But the thing is, if that was not bad enough, some of those on the list that I had eliminated, had been entered with a certain advantage over the others; their youth. Some were no more than boys."

Everyone stared at the Professor, shocked at the revelation.

"Your Mother nearly left me when she found out what was going on, but I managed to persuade her not to. Of course, it helped that at the same time we discovered she was pregnant with you. I of course stopped my gruesome task and returned the money. I never stopped trying to make it up to her."

The small group stared at the Professor, taken totally aback at the confession. Even Mallory, who had grown to immensely respect this maverick scholar, since their adventures on the Titanic and beyond, was stunned into silence.

"Jazmine," said Florence eventually, reaching out to her to give some comfort, but Jazmine was not in the mood to be consoled and pulled away.

"This needs to be reported to the Police!" said Emily. "He is a murderer, and must be brought to account."

The Professor shook his head. "I'm sorry, but that is not possible. The crimes I committed were over two decades ago and I was careful. Each life I took looked like an accident and I ensured that they could not be traced to me. If I were to confess, nothing would come of it. I would not be believed."

"But the man who hired you?" asked Florence.

The Professor smiled. "There was a case of natural justice! The Tontine was down to just two; him and another. Anyway it seems that there was an accident. My 'employer' for want of a better word, fell down some stairs at the theatre and broke his neck." He looked up straight into his daughter's eyes. "I'm so sorry."

"No you're not you cunning old buzzard!" she snarled at him, her stunned silence replaced with sudden anger as the realisation of the truth set in. She turned. "Look! The horses, they're coming!"

Florence and Emily turned also, and for the first time heard the excited rumblings of the crowd around them. Thanks to the Professor's elaborate lie, which had

9

captivated their complete attention, the race was now almost at Tattenham Corner and Jazmine and her Suffragette friends were nowhere near the track; which meant that they could not carry out their plan.

"You lied!" cried Florence.

A big triumphant grin spread across the old man's face. "It was quite a whopper, and one that has put paid to your plan!"

"We can still try," cried Jazmine, as she pulled a small carefully sewn banner from her coat, and started to move towards the track. "Come on girls, lets ...." Her words were cut short as the Professor employed the butt of his walking cane to push her in the back of her knees, sending her staggering. At the same time, Mallory reached forward and caught her as she was about to fall.

"Oh no you don't!" cried Emily. "You will not stop our cause!" With that she reached out and grabbed Jazmine's banner before disappearing off into the crowd towards the track. With a kick to Mallory's shins, Jazmine was free and started to follow. "Emily, stop!"

But it was too late. Emily had pushed her way deep into the throng. Mallory followed, with the Professor not far behind.

Somehow Emily managed to weave through the crowd. Some people even politely moved to one side, under the impression it was a lady trying to get a better view of the race. In no time at all Emily had managed to reach her goal, and was at the tall white rail, just as the horses were rounding the gentle curve of Tattenham Corner.

"Emily no!" cried Jazmine, who was almost within reach of her; but it was too late. Just as the lead horse passed, Emily ducked under the rail and stepped out into the track.

10

About seven horses thundered past, missing her by a matter of inches. Then seeing a small gap she ran out, deeper into the track, as three horses galloped by. As they passed her she reached out to them, trying to grab at them but failed. A little farther down the track another horse approached. Quickly Emily turned and tried to reach out with Jazmine's banner.

"Emily!" cried Jazmine, who had now reached the rail, with Mallory and the Professor behind her, and Florence bringing up the rear. "Move or you'll be ......"

At that precise moment, Emily was struck.

The force of the impact made the horse turn slightly as it, along with the rider, hit the ground and tumbled along. Emily's body too was flung forward, somersaulting over and over again until it came to rest motionless on the track.

CHAPTER 3

For a horrible moment, time seemed to stand still. None of the crowd uttered a word. No-one even moved; all they could collectively do was stare at the sight of the bodies of the woman and that of the horse and rider. Even Jazmine, Mallory and the Professor, who had seen horror and death before, seemed stunned into paralysis.

Then from somewhere nearby a low voice spoke in a whisper. "My god! That was the King's horse! That's the King's horse!" Those who were not staring at the figure of Emily turned to look at the figure of the jockey and the horse, and saw for themselves, for the first time, that the horse which was brought down, but now was back on its feet and moving around, was quite by chance, the Kings horse, Anmer, ridden by Herbert Jones.

11

Suddenly two race officials appeared and ran straight past the fallen jockey, opting to check on Emily who was still lying unconscious on the track. As soon as they got to her they started to check the extent of her injuries. This seemed to spur others into action, because then from the opposite side of the track a few people started to spill out onto the racecourse and over to the scene of the incident. Some headed towards the fallen Suffragette. While others headed towards Jones, who was clearly conscious but, as per the standard procedure for a fallen jockey, remained motionless on the ground.

Then the whole of the track around Tattenham corner seemed to be swamped with people milling around. Even the people by the rail where Emily had ventured onto the track, who had seemed frozen in shock, were now moving in closer to see what was going on.

"Come on," said the Professor to Mallory and Jazmine before they too could move. "We need to get out of here, now!"

"What?" asked Jazmine, looking round slightly confused. She ended up looking at Florence who had turned a dire shade of white and looked as though she was about to be sick.

"We need to get out of here, now," repeated the Professor.

"But Emily," protested Jazmine softly.

"There's nothing we can do for her. She'll be taken to hospital and attended to. Now we need to get you out of here, and fast."

"But I need to stay."

"Oh no you don't," said the Professor, taking the tone of a protective Father. "Your Suffragette movement has just brought down the King's horse at one of the most important race meets of the year. There is going to be trouble. In fact, look over there." He pointed to a couple of police constables who could be seen walking off with a woman between them. She was struggling before starting to yell, "Votes for women!" More Constables were appearing all around, moving through the crowd, looking for further Suffragettes to apprehend.

Jazmine nodded, her mind finally grasping the seriousness of the situation that she was in and had mainly been responsible for.

"Please, can I come with you?" pleaded Florence, looking scared. "I don't want to go to prison for this."

"Alright," said the Professor, "but do exactly what I say."

Florence nodded gratefully.

"Which way do we go?" asked Mallory.

"Under the rail and head over to the opposite side of the track," replied the Professor. "We can work our way back down the course to one of the exits."

With that, Mallory grabbed Jazmine by the hand. The Professor, seeing that Florence was now on the verge of tears, put his arm around her shoulder and started to guide her towards the rail. Quickly they ducked under it and moved onto the track. The unfortunate aspect of the plan was that it of course meant passing almost directly past the scene around Emily's body; as they did so they could not help but look over to her, where they caught the words; "serious injuries." "Damn Suffragettes." "Amazing she was not killed outright." "Blast them! The King's horse." and "I doubt she'll make it," being uttered by the crowd.

"Come on, keep going," urged the Professor, trying to move them along the track. "Oh no, here's trouble!"

Three women in long dresses, holding a banner saying 'Votes for Women,' came bounding over to them.

"Jazmine! Jazmine! What happened? I thought that you were going to be running out."

"I was, Ethel," she replied, "only my Father caught up with us and dropped a fly in the ointment. Emily grabbed the banner from me and ran out before we could stop her."

"I saw the whole thing!" said Ethel. "I was over by the camera people who were filming it. I think that they caught the whole thing!"

"Can you imagine?" said the other girl. "It will be shown in the picture houses! The footage could even go around the world!"

"Is that all you care about?" queried Jazmine. "Emily is seriously injured, she could even die!"

"If she does, she will not be forgotten! She will be a martyr for the cause!"

"Is getting the vote that important to you?" asked Mallory. "You are willing to have the death of a friend used as a tool to be able to vote?"

The woman nodded and smiled slightly. "You look shocked. Well you shouldn't be; there are others, many others who think the way that I do. Getting the vote and other rights is that important. Isn't that right Jazmine?"

"Yes, it is important," she said nodding, "but this was not supposed to happen. I was to run out. We thought that the riders would see someone on the track, then pull up and stop, or take a wide berth round, and the race would be ruined or even be re-run."

14

"But that didn't happen did it?" said the Professor. "If only I could have spun my lie for a bit longer to distract you all!"

"Yes," said Jazmine, her eyes narrowing, "if you had not pulled that little stunt I would have been in position as planned. Emily would not have grabbed the banner and taken my place."

Anger spread across the Professor's face and he jabbed his finger at her. "Don't you dare try and blame me for this! It was a stupid and dangerous scheme you had hatched, that was most likely going to end in disaster right from the outset. All I was trying to do was keep you safe. Of course I'm desperately sorry that your friend was hurt, but I would rather it was her lying half dead on the track than you!"

The sudden outburst took Jazmine aback, giving her Father the chance to address the rest of the Suffragettes, telling them to get away otherwise they would find themselves arrested. For a second it looked as though Ethel was about to reply that that was what they were hoping for. But not wanting to make things worse, they just headed off through the crowd, while Mallory and the Professor continued to lead Jazmine and Florence away.

As planned, they got to the other side of the track, passing the throng of people, who were now moving towards the scene of the incident, and to the nearest exit. They had almost reached their goal when a voice called out. "Oi, you there!" Instantly they turned to see a constable who was making his way over. "I know you two women, you're Suffragettes!"

"No, you must be mistaken," said the Professor quickly. "This is my daughter and my niece." He looked over to

Florence who nodded, trying to confirm the lie. "I can assure you that they had nothing to do with what has gone on here today."

"Do I look stupid?" asked the constable.

"Of course not!" replied Mallory quickly, before anyone else was tempted to answer. "But in this case I think that you are mixing these women up with someone else."

The man shook his head. "Oh I don't think so! I definitely recognise you two. I've seen you both before at demonstrations and on our watch lists. I bet you are mixed up in this somehow." With that he took his whistle out of his pocket and blew it for assistance, attracting the immediate attention of two nearby constables who suddenly appeared. "I am placing you two women under arrest! You are going to have to come along with us to the station!"

CHAPTER 4

Professor Montacute and Richard Mallory waited quietly, sitting on a long bench in the reception of the Epsom Police Station, where the arrested Suffragettes had been brought to be processed before being placed in the cells. Milling about were a number of journalists trying to get information for the evening papers, friends and relatives of those Suffragettes arrested, as well as other police Officers who were desperately trying to keep order.

From behind the main counter a large Sergeant appeared. "Professor Charles Montacute!" The Professor and Mallory stood, and the Sergeant motioned for them to come forward. He opened up a section of the reception desk, allowing them access to the rear office area, where he then took them to one side and into a private interview room.

"Take a seat both of you."

The Professor and Mallory did as they were told.

"My name is Sergeant Dixon," said the Sergeant, as he too sat down.

The Professor and Mallory nodded in response.

"Professor Montacute, your daughter has been arrested in connection with the events that took place today at the Derby. We are aware that she is an active member of the Suffragette movement, having been arrested a number of times, with the suspicion of involvement in a number of other militant acts."

"But, with all due respect," said the Professor with a polite smile, "'suspicion' is not the same as 'proof' is it?"

Dixon paused and nodded.

"There is no denying," the Professor continued, "that my daughter is a Suffragette, and she has been in trouble in the past. But she was not involved in any way, shape or form in what happened today. The reality is that we, that is myself and my daughter, her friend and Mr Richard Mallory here, were just having a day out at the races together."

Dixon raised an eyebrow, clearly not convinced.

"I would like to point out to you," added the Professor quickly, "that Jazmine was arrested nowhere near the incident that took place. I'm afraid that she is a victim of coincidence, strengthened by poor past judgement."

"She is now also," continued Dixon, "facing a charge of assault, as she struck one of my officers as she was being put into the cells."

"Um, er, she has a thing, a phobia about being in enclosed spaces," said Mallory quickly. "Nothing was meant by it. I'm sure it was just a reaction to the thought of being locked up."

"I am presuming then that would explain her language too?" said Dixon. "I've heard swearing before, but in all my years of service, nothing like that from a supposed lady!"

"I'm afraid that she spent some years overseas as a child," ventured the Professor sheepishly. "She may have picked up some creatively descriptive vocabulary from the sailors on some of the cargo ships that we were forced to use as transport, but I'm sure that that whole incident could be overlooked."

"It could, but there is still the matter of the Derby today."

The Professor smiled. "But as I have already explained, she was not part of what happened and there is no proof that she was."

Dixon smiled, then opened a folder on his desk and pulled out a piece of paper. "This is a statement which was given not half an hour ago by a Miss Florence Wilcox. It states quite clearly that she, along with your daughter, was attending the Derby today with the express aim to disrupt the proceedings by sabotaging the main race." Dixon paused to take in the dismay that swept across the Professor and Mallory's faces. "Is that enough proof for you?"

The Professor nodded, then sighed, realising that if he wanted Jazmine to be freed, he would have to reveal the real reason, other than Fatherly concern, as to why they were so desperate to ensure that Jazmine was not charged.

18

"Alright Sergeant, it is clear that subterfuge will not work and I need to be totally honest with you. It is vital that Jazmine is released and it has to be tonight."

"Oh, and why is that then?"

"I assume that you are of course aware of the incidences that have been taking place in Highgate Cemetery over recent weeks?"

Dixon nodded. It had been reported by the Cemetery's caretakers that a number of animals had been found, their throats ripped out and, more alarmingly, their bodies drained of blood. At first it was suspected that it was a fox or a dog. However, in the last week, things had taken a more sinister turn. People were now being targeted. The two victims, both attacked in the night, had escaped unharmed, but the story that they told had caused great concern. The assailant was a man whose principle purpose, it seemed, was to try to cut the neck of his chosen prey and drink the flowing blood. The papers had of course run with the story in the only way they could, claiming that a real life vampire was at large in the graveyard and looking for victims to feed on.

"Well," the Professor continued, "I have been sought out and requested to investigate this incident by your superiors. It is planned that we go to Highgate tonight and try to resolve this matter once and for all, using whatever means necessary."

Dixon looked at the Professor and Mallory with some reservation. "Are you trying to tell me that you are going out to hunt a vampire?"

The Professor looked uncomfortable. "I would prefer it if you would not use that phraseology if at all possible, it gives connotations of romance and intrigue. Let's just say that Mr Mallory, Jazmine and I have wide experience in both natural and supernatural events. It felt that in the current circumstances we would be able to handle whichever it seemed to be, effectively."

Dixon paused, not totally sure if he believed them. "And I suppose that this can be verified?"

"Indeed," said the Professor, reaching into his waistcoat pocket for a card. "This is my official contact regarding the matter. I was under instructions that he was only to be contacted in exceptional circumstances, hence why I tried to persuade you to allow my daughter to be free, rather than tell you the true purpose of what is planned."

Dixon took the card and whistled in surprise. The contact was the Metropolitan Police Commissioner, Sir Edward Henry.

"Sir Henry is a personal friend of mine," added the Professor casually. "He also knows my daughter..."

"Wait a minute! You wouldn't be the Professor who was with him last November when that cabbie tried to assassinate him?" asked Dixon.

Professor Montacute nodded. He had been dining with Sir Henry that fateful night when a disgruntled cab driver had tried to kill the Metropolitan Police's highest ranking Officer; for revenge at the fact his license had been revoked. It was the Professor who had first noticed the suspicious looking man and then sprang into action when he tried to strike. "Of course," said the Professor, "for reasons of my own, I insisted that my name were kept out of the press coverage that resulted."

Dixon nodded, now convinced that he could be telling the truth.

"But regarding tonight's venture in Highgate, it was decided that the whole plan be carried out in secret, with only a few key people knowing. I think that there is a fear that, in the unlikely event that it is a real vampire, it could be dealt with instantly, and then hushed up without anyone knowing the truth."

Dixon looked back down at the card. "Of course I will have to ring the number to check out your story."

"Indeed, please do," said the Professor, who was more than happy for him to make the call.

"But assuming everything checks out, I should be able to let her go, without charge, into your care."

The Professor nodded, breathing a sigh of relief. Dixon stood and started to move towards the door leading to the office where he would make the call, but then he stopped suddenly, a thought occurring to him. "Um I hope you don't mind my asking, but your daughter...?"

"Yes."

"What part is she playing in this attempt to catch this alleged vampire?"

The Professor smiled wickedly. "A very important one. She is going to be used as the bait."

CHAPTER 5

The phone call to Sir Henry had indeed produced the required results. In fact, according to Dixon, Sir Henry acted as though he was actually expecting the call. The Chief of the Metropolitan Police instructed that Jazmine was to be freed at once into the care of her father, and that all mention of her arrest was to be stricken from the record. Sergeant Dixon carried out the orders to the letter, even going so far as arranging for a Hansom Cab to take The Professor, Mallory and Jazmine home.

The journey to the Montacutes' town house in London's Berkley Square occurred in almost near silence. With the Professor glaring the whole time at Jazmine who tried to avoid his gaze, aware of the trouble she was in.

Eventually they arrived home where they were greeted warmly and led inside by the Montacutes' Housekeeper Mrs Paddick. She said that she had a meal prepared for them and would serve it when required, before disappearing off, seeing from the look on their faces that a major argument was about to erupt.

From the hall table, the Professor picked up a copy of the evening's edition of 'The Standard'. There was one story dominating the front page; the events that had taken place that afternoon at Epsom. A look of fury crossed his face and he screwed up the paper, throwing it to one side, unable to control his anger anymore. "What in God's name did you think you were doing girl? You have a brain, you knew the plan you had was foolhardy and extremely dangerous, not to mention the fact that it was going to put tonight's operation in jeopardy!"

"I told you I was not planning on getting caught," replied Jazmine defensively. "I was going to escape. My comrades even said they would do everything possible to ensure I didn't get arrested!"

"'Comrades!'" mocked the Professor, with a hint of sarcasm. "'Comrades!' Are you sure the vote was all you were after? Because it sounds to me as though you were planning the start of a full scale revolution!"

Jazmine gritted her teeth. "I was standing up for what I believe in; just as you taught me."

22

"Don't you give me that!" roared the Professor. "I also taught you common sense, and running out in front of racing horses defies that!"

"But I didn't run out in front of them did I?" pointed out Jazmine, tears forming. "Emily did."

"No that's right and look how she ended up! That could have been you. It was a miracle that she was not killed instantly." He paused, shaking his head sadly. "Not that it really matters. We've seen injuries like that before; we both know she'll pass in a few days."

Tears started to roll down Jazmine's cheeks. "I didn't want for that to happen. Emily was my friend!"

Mallory moved forward and put his arms around her, and she buried herself into his shoulder.

The Professor remained silent, wondering if he had been too hard on her, or perhaps not hard enough, and then summing up the situation he reached a decision. "I think that I need to contact Inspector Todd, call off tonight. Bearing in mind all that's happened I think it's appropriate. We can arrange another date."

"But won't that cause problems?" asked Mallory. "Aside from the fact that there could be another attack, Jazmine was only freed on account of tonight's raid."

"I know," replied the Professor worriedly. "It will look bad, but I don't think that we have any other choice. I'll call Sir Henry and work my magic."

"There's no need," said Jazmine, moving away from Mallory and wiping her eyes. "I know how important this is. What time were we planning on leaving tonight?"

"It has been arranged that we will be picked up here just after eleven o'clock tonight. We should be at Highgate around midnight," said the Professor.

23

Jazmine nodded. "I'm going to go and freshen up and change. If it's all right with the both of you I'll miss supper, I'm not that hungry. I'll be ready for tonight, but I would like to have some time alone first."

The Professor and Mallory nodded in agreement, and Jazmine silently headed up the stairs to her room.

The Professor shook his head in frustration. "Come on Mr Mallory, I need a drink and I expect you to join me!" With that he moved across the hall and into the downstairs sitting room, where he went straight over to a table on which was a selection of decanters. He poured a large glass and downed it in one, before pouring another which he handed to Mallory, who by now had caught up with him. The Professor poured himself another large drink and was about to drink it before seemingly thinking better of it and placing it back on the tray. "I need to be clear headed tonight! Even though that daughter of mine drives me to it at times, I'd better make sure that I keep my eye on the game."

Mallory smiled and made a joke that Jazmine would be able to drive the saints themselves to drink. This made the Professor smile. "I bet at times you wonder if it was worth throwing your lot in with me and my daughter eh?"

Mallory smiled. His life had certainly taken an interesting turn since he met Professor Charles Montacute and his daughter Jazmine. After their adventure on the Titanic, which brought them to New York, Mallory had decided to join them on an escapade to try to uncover a direct link between a mysterious deceased Dr Tumblety, to Jack the Ripper. However, this investigation was dramatically cut short following a message which should have reached them on the Titanic from the Rev Harry Bull, who requested immediate help regarding his house, Borley Rectory, which was being plagued by ghosts and other strange happenings. They of course responded and Mallory again found himself involved in another supernatural adventure; this time battling phantom nuns and the living dead. It was during this adventure that it looked as though he and Jazmine were to become an official couple. However, after she thought she saw him being killed, she decided to end any possibility of romantic involvement. Mallory was devastated, but the Professor had a more pragmatic approach, seeing that his daughter really loved him and that, over time, the two would get together.

Seeing the value of adding Mallory to their number, the Professor secured a small amount of funding from the university, which allowed him to pay Mallory as a 'Freelance consultant'. The three had then embarked on many different adventures, faced many dangers, both supernatural and man-made, which had seen them grow into a tight unit, both on a professional and personal level.

"Well," said Mallory, thinking about what the Professor had said, "I have wondered at times what a quiet life would be like!"

This made the Professor smile. "It would be very boring and when you get to be an old man you would have few stories to tell your grandchildren!"

"Considering the life I seem to be leading now, I doubt that I will get to be an old man. I thought with my army days behind me, even with my work as a detective and insurance investigator, I would be assured of getting to a ripe old age!"

"Don't be so pessimistic Mr Mallory!" laughed the Professor, slapping him on the back. "Look at me! Mid-fifties and I'm still bounding about like a young man, still dodging bullets and the like. Besides, I've kept you alive thus far haven't I?"

Mallory smiled. "I'm sure in the great scheme of things, you getting me into life threatening, mystical dangers, then helping me out of them, doesn't really count." He paused. "Mind you, speaking of which, do you really think that we are going to find a vampire tonight?"

The Professor shrugged. "I'm not sure what we are going to find: an actual vampire; a madman with delusions that he is a vampire; a person who is deliberately taking on that mantle; someone in the process of an elaborate practical joke; or something else. Who can say? What I am sure about is that we will be armed to the teeth and, after tonight, the Highgate vampire will be no more; one way or another."

Mallory nodded in agreement but secretly hoped that out of the options given, it would in fact be a real vampire.

CHAPTER 6

The Hansom cab, which was laid on by the Metropolitan Police, dropped the Professor, Mallory and Jazmine outside the main gate of Highgate Cemetery at exactly midnight. They were greeted by Inspector Gordon Todd. With him was a man dressed in a dark suit and hat, who introduced himself simply as Mr Smith. He had been sent to observe the night's proceedings.

"So," said the Inspector, looking them over carefully, "are you all ready for the task ahead?"

"Oh very much so," replied Mallory who, like the Professor, was dressed in a tweed suit. They both carried with them a shoulder bag that contained a number of items that might be needed for their adventure, including a number of wooden stakes and a mallet. The Professor was also armed with his walking cane, which was in reality a sword stick. Jazmine was wearing a long white dress, with a cream belt and topped off with a large white wide brimmed hat. In her left hand she held a parasol, while in her right a small evening bag. Her attire had especially been chosen to give the idea of a refined, lost, helpless woman.

"It was Jazmine herself who came up with the idea of wearing a white dress," explained the Professor, noting the slightly puzzled gaze at his daughter's choice of clothes.

"Yes that's right," said Jazmine. "It will make me easier to see, both for the so called vampire and for my Father and Richard here."

The Inspector nodded in approval. "A very good idea Miss. If there are any problems they will be able to step in and help you before things get out of hand."

"Oh I'm perfectly capable of taking care of myself," replied Jazmine, and with that she pulled on the handle of the parasol and out came a long thin blade. The sight of the blade made Inspector Todd's eyes widen in surprise.

"It was made by my Father here," said Jazmine proudly. "It will be really useful for tonight, along with this." She held up her evening purse.

"I'm afraid to ask, but what surprise does that have?"

"Quicklime," replied Jazmine, with girlish glee. "The bag had been made especially, so with one sharp movement it will release the contents into the air. Would

27

you like me to show you some of the rest of the equipment I'm carrying?"

"No, no Miss that's quite alright," said the Inspector. "Um Professor, what plan do you have in mind for tonight?"

"Well, the attacks all seem to have taken place among the older Western Section among the Victorian mausoleums. I think that could be our starting point. Our strategy I'm afraid is going to be quite crude. Jazmine will walk ahead through the tombs, while we will follow at a distance ready to step in if required."

"Will you want any help from my boys here?" asked the Inspector, motioning to the group of Constables which were waiting in the background.

"I'm happy for them to follow Mr Mallory and me," said the Professor, "providing of course that they keep well out of our way as per our agreement. Speaking of which, do you have the letter I requested?"

The Inspector nodded then produced an envelope, which he passed to the Professor who opened it, and started to read the contents.

"It's as you asked for, I can assure you," said the Inspector. "An official letter signed by Sir Henry himself, outlining that, for tonight, the three of you are acting as officers of the Metropolitan Police and are offered the appropriate protection by the law."

"Good," replied the Professor, pocketing the document. "After all, if we do end up having to kill this 'vampire,' we certainly do not want to end up on a murder charge."

"But I must stress," said the Inspector, "if it does turn out that it is a vampire, every effort must be made to capture it alive."

The Professor smiled. "May I take an educated guess? There is a group of scientists, probably employed by the government, who are more than eager, in the unlikely event it is true, to get their hands on a live vampire." As he spoke, he casually looked over at Mr Smith and raised a knowing eyebrow.

Mr Smith nodded. "Very perceptive of you, but then from someone with your intellect I would expect no less. You are of course right. If there is such a thing as a vampire, the British government would like to examine it first-hand."

"And is there a vehicle on hand to take the vampire away as soon as it is caught?"

Mr Smith smiled. "I wouldn't worry yourself about the arrangements that are in place Professor, just do what is required of you. If it transpires that there is a vampire, catch it and bring it back alive."

The Professor nodded and smiled, although he had no intention of handing over such a creature. If it did turn out to be a vampire, he was going to kill it at once.

With everyone clear on their roles, they began to put the plan into action. Jazmine set off first through the huge Victorian gates of the cemetery, followed at a distance by her Father and Mallory, with the uniformed officers far behind. The constables had been given strict instructions to keep their distance and to only intervene at a given signal by either the Professor or Mallory.

Having already studied a map of the cemetery, it did not take Jazmine long to reach the old Victorian section which was filled with family crypts and vast dramatic monuments that were the fashion at the time. Once there, it was just a simple matter for her to walk around, looking lost and like suitable prey for whatever was waiting in the shadows.

"I don't like that Smith chap at all," said Mallory, his eyes firmly fixed on the figure of Jazmine in the distance, which had just disappeared momentarily behind a large pink obelisk. "I get the inkling that he could be trouble for us."

"Much more than you think," said the Professor. "I have a feeling that we are now well and truly in the attention of the authorities, which is something that I have always tried to avoid."

"What do you mean?"

The Professor paused. "I had this friend. The government called on him once to do a job. They kept calling on him on a regular basis for the next fifteen years."

"What happened?"

The Professor smiled. "He was on 'holiday' when he was attacked by bandits and killed. Well, that's the story we were told. I have a different theory. I fear that he had outlived his usefulness, or had been deemed as a danger, as he knew too much."

"Would the government do that? I mean, I saw some pretty shady things go on in my army days, but would they go that far?"

The Professor shrugged. "Maybe, let's just hope it doesn't get to that stage. Oh for goodness sake! Where is she going?"

Jazmine had moved off the path and into a group of tall gravestones, where she kept disappearing and then re-appearing through the monuments.

"We need to get closer," said the Professor. "Otherwise we are going to lose her altogether."

30

Quickly, he and Mallory moved forward, trying to keep Jazmine in sight, but then she seemed to disappear altogether.

"Where did she go?" asked Mallory.

"I'm not sure," replied the Professor worriedly.

"Shall we get the constable to come and help?"

"No, not yet, I don't want them coming in until there is no other option. Look, I think I saw something over there!" said the Professor, bounding off. Mallory followed, looking around as he did so, trying to spot Jazmine. Then as the two men navigated around a large gravestone, they spotted her. She continued onwards before she suddenly stopped behind a large obelisk, her distinctive hat visible over the top of it.

"Why is she stopping?" asked Mallory. "I thought she was going to keep moving at all times."

"She was. I think something is wrong," replied the Professor, suddenly moving out and round the large gravestone that they were behind, with Mallory following not far behind. As the two men moved out of position they gained a clearer view of the situation, and realised with horror that it was not a stationary Jazmine they had been observing, just her oversized white hat, which was now resting on top of the column.

CHAPTER 7

"How the hell did that happen?" queried Mallory, staring at the abandoned hat. "Do you think that she has decided to go it alone?"

The Professor shook his head.

"So you think that she has been taken?"

"It would seem so," said the Professor, "and by a cunning enemy who knew that she was being followed and was able to set up a distraction at a moment's notice! Come on Mr Mallory, we need to make an inspection of the scene!"

With that the two made their way over to where Jazmine had disappeared. Nearby they found the sword parasol and the quicklime filled bag.

"What ever happened, it happened so fast, she did not have time to react properly," said Mallory. "Blast it! She's now defenceless!"

"Well, apart from her training in unarmed combat, the dagger she had hidden in her boot and the garrotte which was made into a bracelet," countered the Professor, with a glint in his eye.

"Alright," said Mallory, looking around for a clue as to where she could have gone, "but what do we do now? Shall we get help?" He glanced over in the direction of the Police Constables, but the Professor shook his head.

"No, I don't want them blundering in and getting in the way. Let's just sort this one out ourselves eh?" The Professor looked around trying to see if there was any hint as to where Jazmine could have been taken. "Damn and blast! She could be anywhere by now."

"Do you think that she could be taken outside the cemetery to a nearby house?"

"Possible," said the Professor, hoping that was not the case. If it was, they would stand very little chance of finding her until it was too late. "I think under the circumstances, we have to assume that she is still here, somewhere."

"If I was in the shoes of the 'vampire' I would want to have somewhere nearby, where I could base myself and take someone," ventured Mallory.

The Professor nodded. "Agreed, there are a number of large family crypts to the east, I think that is our best bet. Keep an eye out for anything that could give us an indication as to where they went. If we are lucky Jazmine may have been able to give us a sign of some kind."

So with that they headed eastward, but sadly there were no clues as to where she could be, just row upon row of tombs, monuments and stone coffins.

"I think we have lost our police escorts totally," said Mallory, looking behind.

"Good," said the Professor. "At least something is going our way! I really don't think that they were going to be of any practical use to us anyway. Mr Mallory! Look over there!"

Mallory turned to where the Professor was indicating and there, about thirty feet away, was a strange figure facing them. It was that of a woman who was wearing a shroud-like dress over which was a long cloak which seemed to drag along the ground. She was in her late thirties, with long red, wavy hair. Her face was pretty and very pale. There was no question that this was anything but a supernatural vision, as both men could see straight through her to the gravestones beyond. The ghostly woman seemed to smile at them and with her right hand beckoned them towards her.

"She wants us to follow her," said Mallory, suddenly realising that he felt no fear.

"The Graveyard Guardian," said the Professor. "She is the Graveyard Guardian of Highgate. That's the most likely explanation as to her identity."

"What do you mean?" asked Mallory, unable to look away from the spirit.

"There is a myth that the first person to be buried in a graveyard is charged to oversee it for eternity," explained the Professor.

"Elizabeth Jackson," said Mallory softly, although he had no idea where the name came from.

The Professor smiled. "Yes, I think you're right. I think that when we check the records that will be the first person who was buried here and the description will fit the apparition. But how did you know?"

Mallory just shrugged. "I'm not sure. The name just came to me. I think that she wanted me to know."

They then both looked back at the figure who seemed to smile and beckon them both again, before raising the hood of her cloak to cover her face. She then turned and slowly started to move away.

"I think she is going to help us," said Mallory.

The Professor nodded. "Yes, part of her task is to protect the graveyard and those within from harm, and the issue of a 'vampire' threatening others would certainly fall under that category. As a ghost there are obvious limitations, but I think that she is going to take us to the crypt where Jazmine has been taken, so we can rescue her and stop this fiend. Come on Mr Mallory, let's see where she leads us and pray that we are in time."

And so, the two men followed the ghostly figure. Eventually they came to a section where the obelisks and other monuments seemed to give way to what looked like small buildings, each with decorative entrances. These were the crypts and mausoleums where the very wealthy of the Victorian age had bought and designed elaborate tombs where they and members of their family could be laid to rest.

The ghostly guide continued to lead them, turning every so often to check that they had not been lost through the walkways. Before long they found themselves moving from the well maintained crypts and vaults, through to a section of the cemetery that had almost been forgotten, where grass and vines had been allowed to take over and the tombs had fallen into disrepair and ruin.

Eventually the ghostly apparition stopped and turned towards a certain crypt. She lifted her arm and pointed towards it. She remained there indicating which tomb it was until there was no mistake that they knew exactly which tomb she meant. Then very slowly, before their eyes, the hooded figure began to fade away into nothing.

"When this is over," said the Professor solemnly, "I think it would be appropriate if we were to locate Elizabeth Jackson's grave and lay some flowers there as a mark of respect and as a thank you."

Mallory nodded in agreement. For without the ghostly figure's intervention there was no possible way they could have found the tomb to which they had been brought. The vault itself was set slightly back from the others and there was a small slope leading down to two iron gates and beyond that could be seen a large stone door.

Mallory was about to ask how they were going to proceed when the silence was broken by a shrilling sound which made both men turn to the vault, in time to see a cloud of bats fly out directly at them. With no time to dodge out of the way, the Professor and Mallory brought their arms up to protect themselves. They shut their eyes; however, the bats, for whatever reason, suddenly veered off leaving them untouched.

"Are you alright?" asked the Professor, finally bringing his arms down.

"I think so. The bats, did you see them? They had long fangs!"

"Yes, I have a feeling that they were vampire bats."

"Appropriate for our current situation," said Mallory. "So, what's the plan?"

The Professor shrugged. "The fact that we have lost Jazmine for so long changes things; the idea of using stealth and cunning can be forgotten. We just need to get in there as quickly as possible and pray that we are not too late!"

Moving slowly down the slope to the tomb, they could see that the iron gate was actually unlocked and ajar. Being mindful of anymore bats, Mallory opened the gate and then the two men carefully ventured forward to the large stone door. Mallory took hold of the large iron ring set into the stone and pulled hard.

"Blast! It's shut firm! Professor, is there likely to be another way in?"

The Professor shook his head. "No, tombs such as this only have one entrance, and this is it."

Mallory pulled on the ring again, the Professor grabbing it, adding his strength. But even with their combined efforts the door would not move.

"It's stuck fast Professor. It's not going to budge. What do we do?"

"We keep trying Mr Mallory, because we are Jazmine's only hope!"

CHAPTER 8

Jazmine awoke to find herself laying on the top of some kind of stone table. From the traces of blood, and egg sized bump on the back of her head, she realised she had been attacked from behind and dragged off somewhere. Still slightly dazed, she sat up and took in her surroundings, realising instantly that she had been taken into one of the crypts. The room where she was was quite large. It was lit by flame torches positioned on the wall. Two of which were either side of a doorway with stone steps leading up to another level. In front of her there were four large stone sarcophagus set out in a row, and Jazmine soon became aware that from the last one were muffled cries and frantic scrabbling.

Carefully, Jazmine stood and made her way over to it. She placed her hands on the large stone lid and pushed at it with all her strength. The lid swung freely to one side and, looking inside the coffin, Jazmine saw to her horror that there was a young girl, about sixteen years old, within. Her hands and feet were tied, and she had a gag in her mouth. "Don't scream. I'm here to help you," said Jazmine, as she leant over and took the gag out of the girl's mouth.

"Help me!" the girl begged. "Please get me out of here."

Jazmine nodded, and reached down to her boot to take the knife, which she then used to cut the girl's bonds, before tucking the blade into her belt. "Who are you?"

"My name is Lucy, Lucy Newton," replied the girl.

Jazmine recognised the name at once. The papers had widely reported the disappearance of her when she had gone missing a week before. Now free, Lucy stood and promptly nearly fainted, but was steadied by Jazmine who helped her out of the coffin. "I feel so weak," the young girl said. "My captor kept feeding off of me. He cut my neck and would drink the blood. He kept the wound fresh by rubbing garlic on it, but I thought vampires hated garlic."

Jazmine moved Lucy's long hair to one side to reveal her neck, which had been cut a number of times with some kind of narrow blade. Some of the wounds were fresh, while others were healing. "Garlic is actually an anti-clotting agent," explained Jazmine. "It has been used in warfare for centuries, rubbed onto swords so a simple cut will not heal. This is the work of a vicious and calculated madman."

Lucy nodded. "I can vouch for that, the look in his eyes!"

"Do you know who he is? How did you end up here?"

"I often visit Highgate," said Lucy softly. "It sounds morbid I know, but it is so peaceful here and I like to read the inscriptions. Anyway, on one such walk, I became aware that there was someone behind me. I tried to run, but tripped, and the next thing I knew I woke up here. As for who he is, I've no idea. He's tall, with dark hair and pale skin. He wears black and his teeth, well they are more like fangs. He scares me so much!"

"Then I think that we had better get you out of here," said Jazmine, looking at the frightened expression on the young girl's face.

"I'm sorry, but I cannot allow that to happen!"

38

Jazmine turned and there on the stairs was the figure of the vampire. Despite Lucy's accurate description of him, she was still taken aback. For there, dressed in a long black cloak with black morning suit and white shirt and waistcoat, was the perceived image of a vampire, straight out of a gothic horror novel.

The vampire seemed to almost glide down the stairs, his eyes fixed upon Jazmine the whole time. "Ah, you are awake. First may I apologise for having to bring you here in the way I did."

"You mean knocking me out? Is that how you are forced to get your women?"

"I will choose to let that pass. May I introduce myself? I have chosen to go by the name of John Polidori."

Jazmine smirked. "A chosen name I presume? Well, more original than calling yourself Bram Stoker or Count Dracula I suppose!"

Polidori stared at her intently, while a look of confusion flashed across Lucy's face.

"John Polidori was a physician writer who died in 1821," explained Jazmine. "His short story, 'The Vampyre' has been credited as the first ever vampire story and a template for all that came after it." She looked over at Polidori. "It seems clear that you are a fan. Only you seem to be taking the thing too far."

"Silence!" roared Polidori. "You dare question my providence?"

"Question and deny it!" cried Jazmine. "You are no more a vampire than I am!"

He hissed at her showing his teeth, the two upper incisors were visibly protruding.

"Fake teeth," said Jazmine defiantly. "Easily manufactured and applied!"

"Enough of this!" cried the vampire, as he reached to his belt, producing a long thin knife with a decorated bone blade. "You will submit to me! First I will cut you and then I will drink on your sweet life blood!"

"I'd be more impressed if he could turn into a bat!"

"Don't goad him!" cried Lucy, who had backed away and was now hiding behind her coffin in fear. "You have no idea what he is capable of!"

"Oh, I'm not afraid of this fraud," said Jazmine, who was now feeling more and more confident. "If you are a vampire why do you cut your victims rather than just bite them?"

"Why do some people use a knife to cut into an apple instead of just biting straight into it?" replied Polidori simply. "It is down to personal preference, and mine is to cut rather than bite before I drink. It allows a deeper wound, which is easier to feed from."

"Well I can assure you that you are not going to be feeding on me!" said Jazmine quickly, reaching for her blade which she held up threateningly towards Polidori. "Now, stand aside so Lucy and I can leave this place."

"Never!"

"Then 'vampire' you are going to be in for a bad time. This blade was washed in holy water in preparation and, oh look, it also acts as a cross!" To mock him further she quickly spun the dagger over, catching it by the blade before holding it out in front of her. Polidori stood back, melodramatically wincing.

"Oh please!" cried Jazmine, "stop being so pathetic and melodramatic!"

But Polidori stepped back, continuing the act as though he was in agony and then in a pained voice he shouted to Lucy to come to his aid. Jazmine turned to her to make another quip, but instead was confronted with the sight of the girl charging towards her screaming. In response, Jazmine moved back and Lucy flew past. As she did so, Jazmine kicked out her foot catching Lucy's ankle, sending her sprawling to the floor where the girl, totally overcome, collapsed in a heap and started to sob uncontrollably. Using this distraction, Polidori launched himself over to Jazmine, and in one move snatched the blade out of her hand before staring at her intently for a few seconds. To Jazmine's own surprise, she found that she had no real desire to move or even try to fight.

"Tell me," said Polidori, "have you ever been bitten by a vampire?"

"But you are not a vampire!" replied Jazmine, although she found herself saying this with far less conviction than before. Polidori smiled, then calmly brought up the blade and cut Jazmine's neck. He smiled before moving round behind her, and pulling her close to him. She turned her head to try to call Lucy for help, but only succeeded in exposing her neck to Polidori, who responded by bringing his lips to the flowing blood and starting to drink. Jazmine reached up, grabbed at Polidori's hair and started to try and pull at it. Then after a few moments she became aware that far from trying to detach him, she was actually holding him in place. A strange tingle surged through her entire body, and she smiled as the horrific realisation swept over her that she was actually enjoying being fed upon and did not want him to stop.

CHAPTER 9

"Jazmine!"

The call made Polidori look up, distracting him from his feed. Then a single shot rang out, making Jazmine regain her senses. She grabbed her neck and turned towards her attacker, whose grip on her suddenly loosened, and a look of surprise had spread across his face. In the middle of Polidori's forehead was a small neat hole that was trickling blood. He then collapsed to the ground.

Not totally sure what was happening, Jazmine turned and there, at the top of the stairs to the vault lit by the flaming torches, was the figure of Richard Mallory. He was holding the still smoking gun in its firing position, behind him was the figure of her Father. Both then started hurriedly to descend the stairs, the Professor opting to investigate the body of the vampire to confirm the threat was neutralised, while Mallory went straight to Jazmine.

"Jazmine, are you alright?"

"Um, er, I think so," she replied, as she continued to hold the cut mark on her neck, which was still bleeding.

"Here, let me look at that," said Mallory, turning her head with one hand, as with the other he reached into his pocket for a handkerchief.

"The vampire is he dead?" she asked.

"Very much so," replied the Professor examining the body, with a hint of annoyance. "A very good and necessary shot Mr Mallory, but still an inconvenient situation." Although the death proved that it was not a supernatural creature, it meant the man could not be questioned as to his motives. The Professor then went over to the figure of Lucy, who was now sitting in the corner, her knees tucked under her chin, rocking backwards and forwards slightly. The whole experience had seemingly been too much for her and she had retreated totally into herself. Meanwhile Mallory and Jazmine were exchanging stories of what had happened since they had lost contact earlier that night. Jazmine was intrigued by the Graveyard Guardian and how she had guided them to her.

"Led to the tomb by a ghost, this is going to be difficult to explain," she said, pressing the handkerchief to her neck.

"Not at all," said the Professor, finally joining them. "We will just leave her out of the account totally. I'm just glad that when we got here we managed to find the secret door release. Even if it did take longer than I wanted. How's your neck?"

"Stings a bit, luckily for me he wasn't a real vampire. Otherwise I'd be one of the walking dead by now."

"Nonsense!" replied the Professor. "Vampire law dictates that a vampire cannot just be sired in one bite. No, it occurs over a number of weeks, and even then only if the vampire himself decides it!"

"Right then," said the Professor, "I suppose that we had better get out of here and find our police escorts. Thank goodness they were happy to give me the legal assurance I requested. Do you realise Mr Mallory, that without it, you could be facing a charge of manslaughter?"

"A relief for sure," Mallory replied. "I would not want to have to serve prison time."

However, Mallory's answer went unheard, as the Professor was distracted, noticing his daughter had turned white as a sheet. "Jazmine? Jazmine are you alright?"

"No, look! The vampire, Polidori! He's, he's……."

Mallory and the Professor turned, and to their horror and fascination, saw Polidori now on his feet looking at them, a look of anger across his face.

"But I killed you!" protested Mallory in disbelief. "It was a clear head shot! You should be dead!"

"There are certain methods that have to be used to kill a true vampire such as myself. A mere bullet through the brain, I can assure you, is not one of them," he replied, as he wiped a small trickle of blood away from his eyes. "I, Polidori, have walked this earth for hundreds of years, and I aim to continue to do so for hundreds more."

"Dear lord!" exclaimed the Professor. "Could it actually be that you are what you say?"

Polidori nodded. "I am indeed! I am a vampire and now if you will excuse me, with my secret discovered and my hunting ground now spoilt, I think that I had better leave to find, as it were, new pastures. You may keep the girl Lucy, she was starting to bore me and her blood had an odd taste to it. I don't think she was in the best of health." And with that Polidori grabbed at the sides of his cloak and raised his arms out to the sides. At the same instance the torches that lit the crypt started to flicker. In the semi dimness of the light it almost looked as though the man's form was starting to change, even disperse.

The Professor, dropping his shoulder bag to the floor, drew his sword stick and lunged straight forward into the body of Polidori, who screamed out in pain. Instantly the flaming torches of the crypt seemed to steady, allowing the Professor to see that his aim, due to the darkness, was slightly wide of the heart. He then looked up into the face of Polidori whose expression was no longer that of pain, but something quite different. For a split second Professor

44

Montacute seemed to be caught in the man's hypnotic gaze before somehow managing to tear himself away. Standing back a fraction, he raised his left foot and placed it on the hip of Polidori, and in one movement, both pushed him away and pulled his sword stick free of the man's body. He then made a wild slash with the weapon which connected with the vampire's chin, making him turn away. The Professor then moved in, grabbing Polidori by the shoulder and kicking at his feet. Guiding him to the ground, making sure that his head hit the stone floor hard, stunning him. Immediately, the Professor moved to his shoulder bag, opening it and grabbing a small mallet and one of the sharp wooden stakes. He knelt down by the stunned Polidori and placed the stake directly over his heart. He then raised the mallet, ready to bring it down hard, when a voice called out stopping him in his tracks.

"Thank you Professor Montacute, but I think that we will take things from here!"

Looking round, the Professor saw the figure of the mysterious Mr Smith standing in the vault doorway, where Mallory had fired upon the vampire earlier. To one side of him was Inspector Todd and a number of police constables, who all ran down the stairs and over to the Professor, who, realising that he had no choice, stood up and left the police to their work. Quickly, Polidori was handcuffed and hauled to his feet and led off, while the other officers attended to Lucy.

"What are you going to do with him?" asked the Professor.

Smith, who had now descended, smiled. "He will be taken to a secure location where he will be questioned and examined."

"Examined?"

"Yes, *examined*," said Smith simply. Although it was clear from the way he spoke that the examination that would be taking place would not be pleasant.

"Who are you?" asked the Professor, "and more importantly who do you work for?"

Smith paused, as though thinking whether to reveal his true purpose, then with a sly smile spoke. "Just over thirty years ago an institute was established, dedicated to the investigation of possible extra-terrestrial activity. However, it soon became apparent that a number of these incidences had nothing to do with other worlds, but actually had their basis in the supernatural. So, another organisation was established, one that solely investigates and deals with matters of the occult. I work for them." Smith let the revelation set in. "Now, I thank you for your help. A cab is waiting for you which will take you to wherever you need to go. Needless to say, you must never reveal the events that took place this night. If you do, well the results will be ….. messy."

"Of course they will be," replied the Professor sarcastically.

"Now, if you will excuse me," said Smith, with almost a bow, "an encounter such as this creates a lot of paperwork. I will leave you in the capable hands of Inspector Todd, until we no doubt meet again!" And with that the mysterious Mr Smith turned and headed off, leaving the Professor, Mallory and Jazmine with an uncomfortable feeling that they had found themselves recruited into a mysterious organisation.

CHAPTER 10

The Professor, Mallory and Jazmine eventually arrived back at Berkley Square, at just after four in the morning. Exhausted by the night's events they retired to bed straight away, grabbing a few hours rest before finding they naturally woke at eight o'clock. After washing and dressing they gathered around the breakfast table, which was attended to by Mrs Paddick, who served them with toast, scrambled eggs, bacon and coffee. The air around the table was one of triumph, as the Highgate Vampire had been caught and was no longer a danger. With a young girl saved from a terrible fate and despite the dangers, they had escaped unharmed. The mood was so buoyant that not even the story which dominated the morning newspapers, the events of yesterday's Derby, could disturb the atmosphere. There was even talk of the Professor trying to use his contact with Sir Henry to try to allow Jazmine a supervised visit to her friends in prison.

As the three ate and chatted, from somewhere beyond, the doorbell rang, and then a short while later Mrs Paddick appeared. With her was a middle aged woman, who The Professor and Jazmine recognised at once.

"I'm so sorry to disturb you all," the woman said, as Mrs Paddick left them, "but…"

"Not at all, not at all!" said the Professor, standing. "Please Jane, join us. Can we get you anything?"

"No, no, that's quite alright," she replied, as she moved forward and took a seat at the table.

"Surely some tea?" asked Jazmine. "You look a bit flushed."

"Well, alright, yes."

Jazmine poured some into an empty cup and passed it to her.

"Mr Mallory," said the Professor, as he sat down, "may I introduce to you Jane Quinn. Her husband, Douglas, is an old friend of mine."

At the mention of her husband's name, Jane suddenly welled up and quickly placed the cup and saucer back on the table before grabbing a handkerchief from her sleeve and dabbed her eyes.

"Jane? What's wrong?" asked the Professor.

"I'm sorry," said the woman, composing herself. "Things have been difficult. I did not know who to turn to. The police have not been able to help.......Douglas is missing."

The Professor and Jazmine were visibly shocked by the news.

"For how long?" asked Jazmine.

"I'm not sure; it's all a bit complicated!"

"These things often are," said the Professor gently. "Just start at the beginning."

Jane took a deep breath to steady her. "It started some weeks ago. Douglas was attending a lecture in Vienna, on Renaissance art; he is an advisor to the National Gallery and was invited due to his expertise in the field." The last remark was directed to Mallory, who she realised may not know her husband's occupation. He nodded appreciatively.

"After the lecture it seems that he went off somewhere. Apparently while there, he discovered something which sent him off on an impromptu expedition. He would not tell me where he was going or what he was doing, but he came home a week later in what could only be described as a totally excited state. He was carrying a wooden box. He

48

said that it was a discovery, one that would make him famous, and one that could even change the fundamental understanding of mankind's very existence. I of course asked him what it was and to let me look in the box, but he refused." She paused, taking the time to wipe her eyes again. "Not long after this he headed off again, saying he wanted to do more investigation. That was over a month ago and I have not heard from him since he left London!"

"You mentioned the police," said Mallory. "What did they have to say on the matter?"

Jane shrugged. "They said that they would make a report for the authorities in Vienna which would be sent straight away. They also made the usual enquires here in London, at the gallery, with friends and so on, but they came up with nothing. They said that they would keep me informed of any developments, but they did not sound too hopeful. That's why I came to you Charles. Will you be able to help me?"

"Of course my dear," replied the Professor gently. Although from the situation that she had outlined, there was very little for them to go on. "Now, this box you mentioned," he continued, "do you still have it?"

Jane shook her head. "No, Douglas took it off somewhere before he left. He didn't say where though and the Police have not been able to trace it either. One morning he left very early with it and that was the last I saw of it. I did ask him what he did with it, but he just smiled and said that he was getting the contents verified and investigated."

"Did he ever receive the verification he sought?" asked Mallory.

"I think that he might have," she replied, "a letter arrived which he seemed very excited about. I've tried to locate it, but I cannot find it anywhere. I presume that he took it with him when he went."

The Professor scratched his beard thoughtfully. "It seems that he has done his best to act alone on this, covering his tracks as he went."

"But there must be some way of finding out what's going on and where he is?" said Jazmine.

"Oh there will be," replied the Professor assuredly. "I'm sure there will be some clue; it's just that we have to find it."

"My money's on the box," said Mallory. "If we can find the person or persons who examined it, it could lead us straight to him."

"Possibly," replied the Professor thoughtfully, "but remember he was only getting the contents of it authenticated. There is no guarantee that he told them where he obtained it or where he was going afterwards."

"But the contents of the box could go a long way to explaining what is going on," pointed out Jazmine.

"Indeed," said the Professor, "providing we can find whoever had it and they are happy to tell us. I am sure that they have been given the strictest instructions not to reveal anything, under any circumstances."

"But what of the box itself?" asked Mallory, turning to Jane. "Perhaps that could help us. Jane, can you describe it to us? Were there any markings on it? Did it look special in any way?"

She shook her head. "No, it was just an ordinary wooden box, with a hinged lid, brass lock and a carrying handle. There were no markings or labels that I could see on it."

She then made an approximation of the size with her hands, which was about twelve inches square.

"Did your husband have any problems lifting it?" continued Jazmine.

"No, no trouble at all; he just tucked it under his arm when he went."

"So we know that whatever the contents were, it was light," mused Mallory.

The Professor shook his head. "Now we are clutching at straws! The fact the contents were light does not help us at all. We need something solid to go on, not speculation and guesswork."

"A trip to the National Gallery?" ventured Mallory, thinking that there could be some clue to what was going on at Douglas's workplace.

The Professor shook his head. "No, I wager that if we are going to find anything, it will be in his study at home. Jane, will you allow us to come with you and make a detailed search of Douglas's private study?"

She nodded. "Of course, but what if you don't find anything?"

"Then we will make a trip to the National Gallery and hope that there is something there. If that does not prove productive, there are certain other avenues of investigation that could be employed."

"Such as?" asked Jane.

The Professor gave an uneasy smile. "I do have certain connections with, let's just say, those who do not operate within the full boundaries of the law."

A look of surprise and horror crossed Jane's face. "Do you think that they would be willing help?"

The Professor nodded. "For a price, but let's just hope that it does not come to that. Now, if you will allow us to quickly finish our breakfast we will be yours for as long as required!"

CHAPTER 11

They arrived at the Quinn's house mid-morning. Inside, Jane took them straight to the study. It was a large room, with oversized bookcases filled with volumes on every aspect of art. Opposite the large wooden desk was a table covered with sketches and notes. To the side of this were four easels, on which artworks had been rested. Framed pictures littered the room everywhere. These were works that Douglas had been sent to cast his expert eye over for formal assessment.

"Are these works from the National Gallery?" asked Mallory, looking at a painting of the crucifixion, which had been laid down on the floor.

"Oh no," replied Jane, "the gallery would never allow that. No, these are paintings that were sent by private individuals for him to assess."

"And the owners were happy to just allow him to have them?" Mallory asked in surprised.

Jane nodded.

"Weren't they afraid of a robbery?" he continued.

Jane shook her head. "The room was secured every night and if there was some painting that he thought was especially valuable he would lock it in the vault." With that, she went to a section of wooden wall panel and opened a section of it out to reveal a large safe.

"Have you looked inside?" asked Mallory, thinking that there may be a clue to Douglas's disappearance in there.

"I'm afraid that I don't have the combination," said Jane sadly, "but I was with him when he last locked it and it was empty."

"I'd like to try and open it myself," said the Professor.

"I'm good at these sorts of things. Is that alright with you?"

Jane nodded. "Please feel free. Now if you will excuse me, I will let you get on. I'll arrange some light lunch with cook. I'm sure that this is going to take some time." With that she thanked them again and left them to their work.

"Where on earth to start?" said Mallory, looking around.

"Well I'm going to start with the safe," announced the Professor. "It looks a lot more complex than it is, I'm sure. Jazmine, you start looking through the bookshelves and Mr Mallory you take the desk."

With that, Mallory moved over to the large leather topped pedestal desk. A quick check of the drawers revealed that they were all unlocked and so one by one he pulled them out and placed them carefully on the top, where he proceeded to look through the masses of papers which were kept inside.

"This is impossible!" he said, after finishing examining the fourth drawer. "There is so much here and nothing looks relevant. How are you getting along Professor?"

"Nothing here either," replied the old man, who was now standing next to the open and empty safe. "The combination was easy. It was left on the manufacturers settings, which is a common error." He then broke into a big smile. "Well done Mr Mallory! You are a genius."

"But I haven't found anything."

"Oh you have!" said the Professor, moving over to him. Jazmine, hearing the exchange, abandoned her search and moved over to the desk too, where Mallory was looking slightly confused.

"The drawers Mr Mallory, the drawers," said the Professor excitedly. "Look at the length of them."

He looked down and then saw it. The drawers that he had placed on the desk were significantly shorter than the desk itself. The Professor moved round to the gap where the drawers had been, knelt down and reached inside. "Mmm, solid wood, not a false back." He stood up. "Quick, let's move the drawers. I've an idea."

Mallory and Jazmine picked up the drawers and their contents, and placed them on the floor. When this was done, the Professor grabbed the top of the desk and tried to lift it, but found that he couldn't. "Firmly attached," he muttered. Then he moved round to the back of the desk, running his hand over the lip of the desk and then over the green leather. He stopped, and then ran his thumbnail round the corner of the desk. "Got it!" he said, with a smile. He then very carefully started to pick at the corner, finding the edge of the leather was unstuck. He was then able to pull at it and peel a large section back, to reveal the wood underneath and more importantly a narrow slit at the edge of the desk.

"A vey cunning hiding place indeed!" said the Professor triumphantly. "This desk has been specially crafted to accommodate this nook. Even the leather top was made in such a way that it could be removed and replaced easily without giving away the secret!"

"If we are going to find anything, it's certainly going to be there down in that hidden compartment," said Jazmine, with a smile. "Go on Richard, put your hand inside."

Mallory paused. "Why me?"

Jazmine smiled. "My Father's hand is too big to fit in the hole and my arm is too short to reach the bottom."

Mallory looked at the both of them, sighed and moved round to the slit before taking off his jacket. Then carefully, he placed his fingers into the slot, lowered his hand inside, before suddenly stopping dead. His face contorted in shock.

"Mr Mallory! What's wrong?"

Mallory took a deep breath. "I triggered something. I can feel spikes, or something similar, pressing into my arm!" He tried to move, to retract his arm, but grimaced. "No! I think that they are at an angle. I can put my arm deeper inside, but as soon as I try to withdraw, they dig into me!"

"It sounds like a thief trap," said the Professor. "It's an adaptation to the desk that allows the would-be thief to be captured. The spikes prevent you from removing your arm, unless of course you want to have it ripped to shreds. I think you have been very lucky Mr Mallory. Other versions of this trap involve the arm being severed altogether!"

"Well I don't feel that lucky," complained Mallory. "So what now, how do I get out of here?"

"There must be a release switch somewhere on the desk," said the Professor. "It retracts the spikes. All we need to do is find it! Meanwhile Mr Mallory, keep on! There is a missing piece of the puzzle to find!"

Mallory grunted and put his hands deeper into the cavity, while The Professor and Jazmine searched the desk to find the release lever.

"I've got something!" said Mallory, moments later, "a piece of paper."

"Well done," said the Professor, as he was examining the top of the desk. "Now keep still, I'm sure that we will find the release in a moment!"

But they didn't.

Minutes passed and neither Jazmine nor the Professor could find the release device.

"I would really appreciate it if you could hurry up a bit," said Mallory, with a slight sense of urgency. "It's very uncomfortable bent over like this and I can't help but move slightly, making the spikes dig in!"

"We are doing the best we can," replied Jazmine unsympathetically. "Wait! Got something! Father, take a look at this."

The Professor moved round to where Jazmine was. Under the overhang of the desk at the back was what looked like a small lever, almost flush with the wood.

"Yes, that's it!" confirmed the Professor. "Ah, oh dear!"

"What?" asked Mallory.

"I'm afraid that we have a problem."

"What is it?" sighed Mallory.

"It appears the switch can be moved one of two ways. I presume one to retract the spikes and the other to push them deeper. I have no idea which is which."

"Are there any other options rather than a pure guess?" asked Mallory.

The Professor shook his head. "Sorry, no, trying to tamper with the trap will surely set it off. This is going to be down to chance."

Mallory nodded grimly. "Alright then, do it."

Before anything else could be said or done, the Professor threw the switch.

The desk made a loud clicking noise.

Mallory's face froze.

Jazmine and her Father looked on.

Then, very slowly, Mallory pulled out his unharmed arm, along with a piece of paper.

Mallory unfolded it and looked at the contents. "It's a receipt from The Natural History Museum, for an item deposited. It was signed by a Dr Fredrickson. It's dated just before Douglas's disappearance."

"Does it say what the item is?" asked Jazmine hopefully. Mallory shook his head.

"Well, I think we know that there is only one way to find out," said the Professor with a smile. "You know, I have not been to the Natural History Museum in years!"

CHAPTER 12

The Professor, Jazmine and Mallory arrived at the Natural History Museum's vast entrance hall reception at ten o'clock the following morning. They were met by an eager young assistant who quickly signed them in and then ushered them past the visitors and the reconstruction of the diplodocus dinosaur that dominated the main hall. They went up the large central staircase and through a door marked 'Private' which took them to the areas of the museum that were normally restricted to the general public.

Eventually they were shown into a large room filled with books and benches, on which were placed rows of stuffed birds and animals. They were met by a small balding man in his mid-forties wearing a tweed suit, who announced himself as Dr James Fredrickson. The assistant scurried off. Professor Montacute formally introduced himself, along with Mallory and Jazmine, before getting straight down to business. He explained the situation about the disappearance of Douglas Quinn, and the receipt that they had found hidden in the desk that had led them to the museum. "I'm sorry that I could not explain this over the telephone," he concluded, "but I felt under the circumstances a face to face meeting was required."

"Yes, quite," replied Dr Fredrickson, taking in the information.

"Can you help us?" continued the Professor. "Do you know where Douglas Quinn is?"

"I am afraid that I have no idea of his whereabouts," replied Dr Fredrickson gravely. "I have eagerly been awaiting contact from him myself. But if he has gone missing, that of course explains why I have not heard from him."

"Blast!" exclaimed the Professor, "I was hoping that you would be able to lead us straight to him. Dr Fredrickson, can you tell us why Douglas was in contact with the museum and what did he leave in your care?"

Dr Fredrickson paused, seeming to decide if he should answer, before saying, "Douglas made an important discovery while he was in Vienna. It was, as he put it, 'a clue in a painting,' which he found when looking in a gallery. It led him to travel across the country, where eventually he made an amazing discovery, and please, I do

58

not think that I am being melodramatic here, but this discovery, if proven genuine, as I think it will be, it will without doubt be the most important finding of this century. No matter what is to come! Please come with me!"

Dr Fredrickson took them over to a table on which there was an item completely covered with a large white cloth. "A few weeks ago Douglas came to me with this." Then, almost theatrically, he pulled the cloth away.

On the table, next to a pile of hand written notes, was a large green, crystal skull and next to it a green crystallised brain. The skull looked almost human, apart from the fact that it was slightly larger, having a bigger forehead and eye sockets, and teeth that were almost like fangs.

The Professor, Jazmine and Mallory stared down at it in silence.

"Now please don't let the green crystallisation fool you, although that is remarkable in itself. A crystallisation of this kind can take centuries, but I estimate that this formed in six months, maybe even less. No, the real mystery we are faced with here is the skull itself. I have seen nothing like it before, not quite human and not quite ape, and from all that I have been able to ascertain so far, I believe that it was recently deceased."

"What!" said Mallory, unable to tear his eyes away from the skull. "Are you sure?"

Dr Fredrickson smiled. "Yes! You are by no means looking at an ancient fossil."

Individually the three tried to imagine what the creature would have been like. As if reading their minds Dr Fredrickson started to describe it. "I am estimating that it was about six foot tall, with a larger frame than our own

59

and it no doubt possessed amazing strength. From the teeth, it was undoubtedly a carnivore. I believe that this was a fully grown male, but it's hard to be sure of course, with nothing to compare it to. As for its age, well looking at what I can see through the crystallisation, the way the skull has been formed and comparing it to a human, I would estimate that the creature has some age to it; over a hundred years old."

"A hundred years old?" the Professor found himself asking.

"At least," said Dr Fredrickson, "but there is more here." He picked up the crystallised brain. "As you can obviously see, the brain has been carefully removed and also allowed to crystallise. To my mind this points to some kind of burial ritual, one that would only be carried out by its own kind."

"You mean to say that there could be more of these, these, creatures?" asked Jazmine in surprise.

Dr Fredrickson nodded and carefully placed the brain back down. "Yes, I believe so, somewhere."

The Professor looked down at the items, mulling over the situation. "A crystal skull and brain, the possibility of a new race of beings, this is all hard to take in as real. Are you sure that this is genuine?"

"This is no Piltdown Man fake, if that is what you are getting at."

The Professor gave a smile. "But that has not been proved as a fake - yet."

"Yet," said Fredrickson, with a twinkle in his eye, "but it will be one day."

The year before, fragments of a skull had been discovered at Piltdown in East Sussex. The skull pointed to a creature that could be Darwin's 'missing link' in the evolution of man. It had set the natural history world alight, but others had looked upon the discovery as nothing more than an elaborate hoax.

Dr Fredrickson placed his hand on the skull. "No, as incredible as it is to believe, this is genuine. The green crystal skull here, I believe, belongs to creatures that have remained hidden from mankind for centuries, and I told Douglas as much in a letter."

"That must be the missing verification letter Jane told us about," said Jazmine.

The Professor nodded in agreement.

"Did Douglas tell you the exact location of where the skull was found?" asked Mallory hopefully.

"Sadly, no," replied Dr Fredrickson, shaking his head. "I asked of course, but Douglas was very cagey on this. All I could get out of him was that it was in a mountainous area somewhere in Austria-Hungary, which of course was no real help at all. Other than that he kept the full details to himself."

"Did he give any clues at all?" asked Jazmine. "It's really important."

"Agreed," said the Professor, "my guess is that he went back to wherever it was and that's where he went missing and most importantly of all, where he can be found."

Dr Fredrickson shook his head. "I'm sorry. He just told me that he would make some more personal investigations, and I was to examine the skull and brain and to document my findings."

"And you have?" queried Mallory.

"Indeed," replied Fredrickson, pointing to a large pile of notes and drawings that were beside the tray. "When this

61

discovery is revealed to the world, it needs to be done in the proper manner, with the appropriate investigation and research already done and checked to back it up."

"That would be quite an announcement," pondered the Professor.

"Indeed," replied Dr Fredrickson, "it is one that would literally change our world view as well as turn the scientific community on its head."

Suddenly, from over the other side of the room, the door opened, making everyone look up to see a tall man with blonde hair and piercing blue eyes, dressed in a light suit, enter the room. Over his shoulder was slung a large leather bag and on his belt were a number of pouches. On his head he wore a hat, on which a set of brass goggles were placed.

"I'm sorry Sir, this is a private area, off limits to the public," said Dr Fredrickson, eyeing the strange looking newcomer. "I'm afraid that I will have to ask you to leave."

"Oh, I'll leave," said the man in an Austrian accent, as from his pocket he produced what looked like a modified pistol with some sort of glass cartridge on the top, inside which bright blue sparks danced, "when I reclaim what has been stolen from us."

CHAPTER 13

The man with the strange gun moved forward menacingly. "All of you, put your hands in the air and don't try anything funny. My weapon is set on stun and at a wide burst. The electrical charge it will fire will render you all unconscious for hours."

"What kind of weapon is that?" said the Professor, raising his hands. "I've not seen anything like that before."

"That is none of your concern," answered the gunman dismissively. "Now, all of you move back towards the glass cabinet!"

Slowly they did as they were bid and waited to see what would happen next. The gunman walked forward to the table and looked at the bundle of documents. "Right Dr Fredrickson, I presume that these are the notes you have made on the skull."

Dr Fredrickson nodded.

"Is that all of them?"

"Yes," replied Fredrickson, cursing himself that he had not kept some of the notes in a separate file.

"Are there any copies?"

Fredrickson shook his head. "No, that's all there is."

The blonde man then picked up the documents and placed them into his large bag, followed by the strange skull and the brain; all the time, keeping a close eye on his captors.

"And now," said the blonde gunman standing back, "I must leave you. Our paths will never cross again, but I would like to thank you for your kind co-operation in this matter. I was having problems gaining access to this area of the Museum, where I knew the skull was located. But with your visit I was able to 'attach' myself to your party, so I could reclaim what your friend Douglas Quinn took from us. The assistant who signed you in was more than happy to do the same for me when I told him I was with you, but running late."

The Professor groaned. They had inadvertently brought this stranger right to the skull.

"What about Quinn?" Mallory asked suddenly. "Where is he? Is he still alive?"

"Yes," replied the gunman, watching him carefully, "he is alive, but I am sad to say that neither you nor anyone else will ever see him again. It would be best for you to just put him out of your minds."

"For who?"

"For all concerned," replied the gunman. Then from the man's jacket, there came a strange sound. He reached inside and pulled out what looked like the handset of a telephone and proceeded to speak into it, before putting it away. "That was my colleague," he explained, "checking that all is going to plan. Now I have what I came after, I must go."

"But hold on," said the Professor distractedly, "where was the rest of the telephone? How does it connect into the telephone network? Where are the connecting wires?"

"It is wireless, and it runs on its own special 'network' as you put it."

"Interesting," replied the Professor, clearly fascinated by what he had just seen. "What kind of signal do you get?"

"Depends where I am," confessed the gunman, almost casually. "Tunnels are a problem and sometimes I can hardly hear what the person at the other end is saying, but enough of this small talk! Now, I have to go." And keeping the gun trained on them, he moved backwards towards the door, slamming it shut behind him. Then from beyond, there was the sound of the strange weapon being fired at the lock, which momentarily glowed and then went back to its normal colour.

Professor Montacute was over by the door like a flash. First he touched the handle with his finger, unsure if it was going to be hot. Then, satisfied it was safe to touch, he grabbed the handle to turn it, but it was now stuck fast.

"Are we locked in?" asked Dr Fredrickson.

"More than that I'm afraid," said the Professor. "That gun of his has appeared to have welded the lock shut!"

Mallory moved forward to the door and kicked at it until it flew open, and the small party were able to run out of the room in pursuit.

They arrived back to the top of the staircase that led into the main reception, while their quarry was starting to run across the hallway. With a superhuman effort, Mallory charged down the staircase taking the steps three at a time, with The Professor almost matching his pace and Jazmine and Dr Fredrickson not far behind. At the bottom of the staircase, Mallory and the Professor opted to run down the left side of the giant Diplodocus skeleton, the same side the blonde man had chosen.

"Stop that man someone," called out The Professor, as he and Mallory drew level to the skeletal tail. "He's a thief who has stolen valuable samples from the museum!"

The blonde man, who was now past the head of the skeleton, turned round and again drew the strange gun and fired. Only this time, he aimed his weapon at the reconstruction of the dinosaur itself. For a moment the whole skeleton seemed to light up and strange sparks flew off the structure. Then there was a groaning noise, and the skeleton began to shake and shudder. The supports which held the bones together seemed to disintegrate, sending the bones crashing down and spilling all over the floor, causing Mallory and the Professor, who were now halfway along the dinosaur's body, to dive out of the way. Mallory made it clear, but the Professor found himself pinned under a large section of bones, by his foot.

Around them people screamed and started to run in all directions in panic. Museum staff, unsure what to do, ran forward trying to keep calm. There were cries for the police and someone even yelled out that this was an attack by the Suffragettes.

"Professor!" cried Mallory, arriving at his side.

"Are you hurt?"

"I'm fine," he cried in response, trying to free his trapped foot. "Don't worry about me, I'll be alright! Just get after that man before he escapes. If we lose him, we lose Douglas for sure!"

"Too late Professor," said Mallory, looking into the distance as the mysterious man disappeared out of the door to the museum. "He's gone! I'll never be able to catch him now."

With one supreme pull, Professor Montacute managed to get his foot free, and with the help of Jazmine and Dr Fredrickson, who had now appeared by his side, rose to his feet.

"Damn and blast that man!" cried Dr Fredrickson, looking around at the fallen pieces of the museum's central exhibit. "It will take months to put 'Dippy' back together, assuming of course he is undamaged, which is highly unlikely. By thunder, I hope the board of Directors won't try and use this as an excuse to replace him with that blasted blue whale they keep going on about!"

"There are other concerns here," said the Professor gravely. "We have lost the crystal skull and all the related documentation. Those were the only leads we had to these mysterious creatures, and any chance of finding Douglas. Without them I think he is beyond us."

"How on earth do we break the news to Jane?" enquired Jazmine. "The news he is gone will destroy her!"

"And the world of art and culture would have lost a great man!" added Dr Fredrickson sadly, realising the wider picture. "Did you know that as well as an art expert he was also a talented cartographer?"

"I had no idea," said the Professor, already trying to work out what support they could give Jane.

"His skill at the R.G.S. is going to be missed, as well as the various charities that he supported."

"The R.G.S.?" inquired Mallory.

"Yes, the Royal Geographic Society," expanded Dr Fredrickson. "He was a frequent visitor, helping restore and interpret maps and charts, using his various skills."

A smile spread across the Professor's face. "The Royal Geographic Society, of course!"

Mallory nodded, realising what was going through the Professor's mind. "It has to be worth a look."

"More than that," added Jazmine. "It has to be the answer to the problem."

"Indeed," said the Professor, "I'll wager that on his return to London, Douglas also paid the Society a visit and used its vast archive to research the area where he found the crystallised skull! There is no finer collection in the world of maps, charts and travel accounts."

"So, all is not lost?" queried Dr Fredrickson.

"No, not yet anyway," replied the Professor with a smile.

CHAPTER 14

The Professor made a lengthy telephone call to the Royal Geographical Society, from Dr Fredrickson's office. It seemed that they had no idea that Douglas was missing and on hearing that the Professor was conducting a private investigation, they immediately offered any assistance they could. And so an appointment was made for that very day for the Professor and Mallory to pay them a visit in the hope of finding a clue as to where Douglas could have gone. While, in the meantime, Jazmine had decided to stay at the Natural History Museum to help Dr Fredrickson explain what had happened and to lend a hand with checking the condition of the remains of 'Dippy'.

At around two o'clock the Professor and Mallory arrived at the Royal Geographical Societies new headquarters, 'Lowther Lodge', which was located in South Kensington. They were promptly admitted and taken straight to the main library and reading room, an area that was stacked floor to ceiling with books, covering every conceivable subject connected to the geography of the earth; everything from directories listing the latest population statistics, to hand written individual accounts, to travellers who had submitted their observations to paper and had passed it onto the society.

In preparation for their visit, Douglas's most recent official work with the Society had been gathered and laid out on a table for viewing. Left alone, the Professor and Mallory quickly looked over the documents, but had to dismiss it as not useful to their search, as the material brought to them related to areas of the South Pole. Information which was gathered the previous year on what should have been a scientific expedition, but had turned into something much more, a race to the South Pole, which ended in a terrible loss of life.

"So what do we do now?" asked Mallory, carefully placing down Scott's journal, which he had been looking through.

"We have to turn our attention to the wider library," replied the Professor, looking around, "focusing at first, of course, on the area relating to Austria-Hungary."

Mallory groaned. "That could take some time, there are a lot of books here and we still don't know exactly what we are looking for."

"Well initially," said the Professor, "I think we need to check to see if there is anything obviously out of place; such as books missing or signs that there have been any removed and put back out of order and the like."

"But if there is, that does not mean that it was down to Douglas. After all, other people use the library as well," pointed out Mallory.

"Agreed," replied the Professor. "This is very much chancing our arm, but it is that or having to read books one by one, although that option still could lie ahead of us."

And so the search began, as the Professor had instructed, with any suspicious book or journal being removed and examined more closely in the hope it would give them the clue that they were hoping to find. After twenty minutes it was Mallory who discovered what they were looking for. Volumes one and two of 'A Provisional History of Austrian villages 1836 - 1900' were set back slightly from the other books on the shelf, indicating that one, if not both of the books, had been moved and then replaced at some point. Looking more closely, Mallory found the clue that they had been searching for, and triumphantly called to the Professor who met him at one of the reading tables.

"I found this tucked in the pages of volume two," observed Mallory, as he held up a piece of paper.

The Professor took it to examine more closely. "Why, it's a pamphlet from the Natural History Museum advertising an upcoming exhibition which actually started two weeks ago. Douglas must have picked it up and used it as an impromptu book marker. Good work Mr Mallory. This is indeed the clue that we have been searching for." Putting the pamphlet aside, the Professor then turned his attention to the page where it had acted as a book mark. The title of the chapter jumped out at him. 'Karlstad.' Immediately he started to scan over the chapter.

"Well Mr Mallory, it says here that Karlstad is a large town near to the border with Switzerland. It is well known as a tourist retreat, attracting people from all over Europe and even beyond. Above it, in the mountain, there is a large fortress left over from the early Middle-Ages, which has now long since been abandoned.

"That fortress does seem to offer some tantalising possibilities," said Mallory.

"Indeed," said the Professor, scratching his beard thoughtfully. "It could be a perfect location for the creatures to hide or it could even serve as a prison."

"You don't think that Douglas could be being held there?" replied Mallory in disbelief.

The Professor shrugged. "It's possible, but of course there is only going to be one way to find out for sure."

"A visit to Karlstad?"

"Yes, a visit to Karlstad. Once there we will be able to make some enquiries. Ah, now, this is interesting!" said the Professor, looking intently at the page he had open. "This section goes into the history of the town and there is an illustration of the main street, showing one of the main buildings, a hotel called 'Post,' one of the oldest in the town. Underneath it there are some dots where someone had rested a pencil."

"They must have been made by Douglas," said Mallory. The Professor nodded. "It seems likely. He would have to stay somewhere in the town. I think we have our starting point! I wager that's where Douglas stayed when he visited Karlstad, but my gut tells me that the answers we seek are going to be far above the town, maybe even in the mountains themselves."

Mallory nodded, it seemed a logical conclusion. "I have a feeling that we are going to end up doing some climbing. How are your mountaineering skills Professor?"

He shrugged. "Not as good as they used to be I'm afraid. I think that we are going to have to enlist some help with this venture."

"A local guide?" suggested Mallory.

"No. We are already aware that there is a campaign to keep Douglas hidden, so I have a strong suspicion that we would not find anyone willing to help us. We are going to have to recruit help here and take them with us."

Mallory paused. "I've got a distant cousin, George. He's a teacher at Charterhouse. The summer holidays are coming up in a few weeks and I'm sure he'd jump at the chance to help us. He is always up for a challenge and, most importantly of all, has a natural talent for mountain climbing."

The Professor paused. The idea was sound, but he knew that Mallory had overlooked the obvious choice. "There is of course…" he left the sentence hanging.

Mallory paused. "Yuri Romanovsky?"

The Professor nodded. "No disrespect to your cousin, but no matter how good he is, it is safe to say that Yuri will be better. He can handle himself in almost any situation and is an expert marksman, can speak the language and has the stamina of an ox."

Mallory paused. They had worked with the big Russian the previous year. His skills were not in question and he would be ideal for any mountain expedition, but there was one key underlying issue. Yuri was a larger than life character, partly fuelled by the large amounts of vodka he regularly consumed. It was a problem that had gotten him into a lot of trouble in the past, and his appetite for alcohol had only got stronger.

"But we don't know where he is," said Mallory.

"I do," said the Professor. "He's been working as a security guard at Marshall & Snelgrove Department Store, here in London, for the past six months"

"A far cry from his former life in the Royal household at the Tsar's Palace," remarked Mallory, finding himself almost feeling sorry for the big Russian.

"Indeed," said the Professor, "but I am sure that one day he will be able to return home and to regain all that he has lost. Who knows, this could be the very first step!"

"Do you think that he will join us?" asked Mallory.

The Professor smiled. "There is only going to be one way to find out! Mr Mallory, I think we need to go to Oxford Street for a shopping trip!"

CHAPTER 15

Professor Montacute and Richard Mallory arrived at
Marshall & Snelgrove Department store, which was
located on the north side of Oxford Street, a few hours
later. They entered the building and found themselves in
the women's section, which consisted of various counters
and displays showing off perfume and fragrances, as well
as ladies accessories like hats, gloves and scarfs. The two
men, clearly feeling out of place, looked around in the
hope of seeing Yuri, but across the vast sales floor he was
nowhere in sight.

"No sign of him," said Mallory. "What if it's his day
off?"

The Professor shook his head. "No, he works weekdays
through opening hours. He must be here somewhere."

"Are you sure that he's on the ground floor?"

The Professor nodded. "Yes, he told me that he was
particularly hired to work this area due to the amount of
small items that are easy to take, as well as to ensure that
the women who work here were not harassed in any way
by male customers."

"Judging by some of her recent activity and views, I'm
sure Jazmine would have something to say about that
concept," said Mallory with a smile, "and none of it
pleasant!"

"Yes, well, hopefully after the events of Epsom, she will
have a rethink about the methods used to attain her chosen
goal. Things are certainly unbalanced regarding the gender
divide and need changing, but I can't see it happening
through the methods that they currently employ."

"So what would change things?" asked Mallory curiously.

The Professor shrugged. "Either small changes over a long period of time, and I am talking decades, or some major event that will shake up the entire country."

"Let's hope it's the former rather than the latter," said Mallory.

"I agree," replied the Professor, still looking around for the Russian. "Oh blast it, where could he be? We'll just have to ask someone." With that, he went over to the nearest counter and was greeted by a young sales assistant. "Excuse me Miss, I wonder if you could help. We are looking for a friend of ours who works here, a Security Guard, Yuri Romanovsky."

She smiled. "Yes, you have just missed him. He went rushing off to the women's wear section on the first floor." She pointed over to a grand looking staircase in the middle of the store. "Just follow the stairs up."

"Thank you Miss," Replied the Professor and, with that, he and Mallory headed towards the staircase.

"Sounds a bit strange," said Mallory, "him having to 'rush off' as she said."

"Yes, I wonder what he was doing. Well we'll find out soon enough."

It did not take them long to get to the Women's Wear section. As soon as they stepped onto the shop floor from the stairs, they spotted the figure of Yuri, who was trying to hide, and failing to do so miserably, behind a mannequin of a woman in a green dress.

The Russian, who was dressed in a standard Marshall & Snelgrove guard's uniform, was six foot two tall. His dark short hair was parted to the right and he sported a large black moustache. He was in his late thirties, but his weathered face gave him the appearance of being a decade older.

Just as The Professor and Mallory were about to move forward, the Russian looked round and spotted them. He gave them a big grin, then put his fingers to his lips and beckoned them over.

"Professor Montacute, Captain Mallory," he greeted them in a whisper, as they sidled up to him, "'Tis good to see you again, but hush now! There is trouble!"

"What's going on?" said Mallory, noting that Yuri's broken English had not improved through his time living and working in London.

Yuri pointed to a young man in a brown suit and cloth cap lurking near the long counter where the till was located. "That man is ex-boyfriend of sales assistant. She broke things off but yet he continually comes in to bother her."

"So where is she?" asked the Professor, looking round. "I don't see her."

"She is gone on tea break, but back soon. He will try and speak to her and make a scene. Then Yuri steps in! I will ask him to leave politely. Then if he refuses I will have to be more forceful. Look there!"

From round a corner a pretty young girl in her late teens appeared and the man, on seeing her, rushed forward, calling her name, but stopped in surprise as Yuri moved out from his hiding place and started to walk towards him. "Hey! You there! Stop!"

The man turned, eyeing the Russian. First he was surprised, but then a look of anger and desperation crossed his face. He reached into his pocket and pulled out a knife.

On seeing the blade the female assistant he had come to see let out a scream, and then ran off to hide.

"No, no," said Yuri calmly, walking forward. "You don't want to do that. Put knife down. No sense in doing something stupid. I used to be in the Tsar's Private Guard! You don't stand chance!" Seeing the big Russian approach him the man paused, swore, then also ran.

"Ha! You not get away that easily!" said Yuri, heading after him. Not wanting to be left behind, Mallory and the Professor joined the chase.

The knifeman ran down the walkway heading towards the back of the store. As he did so, he momentarily stopped to topple over part of the display onto the customer walkway, but this obstacle was of course no real hindrance for his pursuers who simply jumped over it.

"He's heading for the lifts," noted Mallory, seeing a directional sign overhead.

"No problem!" said Yuri. "They take ages to be called. We have him!"

However, just as the man reached the customer lifts, to his right, two doors that had a sign saying 'Staff Only – Service Area', under a glass viewing window, suddenly swung open and a large wire framed cage appeared filled with stock. Seeing his chance, the knife man grabbed the cage and pulled it through the door along with the startled sales assistant who was innocently taking out the replenishment stock to the shop floor. The knifeman then turned the cage around towards his pursuers, and pushed it hard at them, also sparing the time to quickly turn and push the sales assistant away. He then threw himself through the now slowly closing doors of the stock area, where they slammed shut behind him. Yuri, the Professor and Mallory arrived a few moments behind, having dodged round the cage of stock. Through the window, the knifeman stared out at them and smiled triumphantly.

"Blast it!" cried Yuri. "He is in what we call 'Lift Area'. In there are large rubbish bins and two lifts for staff to use for stock and the like. Doors to Lift Area have combination lock so customers cannot enter."

"What's the combination?" asked Mallory, looking at the numbered lock.

Yuri shrugged. "I don't know! I never remember. My memory is not what it used to be."

"More of a case that you are too drunk to remember!" interjected a sales assistant, who had now joined them.

"That not true," protested Yuri. Although in reality, he knew that he was relying more and more on his beloved vodka.

"Do you know the combination?" Mallory asked the sales assistant. Glancing over, through the glass, he could see that the knifeman was now standing calmly at the concertina door of the right hand lift, having pressed the button which would summon it.

"It's 63254," said the assistant, casting a disapproving glance at Yuri.

"Good," said the Professor. "Now get yourself clear and make sure that the police have been called."

The assistant nodded, and then disappeared off.

Mallory moved to the door and entered the numbers on the small keypad. As he did so, inside the lift area, the stock lift had arrived and the knifeman had already started to pull back the concertina doors ready to enter. "There, done!" cried Mallory, as he started to reach for the handle of the door, but Yuri was there before him, grabbing the side of the door and throwing it open before diving through.

In one quick movement the knifeman threw himself into the lift, slamming the doors shut behind him, before reaching over to the control panel. He pressed a button and the lift started to ascend leaving Yuri, the Professor and Mallory behind.

CHAPTER 16

Swearing in Russian, Yuri hit the call button to the lift on the left hand side and a few moments later the sound of it could be heard descending. "Lucky for us he take right hand lift," he explained quickly with a smile. "That has only one stop on top floor. If he take this left one he could stop on any floor and we lose him."

"What's on the top floor?" Mallory asked.

"Maintenance workshop and Visual Display Department," replied Yuri.

"Visual Display?" queried Mallory.

"Yes, where they keep dummies and props for displays throughout store and main window. There is even Santa's Grotto there. Ah! Here is lift." With that Yuri took hold of the door handle and opened the outer door, followed by the inner concertina door and the three entered the service lift. Yuri closed the doors behind them and pressed the button that would take them to the top floor. "Now," said Yuri, as the lift started to ascend, "it good to see you both again, but I presume that your visit is more than to exchange pleasantries and talk of old times."

"Indeed," said the Professor, "a friend of ours has going missing and we are going to mount a search to find him. We have traced him to a town in Austria-Hungary called

Karlstad and we believe he might be in a mountain fortress."

"And you think that I might be of use with my climbing skills?"

"Exactly."

The Russian nodded and smiled. "Sounds like fun. I could use break. I have holiday time owing and could do with time away from my Manager. He does not like me!"

The lift suddenly came to an abrupt halt, Yuri opened the doors and they all stepped out into a narrow section of corridor. The first thing Yuri did was to look at the other lift the knifeman had used. The doors were open and the empty lift was there.

"Good!" said the Russian, "he here. Small possibility he arrive and then go back down. As lift still here this only place he can be."

"So where would he go?" asked Mallory.

"Either in Workshop," he pointed to two doors almost in front of them, "or in Visual Display." He then pointed to another set of double doors at the end of the corridor. Then the Russian moved forward to the doors of the workshop and gently pushed them. "Locked," he said.

"Is there any possibility he could have gone in and locked them from the inside?" asked Mallory.

Yuri then reached up to the top of the door frame and felt around, and moments later produced a key that was hidden on the wooden lip. "No, he not in there. Workshop kept locked when not in use and this only key. He must be in Visual Display room. Come on."

The three of them, Yuri leading, headed towards the end of the corridor, where he placed his hand on the door and slowly pushed it open, half expecting some sort of attack, but none came. Then carefully the three of them entered the large room and allowed the door to swing shut behind them.

The Visual Display room itself seemed to be run on organised chaos. Although the contents did seem to roughly be placed into sections, nothing was placed neatly or in order. Behind the door they came through, to the left, along the wall, was a large shelving unit with small compartments that was filled with different types of ticketing that was used to display prices in the sales. In front of them, to the left, was an army of mannequins ready to be taken to the shop floor and dressed. Along the wall in front of them was a large shelf unit, on which there were props; everything from vases and dolls to tins that were used to help show off the products of the store. Leaning against the edge of the shelf unit were rolls and rolls of various materials and decorative papers, again all used to enhance the displays. Most of the room, however, was taken up with display plinths and the larger items that would be used in the main displays. There was a selection of small stuffed imitation animals, a side of a carriage, a guard's sentry box, fake trees, deckchairs and even a giant clock face.   Behind this at the very back of the room they could just make out large fake trees, part of what looked like a log cabin and a number of fake Snowmen and penguins used as part of the Christmas displays.

"This place is oddly unsettling," said Mallory.

Yuri nodded. "Yes, I think it has something to do with mannequins, especially where there is only head." He pointed to a shelf which had a row of mannequin heads, the faces staring back at them blankly.

"Right," said Mallory with a shiver, "the sooner we find this knifeman the sooner we can get out of here!"

"Agreed," said Yuri, "he can't be far. But be careful, when cornered wild animal the most dangerous! I know from my hunting trips in Russia."

With that the Professor swiftly removed the blade from his sword stick and held it up with a smile. "Not a real problem. I always come prepared."

Carefully the three of them started to make a search of the room. However, after a few minutes the knifeman remained undiscovered, despite the lack of apparent hiding places.

"I can't understand it," said Mallory, who joined the Professor and Yuri towards the back of the room, which had been designated for all the Christmas displays. "He doesn't seem to be here."

"Well he could not have slipped past us," said the Professor. "For one thing we haven't heard the lift being activated. Yuri, is there any other exit here?"

"No, unless he decided to climb out of window, but all of them locked closed," said the Russian, blinking and wiping his eyes.

"What's wrong?" asked Mallory.

"Nothing, I think I had too much vodka on morning break. I swear Santa moved," said the Russian, pointing to a large throne just by them on which was sitting a large stuffed figure of St Nicholas dressed in a red robe which had white trimming and a facemask to which a beard was attached.

On seeing the mannequin, the same thought crossed Professor Montacute and Richard Mallory's mind, but before either of them could say anything, the figure of

Santa Clause let out a yell and sprang forward from the throne. His target was Mallory, who he reached and grabbed hold of, turning him round before anyone could react, and placed the knife against his neck. "Nobody move, or I'll slit his throat open! Now back off!" Then seeing the Professor and Yuri move out of his way, he started to slowly move towards the door, taking Mallory with him.

"Yuri?" said the Professor, seeing the Russian hesitate. "Yuri, come on! Pay attention! Do something!"

"I can't!" he replied. "It Santa Clause! I can't attack Santa!"

"It's not Santa Clause you fool!" barked the Professor, moving forward. As he did so, the knifeman pressed the blade harder into Mallory's throat. However, that act seemed to snap Yuri back to reality and he shot out his left hand and seized a nearby small red pot, which was placed on a plinth, and then hurled it through the air. Before the Santa-knifeman had a chance to react the pot hit him square in the face. He immediately let go of Mallory and the knife, falling backwards, crashing to the floor. His head hit the concrete surface with a thud, knocking him out cold.

"Well done Yuri!" cried the Professor, giving the Russian a hearty slap on the back. "Although you had me worried for a moment. That was an excellent throw."

"Um, er, actually I was aiming past him," confessed the Russian, looking a bit sheepish. "As I said, too much vodka on morning break. Put aim off slightly, still all good!"

"Apart from the fact I nearly had my throat slit," said Mallory with annoyance, coming over to join them while rubbing his neck.

Yuri shrugged. "You have just small cut. Sure you have done worse shaving in morning." He looked down at the knifeman. "When police arrive they will take him away and no doubt he will go to prison. At least he won't be harassing that young girl anymore."

"Indeed," said the Professor, "and after he's dealt with, you can have a chat with your boss about getting a couple of weeks off."

Yuri smiled. "Yes, I can almost taste the orange schnapps!"

CHAPTER 17

With the likely location of the missing Douglas Quinn discovered and the recruitment of Yuri Romanovsky to their cause, Professor Montacute then put in motion the necessary arrangements for the visit to the mysterious town of Karlstad. The final element to this was a farewell meal at Berkeley Square to which Dr Fredrickson, along with Jane Quinn, had been invited to attend. There was one noticeable absentee at the dinner table though, as Yuri, who despite his assurances that he would be on time, had not arrived.

After waiting for an hour, it had been decided that the meal Mrs Paddick had prepared would have to be served, to avoid being totally ruined. The roast dinner was duly eaten, while they engaged in small talk. Although the subject of why they were all there seemed to be skirted around, not wanting to address the issue until Yuri was present. Lucy and Jazmine got on particularly well, and Lucy was enthralled to hear about Jazmine's involvement in the Suffragettes, as well as the events of the Titanic, Highgate and her other adventures.

As the main course was finished, Dr Fredrickson turned the attention to the empty chair. "Look, I really hate to be the one to say it, but it looks as though this man of yours has abandoned the venture before you have even started."

"No," said the Professor quickly, "I have every faith Yuri will turn up. His time keeping is a little errant occasionally that is all."

Then, as if on cue, a rapid hammering could be heard from outside the front door.

"There," said the Professor with a hint of relief, "I told you he would come. Mrs Paddick, would you mind?"

In response Mrs Paddick, who had been in the process of starting to clear away the plates, turned and left to answer the door and a short while later Yuri burst into the dining-room. He looked dishevelled and had a newly formed bruise across his brow. Snapping his heels together he stood to attention before announcing himself. "Good evening, I am Yuri Alexander Romanovsky. I must first apologise for being late. It has been an interesting afternoon." With that he went over to the table, took the empty seat and immediately poured a large glass of wine before starting to help himself to the remaining food that was in the various serving dishes.

The Professor formally introduced the Russian to Jane and Dr Fredrickson before asking him why he was late.

"I had disagreement with my Manager at Department Store," said Yuri with a wry smile. "He was not keen on giving me time for our trip, we argued and he called me a drunkard."

"Please tell me you didn't hit him!" exclaimed Jazmine.

The Russian smiled and shrugged. "I tried to throw gentle punch, but missed, fell over and hit my head; all quite embarrassing. Anyway, good news is that I don't have to worry about going back there, so does not matter how long this venture take. Mallory, pass me the horse radish sauce if you please."

Slightly shocked, Mallory did as he was requested. His look was reflected on the faces of Jane and Dr Fredrickson. Seeing the uncertainty, the Professor quickly tried to move things along. "Right, now that we are all here, I think that it is time we got down to business, don't you? Now the plan is as follows. Mr Mallory and Yuri here will travel to Karlstad and book themselves into the hotel Post where we believe Douglas stayed. From there they will be able to make a few discreet enquiries about his visit there and where he could be."

"Why you and Jazmine not coming with us?" asked Yuri, as he took a bite out of a bread roll.

"I'm afraid that the University simply could not grant myself and Jazmine immediate leave," replied the Professor, with more than a hint of disappointment in his voice. "They have always been very flexible with my little excursions before, but sadly on this occasion, they just cannot accommodate me, and of course as Jazmine is my assistant, she will not be allowed to leave either. It is an inconvenience but not the end of the world. I don't want to delay things so it will be up to you and Mallory, until we can catch you up."

"When do you think you will both get to Karlstad to join us?" asked Yuri.

"Best possible scenario, two to three weeks," replied Jazmine. "But it may be a little longer. We will get to you as quickly as we can,"

"Of course there is the possibility," said Mallory, "that we could end up finding Douglas before you arrive."

"That's what I am secretly hoping for," said the Professor with a smile, "but I somehow doubt it. By our conversation with that mysterious blonde man at the Natural History Museum we can assume that things are not going to be straightforward at all."

"What if the research indicates Douglas is at this Upper Karlstad you mentioned?" asked Dr Fredrickson. "Will Mallory and Yuri venture up there?"

The Professor shook his head. "No, I have a strong feeling that this adventure will take us up to the fortress, and even the mountains beyond, but I want to be there when that happens."

"Ah, I bet you are thinking of the mysterious creatures," said Fredrickson excitedly.

The Professor nodded. "Yes, and that is the secondary part of the mission, well, depending of course how finding Douglas works out."

"But if these creatures exist, and it seems that they do," said Fredrickson, "you will bring back some sort of proof?"

The Professor nodded. "That is the hope, although we don't know what form that would take."

"Another crystallised skull would be ideal," said Dr Fredrickson with a smile. "I could make another examination of it and would have something to show the scientific community."

"Yes, it would," replied the Professor. "But that cannot be guaranteed, although we will try and bring back some physical evidence, if we can find it. However, we do have other methods in mind, isn't that right Mr Mallory?"

"Yes," replied Mallory, "we intend to take with us a Kodak camera. What we want is to try to bring back photos of the creatures, assuming of course they do exist."

"That's a good idea," said Dr Fredrickson, with a hint of uncertainty. "But surely you don't think you can expect one of them to stand and pose for a photo do you?"

Mallory smiled. "I'm sure that with a bit of luck we can manage something."

"But even if you get a decent photo," continued Dr Fredrickson, "it will be questioned, scrutinized and most likely disbelieved. People may just think that it was someone dressed up in a costume, or that the photo was faked in some other way. Did you know that the photos of the 1906 San Francisco earthquake were reported to be falsified? The Mayor wanted to convince the world that it was not as bad as it seemed, and so damage was actually removed and even destroyed buildings were added back in."

"I heard that too," said the Professor, "but the photos are the best option, short of a live specimen, another skull or something else. At the very least I am hoping that a photo, backed up by a sworn statement that you had a skull in your possession, would be enough to tweak the interest of sponsors here in London. Hopefully then we could mount a proper investigation with the required resources behind us."

"A full expedition eh?" said Dr Fredrickson with a smile. "Well the locals won't like that. Think how they sent someone to come all the way to London to ensure that all evidence of the creatures were secured, and that factor will no doubt play a big part when you arrive there and start asking questions."

"We are not expecting an easy ride of things," said Mallory. "But I am sure we will be able to cope."

"Indeed," continued the Professor, "especially with the added skills that Yuri will bring to our small team."

"That is of course assuming that he is able to stay sober and awake long enough," said Dr Fredrickson, nodding in the direction of Yuri, who was now fast asleep in the chair.

Professor Montacute groaned inwardly. "Um, yes, he will be fine. Mrs Paddick, would you be kind enough to bring in the coffee? Oh and you had better leave the pot. I have a feeling that it will be needed."

CHAPTER 18

The following Friday evening, Mallory and Yuri arrived at Karlstad's railway station just as the big brass clock, with ornate open workings, struck eight thirty. Carrying their luggage they walked down the road from the station. They soon found themselves passing a large church before entering the town square which was lined by three storey houses with long sloped roofs, in keeping with the Tyrolean style. Each had a wooden balcony, from the front of which hung flower boxes that were filled with all kinds of blooms. Most of them looked to be hotels or cafes. Many of them had tables and chairs out the front for patrons to sit outside and eat. Two of the buildings looked very plain. Both had signs outside indicating one was a Post Office and the other was a Pharmacy. Outside the Post

Office was a man with a small stand selling newspapers. He was easy to see due to the brightly coloured patchwork coat he was wearing. One particular building stood out from the rest. The outside was blackened, the windows boarded up and the roof partially collapsed. It had clearly been ravaged by a recent fire. Slightly down from this, there was a small queue lining up in front of a man who was operating an elaborate looking machine housed in a small hut. The machine had three large brass barrels which was powered by a large pump. At the request of each customer he would go to a barrel, open a valve that was on the front, and dispense a large portion of what looked like ice-cream into a cone or tub from a central tap. A number of people were milling around the square, many of whom seemed to be wearing hats with goggles attached, as well as various leather pouches that hung from belts and bandoliers. Mallory and Yuri then turned their attention to the main street that branched off the square, where their hotel was located.

The Hotel Post, which dominated the end of the street, was really two large buildings that had been joined with a smaller structure in the middle, which served as a main entrance. Mallory and Yuri entered through the main doors and found themselves standing in the hotel foyer. On the right was an open area filled with lounge chairs and tables. On the left was the reception desk, behind which was a woman in her mid-thirties with blonde hair and blue eyes. She was dressed in traditional Tyrolean attire, which consisted of a long red Tyrolean dress called a Dirndl, and a low cut trachtenblus'n blouse with a long pinafore which went down to her ankles. Although, unusually, around her waist was a brown leather belt that had three large brown pouches hanging from it and on her head she wore a small pair of brass goggles.

"Einzelzimmer zwei, bitte," said Mallory.

The woman smiled. "Would you prefer that we speak in English?"

Mallory nodded and returned a grateful smile. "Yes, please. I'm afraid that my Austrian is not very good!"

"Oh that won't be a problem here," she replied. "Practically everyone here speaks English."

"They do?" said Mallory in surprise.

She nodded. "We have to, also French and Spanish, due to the amount of visitors to our town. My name is Heidi by the way. My family owns the hotel."

"Pleased to meet you, my name is Richard Mallory and this is my friend Yuri Romanovsky. We would like to book two rooms."

Heidi put the goggles over her eyes and began to flick through the register. "I'll see what I can do. We are busy due to our famous Dumpling Festival on Sunday. I'm not sure what we have left."

"Dumpling Festival?" repeated Mallory.

The girl nodded. "The main street and town Square is turned into an open air restaurant, where various dumplings are served all day. There is also a small fair and various other entertainments." She continued to flick through the book. "How long did you want to stay for?"

Mallory shrugged. "Two weeks?"

"Well, I can book you and your friend into a twin room for four days. I might be able to shuffle things around later, but that's all that is possible at the moment."

"That's fine, we'll take it. We also have friends who will be joining us at some point," said Mallory, thinking of the arrival of Jazmine and the Professor. "Will they be able to get rooms?"

Heidi smiled and nodded. "I'm sure we will be able to accommodate them. Just let me know, as soon as you can, when they will be here. Now, that will be five shillings a night each; that includes a buffet breakfast and an evening meal. I'm afraid that you have missed tonight's sitting, but our Strube, what you would call a bar, does have a limited menu. Or the town does have some good restaurants, which will serve right up to midnight."

"That's fine. We ate on the train a little earlier," said Yuri, with a smile.

Heidi tapped down to the big hotel register that was on the counter. "Could I just get you to sign the hotel register, please?"

Mallory picked up the pen on the desk and started to sign in.

"Um, interesting glasses you have there, if you don't mind me saying," said Yuri, who had been fixed on the goggles since they had arrived.

Heidi smiled. "Yes, they are a bit unusual. We have an optician here in the town that makes them to his own design. Quite a few of the residents here have them."

At that point a telephone on the counter behind Heidi rang and, excusing herself, she turned to answer it. Taking the opportunity, Mallory quickly flicked back through the hotel register trying to find the details of when Douglas had signed in. To his surprise he found a page of the register had been removed, neatly cut out of the book, at around the time it was suspected that Douglas would have stayed there.

"Yuri, you see this?"

The Russian nodded, realising the implication. The owners of the hotel were trying to hide the fact that Douglas had stayed there.

Then from directly behind them was a growling sound. Mallory and Yuri turned round to find that they were being looked over by two angry looking German Boxer dogs, who had positioned themselves a few feet away. Both of the dogs seemed unhappy at the presence of the men, and were not afraid to show it.

"Sorry, don't mind them," said Heidi, who had finished the phone call and returned to them. "They are our pets, Felix and Casper. They look far fiercer than they really are! It's almost time for their food. I expect that they are just hungry."

"I think we have been chosen for main course!" said Yuri, a little worriedly.

"Oh not at all!" said Heidi. "The only danger you would be in from them is from being licked to death!" She then looked at the dogs sternly and in a sharp voice spoke to them. "Felix, Casper – to your beds now!" The two hounds barked in response, before running off up the staircase, which was just by the reception desk.

"What fine animals," Mallory found himself saying, almost with relief, as for a split second he thought the animals were going to attack.

"Yes, they are sisters. We have kept dogs here in the Hotel Post for generations. They are actually direct descendants from a dog brought to the hotel in 1701. Have you signed in?" She glanced down at the book, noticing that Mallory had turned back to where there was a missing page. She looked back up and gave a quick, nervous smile. Mallory, aware that he had been caught out, returned to the front of the register and proceeded to write in his details before passing the book to Yuri to do the same. Heidi then took the register and looked at it for a moment, scrutinising what had been written, before writing in it as well. "Right," she said, trying to sound normal, "you and your friend are on the first floor, room number five. Would you need any help with your luggage?"

"No that's fine," said Yuri, stooping down to pick up the bags.

Heidi reached to the nearby key rack, where she took the room key and handed it to Mallory. "I hope that you enjoy your stay here at the Hotel Post."

Mallory smiled and as he did so, caught the strange look in Heidi's eye which sent a chill down his spine.

CHAPTER 19

Mallory and Yuri headed up the hotel's main staircase, turning off onto a small corridor on the first floor. This led them to a small landing, where not only was their room located, but they also found a small staircase which had a sign pointing down indicating it led straight to the Strube. After dropping off their luggage and freshening up, they decided to get a drink from the Strube. Back on the landing a large painting caught their attention. It showed a man dressed in an old style suit, dating to the late 1800's, sitting at a writing desk. Beside him on a small table was a green crystal skull and closed book. Above the table was a window that showed a mountain scene.

"Well," said Mallory, "this shows we are very much on the right track."

Yuri nodded. "This painting, the hotel register, the phone Heidi used."

"What about it?" Mallory asked quizzically.

"I watched Heidi when you were looking in register. No wires attached to it, like the phone you saw at Natural History Museum."

"This is getting more and more interesting by the minute," said Mallory, stealing another glance at the painting. And with that the two men headed to the staircase where, going down it, they found themselves in a small bar & restaurant area. They took one of the booths located along the left hand wall. Almost as soon as they were seated a waitress appeared, who introduced herself as Anna. She was in her late-twenties, and wore a long yellow dress which had a number of brown leather pouches hung from the belt. After taking their order, which was elongated by Yuri insisting on Russian vodka they did not have, before settling reluctantly for a local beer, she promptly left.

"Nice girl," commented Yuri with a smile.

"Yes," replied Mallory, "from the looks of her I would say she was related to Heidi, I would guess her sister."

"Or maybe cousin?"

"Could be, we can find out later," said Mallory, taking a good look round at their surroundings.

The Strube was fairly busy, with a combination of tourists and locals, the latter of which was easily identifiable by the wearing of Austrian style clothing. It was also noticeable how many of them wore brass goggles and had various brown leather pouches and additional belts on their clothes. Those of them who smoked seemed to be doing so from strange circular tubes, instead of from

94

traditional cigarettes or pipes, which gave off strange clear vapour that dispersed almost at once.

To the right of the stairs, which led to the first floor landing, there was a small bar area and beyond that could be seen a kitchen. On the opposite side of the wall to where they were sat was a large wood burning stove, set in the remains of a large fireplace, which burned brightly. Over the fireplace were a number of paintings showing scenes and episodes from Karlstad's history with captions underneath. Two of them particularly stood out. One showed an ape-like creature standing tall, wielding a double edged war axe. While another showed two similar creatures seemingly climbing a mountain.

After a few minutes Anna returned to them and placed two steins filled with beer on the table.

"That's a strange creature Miss," commented Mallory, nodding over to the pictures over the fireplace.

She smiled. "Yes, it is isn't it?"

"What is story behind them?" asked Yuri.

"They are something out of folklore;" she replied dismissively, "creatures that were supposedly spotted over a hundred years or so ago in the surrounding mountains."

Mallory smiled, this story further reinforced the idea of the mysterious creatures they believed to be here. "Oh, by the way," he said, remembering something he had seen earlier, "what happened to the house across the square?"

"A fire," replied Anna. "It was only a few weeks ago, they are still not sure what caused it."

"Anyone hurt?"

Anna shook her head. "No, everyone got out alive and unscathed. It was a miracle. Is there anything else I can get you?"

The two men shook their heads, and with that she left them to return to the kitchen for the next order.

Yuri took another swig from the stein and pulled a face and slammed the glass down. "I do not like what they call 'beer' and I don't like their version of chess either."

"Chess?" enquired Mallory.

"Yes," replied Yuri, nodding to the table over the other side of the room, "don't you see it? It played with discs, not proper pieces, and there are extra pieces too."

Mallory frowned, impressed that the Russian had picked up on this detail. "Perhaps it is a regional variant of the game?"

"It is CHESS," spat Yuri passionately. "There are no other versions, just the one! I should know. I am chess expert! Back in Russia I won hundreds of games and competitions before I was forced to stop playing."

"Forced?"

Yuri nodded slowly, recalling his downfall. "There were incidences, one even a full blown fist fight with opponent and I was banned from entering official tournaments. Then others refused to play me."

"Why?" asked Mallory, but as soon as he asked the question he realised the answer. Yuri picked up his tankard and downed the rest of his drink in one go before again slamming it down. "Vodka," the Russian replied simply, "that was the problem; too much Vodka ... or maybe perhaps too little?" With that he managed to get the attention of another waitress, and ordered another stein of beer.

As Mallory and Yuri sat and chatted to each other, they could not help notice a change in the atmosphere in the Strube. From the kitchen area the staff kept looking over at them, a fact also mirrored by some of the locals, who quickly turned away when either Mallory or Yuri tried to catch their eye.

Much to Mallory's annoyance Yuri continued to order beer after beer, and it was clear he was slowly getting drunker and drunker. The Russian slammed down his eighth empty stein on the table. "This muddy water is making me thirsty. Where is waitress gone?"

"It seems everything makes you thirsty," remarked Mallory. "Shall I get you a jug of water?"

Yuri looked at Mallory, with a hint of anger in his eye regarding the comment, but then the flash of annoyance turned into a smile and he leant across the table and thumped Mallory on the shoulder. "Ha! I like you Mallory. Not many have the balls to make comments to Yuri like that." And with that he stood and strolled over to the small bar area and, pushing one of the locals aside, started to thump the stein on the wooden counter. "Beer! Where is how you say – wench? I am dying of thirst here!"

"Dying for a lesson in manners!" replied the local, who had just been shoved out of the way.

"Manner? Manners? What could you teach me about manners? Where is manners when you keep loyal customer waiting?"

"I could teach you a lot actually!" replied the man, sizing the Russian up. By now, the rest of those in the Strube were looking at the two men, some clearly anticipating a brawl. Mallory, sensing what was about to happen, sprang from his seat and over to the bar area. He grabbed Yuri by the arm and pulled him back. "Sorry friend, you will have to excuse my associate here. It's been a long day. We have spent most of it stuck on a train. There were delays and we almost lost our luggage." Quickly he reached into his pocket and pulled out some money and placed it on the counter. "Here, have a drink on us by way of an apology." And before the local could respond, Mallory pulled Yuri away back towards their seats. "Are you trying to get us in trouble Yuri?"

"I'm sorry," the Russian whispered back, realising that he had overstepped the mark. "I get annoyed and passionate at times!"

"No you get…" Mallory's words trailed off. Back at their table, on the seat where he had been sitting was a folded up piece of paper. Mallory picked it up as he took his seat.

"What does it say?" asked Yuri, leaning forward. Mallory unfolded the paper and read it. "It just says, 'Meet me in the church on the edge of the town square at midnight.'

"I wonder who put it there?" said Yuri, looking around. Mallory sighed. "I guess we will find out at midnight."

Yuri paused. "I think I will have that jug of water now. I think I am going to need a clear head!"

CHAPTER 20

The Strube closed at eleven thirty, and Mallory insisted that they briefly return to their room before going to the church, to fetch his service revolver, just in case there was trouble. As they stepped onto the first floor landing, Yuri immediately noticed that something had changed. "Look Mallory! It's gone!"

"Yes, you're right," Mallory replied. "Now that is interesting!"

The portrait of the man and the crystal skull they had looked at a few hours before was now missing, and had been replaced with a visibly smaller painting of a red fox on a snowy hillside.

"I'm guessing there was something on there that we were not supposed to see," said Yuri.

"Agreed," said Mallory. "In London Dr Fredrickson said that Douglas discovered 'a clue in a painting' in Vienna, which started him off on his search. I'm guessing that that and the portrait we saw earlier are connected somehow."

"I wonder where painting is now?" pondered Yuri.

"It could be anywhere," said Mallory glumly. "There are lots of places in the hotel it could have been moved to, assuming of course it wasn't taken to another location altogether. We can worry about that later though. We need to get to the church."

So, eager to make the meeting on time, they put the missing picture to the back of their minds, instead heading to their room where Mallory armed himself. Then the two headed to the main staircase of the hotel, down to reception, and out onto the main street, before making the short walk across the town square and to the large church which dominated the skyline. Unsure what to expect, Mallory pushed on the large wooden door of the church, which opened with a creek, and then he and Yuri stepped inside.

The church itself was almost empty except for a couple of hunched figures in the pews who had come there for late night personal worship. The denomination of the church was Catholic, and like all such churches it was richly decorated. The high alter was dominated with a backdrop adorned with rich gold leaf and in the centre of it was a large crucifix. Running down the walls at regular intervals were a series of brass etchings which depicted the events of the crucifixion of Christ that looked almost three dimensional. On the right hand side of the church was a large wooden confessional box, which looked like an oversized wardrobe. The light over the two doors was on, indicating that there was a priest available and waiting in the left hand section, to hear and absolve someone's sins.

"So what do we do?" asked Yuri.

"I'm not totally sure," replied Mallory, who had hoped their mysterious contact would have greeted them as they arrived. "I'll go in and wait. You stay here by the door. If anything goes wrong, you can step in."

Yuri nodded and Mallory moved into the church, where he walked down the central aisle before taking a seat on one of the pews and waited. He looked around, eyeing those in the church, wondering if any of them was the origin of the mysterious note. He waited for a few minutes, but nothing happened. He was about to go and try to speak to one of the worshippers, when he noticed that the light over the door of the confessional started to flash furiously. Quietly he stood and walked over to the wooden structure and cautiously opened the right hand door, to find it empty. He then went inside, closing the door behind him and seated himself on the wooden chair. "Um, forgive me Father for I have sinned." He was not sure on the exact form of address, but remembered it was something along those lines from his time in the army. Suddenly a screen in the dividing wall of the confessional slid back and Mallory was able to see the outline of a figure through the wire grating, which spoke to him in English. "I can assure you my son that any sins that you have committed in your lifetime pale into insignificance to the sins that this town have been committing on a daily basis for centuries!"

That statement took Mallory by surprise. "What do you mean? Who are you? Are you a priest?"

"Not quite, I'm a Curate, sent here for training from the City of Graz. I have been here for six months, and in that time I have come to discover that things are not right here in Karlstad."

"How so?"

"There is an air of secrecy," came the reply, "coupled with mysterious things."

"Like what?"

There was a pause. "There are devices that exist here which should not be, and even normal looking things that work in a way that shouldn't."

"Brass goggles that are glasses, cylinders that act as smoking pipes, telephones without wires and strange machines that serve ice-cream?" ventured Mallory, recalling the things he had seen since their arrival in Karlstad.

"Yes, yes," replied the Curate, "but there is so much more than that. You cannot begin to imagine what is here. I fear that this town is aided by forbidden knowledge, knowledge that only comes from one source."

"Which is?"

"The creatures!"

"Creatures?" repeated Mallory.

"Yes," continued the Curate, "creatures! They are hidden by the locals and are never spoken about openly, but they are the source of the things that should not be. They fuel this town's success!"

"Have you ever seen one of these creatures?"

"Yes, so help me I have! I was not supposed to, but I have seen a number of them."

"A number of them? How many of these things are there?"

"I saw five, but there are many, many, more!"

"What do they look like?"

"Monsters! They look like apes, but are certainly not primates as you would recognise them."

Mallory let out a whistle, the description matched the pictures he and Yuri had seen in the Strube above the fireplace.

"These are not of God," continued the Curate, "but even so, the town continues to align themselves with them. I fear for those here, they have made a pact with the devil which will have to be paid. The bible says such things are forbidden, but it happens and God will surely punish us all!"

Mallory remained silent, it was very clear that the Curate was in the middle of some personal religious crisis, brought on by finding out the existence of the creatures which no doubt challenged the very core of his beliefs.

"You and your friend are in great danger," continued the Curate. "I saw the way that the locals were looking at you. You must leave this place at once. First thing tomorrow you must get on the first train out of Karlstad and leave straight away!"

"I'm not sure we can do that," replied Mallory. "The reason I and my friend came here was to find out what happened to someone who went missing some weeks ago."

"Who?" asked the Curate. "It is common for people to disappear from here without trace."

"Douglas Quinn."

"Yes, Douglas Quinn, I know that name."

"Do you know where he is?" asked Mallory hopefully.

"No, I am sorry," came the reply.

"Could he be up at the mountain fortress?" suggested Mallory.

"You must never speak of that place, it is evil!" hissed the Curate through the grating. "Forget that it even exists, if you value your soul!"

The outburst stunned Mallory into silence. He was not sure what to say next, when the Curate spoke. "Now I must go. While you are here would you like to make a confession?"

Mallory thought for a moment. "Um, er, no, not really. I'm afraid that I am not really that much of a believer."

"At the moment my son I can assure you that your faith is actually stronger than mine. Now I must go. Take care!" With that the small hatch door closed, putting Mallory into semi darkness. Quickly he opened the door and left the confessional, to see a figure in black, the Curate, hurrying away, before disappearing into a side door. With that Mallory looked round and realised that Yuri was nowhere to be seen, so he headed towards the big wooden doors that would take him back out onto Karlstad where he would hopefully find the Russian.

CHAPTER 21

Yuri soon became bored.

After watching Mallory look around the church, and then disappear into the confessional, there was nothing more for him to do but wait. He took a stroll around the church and looked at a couple of the paintings before ending up back at the main door, which he opened to look out onto the quiet scene of a night time Karlstad. Soon his mind started to wander, wondering what was happening at home in Russia and if he would ever be able to return there. His thoughts also turned to his younger sister who, of all the members of his family, he missed the most.

"Well, are you in or out?"

Yuri was snapped back to reality and found himself being glared at by an elderly woman in a dark knitted shawl. "Well are you in or out?" she repeated, tapping the door with her walking stick. "It may be summer, but there is still cold at night, and you keeping the door open is letting the heat out!"

"Um, sorry," he replied, moving outside the building. The woman threw him a look of further distain, before grabbing hold of the church door and slamming it in the Russian's face. Yuri paused, and then let out a loud deep laugh. Here was the great Yuri Alexander Romanovsky, allowing himself to be pushed around by a little old lady! Surmising that Mallory would be safe, and not really wanting to venture back inside to face the old woman again, he decided to take a stroll around the churchyard and look at the graves that encircled the building. The tombs were all similar sizes and style, being rectangular and made from a white marble. As well as the usual inscriptions, Yuri noticed that most of the graves had actual photographs on them of their occupants. The pictures were mounted in small oval frames attached to the stone, which was quite unsettling. Then after a while it struck Yuri that something was very odd about the graves. Slowly he moved around the graveyard again, checking the inscriptions and photos carefully, to see if he had missed something, but he had not. There was a total absence of infant deaths, nor for that matter could he find any grave of anyone who had died as a youth or in their twenties, thirties or even forties. In fact, making a quick estimate of the graves, Yuri worked out that the average life expectancy for a male resident of Karlstad was seventy five and for women eighty, which was well above that of Russia or even the United Kingdom.

Then, from behind, there was a tap on his shoulder, making him turn round. "Mallory! Do not do that!" Mallory smiled. "Sorry, I did not mean to make you jump."

"How was meeting?"

Mallory shrugged. "Interesting, it turned out our contact was a very alarmed Curate. He couldn't tell me anything about Douglas, but it seems that the creatures do exist, and they seem to be highly advanced and supply the town with futuristic technology."

"Well I find something strange here too," replied Yuri, who then went on to explain to Mallory his discovery in the graveyard. His curiosity stirred Mallory too. He went to look at the graves and when he had finished inspecting them for himself, the two found themselves standing at the east side of the church. To their right, outside the churchyard's iron railings, was the road which was lined with buildings that linked into the town's main square. Stretched out between the church roof and the buildings opposite was a banner advertising the Dumpling festival, which was going to be taking place that weekend.

"I'm guessing that there must be another graveyard somewhere," Yuri concluded, looking round.

"That seems likely," replied Mallory. "A town of this size must have another place for burials, bearing in mind

105

the population and the fact that it has been around for hundreds of years."

"Even so," said Yuri, "it is very unusual that there are so many deaths taking place in old age."

"Agreed," said Mallory. "It would seem that this advanced technology seems to stretch out into medicine as well."

"I'd be impressed if they find cure for common cold!" said Yuri with a laugh. The Russian was about to say more when, from above, he felt something hit him on the head and shoulder. It felt like a grain of dirt or dust, but it was more than enough for him to instantly react. "Mallory look out!" and with one shove he propelled Mallory to one side, and using the momentum allowed himself to be driven backwards also. Then, just where the two had been standing, a large chunk of masonry from the church roof smashed into the ground.

"You alright Mallory?"

"Yes, thanks," he replied, steadying himself from the push, "you?"

The Russian nodded, then both men looked up to see where the debris had come from, and for a second they both thought that they saw the figure of something against the skyline, which quickly moved away from the roof's edge.

"Did you see that?" asked Mallory in surprise.

"Yes, I think so, but you say it first. I sometimes see things I shouldn't due to too much vodka."

"Well that was certainly no pink elephant!" replied Mallory. "It seemed to be covered in white fur. I think it was one of the creatures!"

"That's what I thought too. Look, there it is again!" cried Yuri, as the figure came back into view. The creature briefly looked down at them before moving towards the small tower, capped by an onion style dome, on the side of the church. Carefully, despite the fact it seemed to be burdened by something under its arm, it climbed up onto the dome where it stood upright, giving Mallory and Yuri a clear view of it, where, illuminated by the full moon, they could see the creature in perfect detail. It appeared to be over six foot tall with its whole body covered in short white hair. The head was slightly larger than a human's, fitting the shape of the skull that Mallory had seen back in London. The skin tone of the face and hands seemed to be blue, almost grey, in colour. The creature gave a roar, and momentarily they could see its fang shaped teeth, before it stared down at them with its large blue eyes.

"By the saints!" muttered Yuri. "I never have seen anything like it in my whole life. How it possible such a creature even exist?"

Mallory shook his head. "I have no idea!"

By now the creature had taken the thing that he was carefully carrying, another piece of masonry, into both hands and had lifted it high above his head.

"Get ready!" called Mallory. "It's going to try again!"

Both Mallory and Yuri watched the creature intently. It looked from one to the other, seemingly choosing its target, then using its raw power it hurled the stone downwards. The stone tumbled towards him in a blur, but flew behind them, landing on the top of a tall weeping stone angel which was positioned on the top of a sarcophagus. The masonry, and the stone angel it landed on, shattered into fragments showering both Mallory and Yuri with large

107

chunks of flying debris which knocked both men to the ground.

"Are you alright?" said Mallory, as he struggled to his feet.

Yuri grunted in reply, also standing to his feet. "Yes, I think so. Mallory, give me your gun."

"Alright, but just a warning shot, we don't want to kill it." Mallory reached into his jacket and produced his service revolver, which he handed to the Russian.

Yuri nodded and looked over the weapon approvingly, before letting off the safety catch and aiming the weapon upwards at the creature that was still standing on the onion roof, and let off a single shot, deliberately wide of the beast.

The creature did not even flinch, but instead produced another piece of masonry it had kept in reserve and hurled it downwards. The rock hit the gun with such force it was knocked out of Yuri's hand. On picking up the weapon from the ground, the Russian noted that the gun had been damaged and was not safe to fire. Looking up, the creature somehow aware that it had left them defenceless, raised his arms in the air and roared triumphantly.

CHAPTER 22

The creature let out a second roar before calmly stepping off the church's onion tower and letting himself fall some twenty feet, landing lightly on a lower ledge of the church building. Suspended from this ledge was a rope, which stretched out from the church over the street and was anchored to the building opposite. Hanging underneath was the large banner advertising the Dumpling Festival. Then the creature placed its foot on the rope, paused and stepped out on it, throwing its arms out for balance and walking across it like a tightrope.

"Impressive," said Yuri, looking up at the creature that was now almost half way across the street. Then, without a word to Mallory, the big Russian reached into his sleeve, where he produced what looked like a long handle and, pressing a small button, a long blade suddenly shot out. With a well-aimed overarm throw, the flick knife flew upwards, high over the church's iron railing towards the creature, where it hit and lodged itself in its left leg.

The creature let out a strange yell, lost its balance and started to fall, but grabbed the rope as he did so, so it ended up hanging in the middle of the street against the banner. It let out another cry, this time one of anger, before continuing on its way, hand over hand towards the building opposite the church.

"What did you do that for?" cried Mallory, annoyed. "I said not to kill it."

"I aimed for its leg, not head or heart."

"It nearly fell!" pointed out Mallory.

"It would be fine!" said Yuri dismissively.

"What did you expect it to do, bounce on the ground then get up again?"

"Ha! I like you Mallory; you have good sense of humour! No, that creature not going to die easily, it would have been alright. Come, we go! It getting away!" With that, Yuri turned to run back through the graves of the church, heading towards the main gate with Mallory, still annoyed at the Russian's actions, following close behind. Outside the church the two men turned left and headed back round on themselves to the street where the banner was suspended. By now the creature had safely made it all the way across and had climbed onto the top of the building opposite, where it now stood, staring down intently at the two men, before reaching down to Yuri's knife, still stuck in its leg and pulling it free, then throwing it to one side.

"Blast! That was a good knife! Come, Mallory," cried Yuri, eagerly. "This not over yet! Look over there, side of building it is an easy climb to roof. I go up after it."

Mallory stared to the shop front where Yuri was pointing. He was indeed right, there was a small green canopy and above that a balcony with wooden columns and ledges eventually leading up to the edge of the building and the roof. "No Yuri, don't even think about it. You would be a sitting duck as you climb up."

"Pah!" replied the Russian. "You never get anywhere with that kind of attitude, my friend" He then ran to the shop and quickly started to climb with, as Mallory noted, assurance and confidence. It was clear that the Professor's confidence about Yuri's mountaineering skills were indeed totally justified.

Then, predictably, the creature who was watching Yuri's actions with keen interest, acted in the only way possible; disappearing for a moment he returned to the roof's edge and started to throw something straight down onto Yuri. The first roof tile flew past slightly to the left of the big Russian, making him wince. Then another whizzed by, this one going to the right. Then more tiles were dropped, one after another, designed not to hit but to intimidate and toy with its pursuer. The creature seemed intent on getting some warped revenge on the Russian for his attack, before inflicting the coup de grace.

Then when Yuri was almost at the rooftop, the creature lunged down, trying to grab at him, but instead he clutched mid-air as the Russian managed to dodge to the side, and then made a response of his own by punching upwards. The blow connected with the creature's face, sending it sprawling backwards onto the roof. Taking full advantage Yuri then quickly completed the rest of the climb onto the rooftop where he disappeared out of view.

Mallory strained to try and see what was happening. From above he could hear strange yelps of pain from the creature and then Yuri's voice yelling out expletives in Russian, as well as his odd cry of pain.

The figure of Yuri suddenly rolled into view and off of the edge of the roof. Mallory gasped in horror, but as the Russian fell he managed to throw out his hand to save himself and ended up dangling by his left hand facing towards the building. Then the creature appeared, and stood over Yuri. With a grunt it lifted its foot and brought it down sharply, aiming for Yuri's hand, but the Russian was not going to allow himself to be defeated that easily. In an amazing move of dexterity he shifted his hand and himself entirely to the side, and the creature's foot crashed down missing him by inches. The creature then tried to stamp down again, but with his free right hand Yuri reached upwards and caught the creature's foot in mid-air and held it, trying to push the monster off balance. Sadly it was a battle that the Russian could not hope to win. The creature pulled his foot back and Yuri was again momentarily hanging by one hand before the monster moved forward for another attack. This time Yuri swung his free hand up high and grabbed onto the creature's lower left leg, clinging onto the short fur. For a moment it

111

seemed to almost lose its balance, and threw out its arms to steady itself from the sudden extra weight. The creature started to shake and kick out its leg until Yuri had no option but to let go, but this time, with his right hand, he grabbed onto the edge of the roof.

The creature stared down at him and then let out a roar. It then leant down and punched down hard, hitting Yuri on the side of the head, but impossibly the Russian took the blow and managed to hang on. The creature grunted, and then punched down again. This time, finally, Yuri could not sustain the assault and let go and started to fall.

The Russian's descent lasted no more than a second or so before he landed on the green shop canopy which bowed, before momentarily throwing him directly up into the air, around two feet, before gravity again took over and he fell back onto the awning where this time he stayed. Alive and unhurt, Yuri rolled to the side of the green canvas and grabbing the edge flipped forward, landing on his feet on the ground below. Talking angrily in Russian to himself and waving his arms in annoyed gestures he walked over to Mallory. As he did so, the creature who was now standing up let out a howl of frustration on seeing that his foe had escaped unharmed, before turning and disappearing from view away over the rooftop.

"Yuri, are you alright?"

The Russian nodded. "Yes, but angry with myself. I nearly had him! I hold onto him by the leg!"

"Er, true," said Mallory, sceptically, "but as you were hanging off a building at the time I'm not totally sure if that qualifies as you nearly capturing him. Just count yourself lucky to be alive, that fall could have been fatal!"

Yuri waved his hand dismissively. "That nothing; like fall off trapeze onto safety net when I spend summers with circus as small boy!"

"Well, at least there is one good thing."

"What?" replied Yuri.

"We know for certain that the beasts of Karlstad exist." Yuri spat on the floor in disgust. "Some consolation! Come! We go back to hotel. I need a drink and have bottles of vodka in luggage."

Despite the lateness of the hour and the fact he was trying his best to dissuade Yuri's drinking habit, Mallory could not help nodding in agreement. After the night's events he decided that he needed a stiff drink too.

CHAPTER 23

The Hotel Golden Rose was located at the far end of the main street of Karlstad, far away from the town square, just by the railway line and level crossing. It was in this hotel that the Higher Council of Karlstad met. The location had been chosen as it was away from the hustle and bustle of the town, and its close proximity to the cable car, which served as the main link to Upper Karlstad, allowed greater ease for those from the upper fortress to visit and attend meetings, like the one that Fritz had now called. With all the members of the Council assembled in the meeting room of the hotel, located far away from the guests that were staying, Fritz began to address them. "Thank you for coming at such short notice. I would not have called you out at this late hour if it were not absolutely necessary."

"Is it Zidal?" asked Anton eagerly, who was the Editor of the local newspaper. "Are there any developments?"

"Sadly not," replied Fritz. "There has been no sign of him for weeks."

"This is worrying," said Karl, who owned the local Butchers, "I really think we need to consider calling off the Dumpling Festival."

"Impossible," said Stefan, who was the Post Master, "this was discussed at the time and it was decided that with the hotels full, schedules planned, invitations sent out etc it was too late to do anything, let alone now with it being a day away. Besides, what possible excuse could be given at this late stage?"

"But what if there is an incident?" said Karl worriedly. "What if he were to return to the town in the middle of the festival in his current savage state? Can you think of the consequences of that? Netvor, I blame you for this; you promised us that this would be dealt with and yet he is still at large."

All eyes turned to the end of the table, where one of the creatures was seated. He was covered from head to foot in silvery white hair. Over his shoulder was a sash on which a number of leather pouches hung and on his head was a brown top hat on which was resting a set of brass goggles. Netvor was the official representative of the creatures who lived in the fortress of Upper Karlstad. "I can only apologise again," he said in their language, as he shifted awkwardly in his chair. "I fully admit we were caught off guard. Nothing like this has ever happened before. When Zidal fell ill we assumed that it was just a simple fever. We had no reason to expect that he would be gripped by madness or bloodlust, or even try to escape the way he did. The whole situation is a mystery to us, despite our attempts to try and discover what is going on. Anyway, the fact is that he has not been sighted for weeks, so it can only be assumed that he has gone off somewhere quietly to die."

"That does seem more likely, bearing in mind the time that has passed," said Fritz, "and you are right Stefan, there is no way the festival can be cancelled at this late stage, even if there was an active risk. As a precaution, however, we will send out some patrols to see if Zidal can be found. If not, we can place people at the most likely entry points into the town, and we can also discreetly have some of our people armed at the festival, should the very worst scenario occur."

There was a murmur of agreement around the table. Under the circumstances, that seemed the only course of action open to them.

"Good," said Fritz, "that's settled; I must turn to the reason that I summoned you all here." He moved uncomfortably in his seat, aware that he was partly at fault for making the situation worse. "Heidi has informed me that two men have booked into the hotel this evening. One is a Russian, the other is Richard Mallory, one of the men that I encountered in London while retrieving the crystal skull. I am afraid that they are already asking questions regarding the whereabouts of Douglas Quinn."

"What!" cried Karl, "How could they have traced him here?"

"I have no idea," said Fritz, who had been trying to work that out himself since he heard the news. "I was careful to ensure I left no traces of my identity, and Douglas of course has not contacted them, but somehow they have made the link to Karlstad and are here. They have already indicated that the others I encountered in London will be following shortly."

"The timing is not good," remarked Stefan, "but I am sure we can deal with them. We can keep them under close observation; restrict their movements and communications with the outside world. Worst case scenario, we can always employ our usual 'Ultimate plan' to deal with them. After all, we are more than experienced at keeping the secrets of Karlstad safe." He looked over at Netvor with a smile.

"I am afraid," confessed Fritz sheepishly, "that on my trip I was less than careful when I encountered them. They openly saw my electronic blaster and my portable phone device."

"Now that is a problem," said Stefan. "They are bound to notice our other technologies here and ask even more questions."

"Well, I have said for a long time that we were being far too obvious and we should have been more discreet, even restricting technologies solely to Upper Karlstad!" said Anton.

"Funny," said Karl, with a hint of accusation in his voice, "I didn't see you protesting too much when Netvor told you they had found a way to print that scandal sheet you call a newspaper in colour."

"Oh I know what this is about," replied Anton hotly. "You are still upset about my exposé on what kind of meat you were actually selling to the public in those flat meat patties of yours! Well, I would like to point out, you were more than happy with the colour advertisement we designed for you."

"And you were more than happy to overcharge me for it!"

"Why you …."

"Gentlemen please!" interrupted Netvor. "Arguing amongst ourselves like this will do us no good. We have done our best to ensure that the inventions we have provided for you are mostly 'hidden in plain sight'. Look at the bath chair we have provided for Fritz's niece for instance. Although different to the traditional design, no one would suspect it is powered by electrical cells, rather than by rotating hand cranks."

"True Netvor," said Fritz, "but even you have to admit that Karlstad is starting to stand out. You should hear some of the things that the surrounding villages say about us."

"Then perhaps," replied Netvor, "it is time we tell the world some of our secrets. Not the existence of my kind, of course, but it would be possible to disseminate some of our technologies out to the villages, and far beyond. It pains me to know that millions die of simple infections and illness all over the world, when we have here at our disposal a simple green fungus that can cure that and so much more."

Fritz shook his head. "If we expose the technologies, then it will ultimately end up in having to reveal the source of them, and the world is not ready to know the existence of your kind."

Just then there was a quiet knock at the door and a young girl entered. She moved over to Fritz, dropping him a folded piece of paper, before disappearing off. Fritz opened the paper and read the contents. The blood drained from his face.

"What is it, what's wrong?" enquired Stefan, seeing that it was bad news.

"Well," said Fritz, struggling to find his voice, "it appears that our friends from England have encountered Zidal at the church in the centre of town. There was a fight, after which Zidal returned to the church where he attacked and killed the Curate."

There was a long pause before Netvor spoke. "I will make arrangements immediately to mount an extended hunt for Zidal in the surrounding area. He must be hiding somewhere close. We have a day to find him before the Dumpling Festival starts."

"And what if he's not found?" asked Anton.

"Then," said Fritz solemnly, "we arm everyone we can and pray that he does not venture to the town, for if he does, the secrets of Karlstad will be exposed to the world for certain."

CHAPTER 24

At about nine the following morning, Mallory and Yuri ventured out of their room to head down for breakfast, having slept in later than planned.

In the main dining room Mallory and Yuri, as directed by one of the waitress's on duty, made their way to the buffet at the end of the room where they helped themselves to a selection of cold meats and cereals which were laid out across two tables. On a third table was a selection of newspapers that guests could borrow to read with their meal if they so wished, as well as a hotel produced newsletter outlining local news and events.

The dining room was half empty; many residents having already taken their morning meal. So they had no problem finding a seat, where upon Anna appeared, this time in a much friendlier mood. Strapped on her back were three small brass cylinders, attached to which there was a hose with a nozzle on the end. Anna explained it would dispense tea, coffee or hot chocolate on demand. Mallory opted for tea, while Yuri asked for hot chocolate, and Anna promptly filled their cups before heading off.

"Dumpling Festival looks interesting," said Yuri, as he took a closer look at the hotel newsletter, which outlined the details of what was planned. "I like the sound of the evening candle parade."

Mallory nodded, trying to look interested, but his head was still hurting from the drinking session the night before. "Don't you ever get a hangover?"

Yuri paused. "Sometimes when I sober up, so I ensure I never sober up!" With that he reached into his jacket and produced a small silver flask which he opened and poured over his cereal.

"You are one stage up from an animal! I bet even that creature we faced last night has more manners," said Mallory, shaking his head.

Yuri smiled, raised his spoon as though he were making a toast, and then started to eat.

"May I join you for a moment?" asked a voice.

"No, this is private table," said Yuri, without even looking up to see who had spoken.

"No Yuri," said Mallory, who had taken the time to see to whom the voice belonged. He then beckoned the newcomer to sit at the empty chair at their table.

"You of course recognise me from London?" said the man, as he took the seat.

"Yes," replied Mallory. "Yuri, this is the man that we told you about, who we met at the Natural History

Museum; the gentleman who took the skull of the creature, the notes and tried to kill the Professor and me by dropping a dinosaur on us."

"Dinosaur?" replied Yuri. "This vodka of mine is stronger than I thought!"

The blonde man smiled at the interaction. "First I would like to point out that the skull was originally stolen from us. I was just taking it back. I also warned you not to pursue this matter of Douglas Quinn any further didn't I? But you seem to have ignored my advice and here you are. I might as well introduce myself. I am Fritz. I of course know who you are, but have not met your friend."

"I am Yuri Alexander Romanovsky," responded the Russian, trying to sound as impressive as possible. "Former Palace Guard to the Tsar, Former Chess Champion, and Former Security Guard at one of London's top Department Stores!"

Fritz eyed the Russian up and down "There are quite a lot of 'formers' there aren't there? Life does not seem to be going your way does it? I wonder why?" He then eyed the vodka soaked cereal suspiciously.

A look of anger flashed across Yuri's face. "I am able to do things better drunk than sober, like take on one of your beasts!"

Now it was Fritz's turn to show anger. "Yes, you did take him on didn't you? And do you know what the result was? After you and your friend here returned to the hotel to the safety of your beds, the creature returned to the church, broke in and killed the Curate."

Yuri looked at Mallory in stunned silence.

"Your little excursion cost a man his life and has caused us no end of trouble!" said Fritz.

"But why attack Curate?" asked Yuri.

"I think I know," said Mallory. "The creature was on the church roof, somehow he must have heard the conversation in the confessional and decided to come back to take care of the Curate."

"Creatures hearing must be good."

But Mallory did not think so, he had heard of 'listening pipes' secretly installed into confessional boxes so other people could listen in on the floors above. He thought that somehow, even though the creature was on the roof, it had somehow managed to listen in this way. He was about to voice his theory, but was distracted as Fritz had reached into his pocket and dropped a folded piece of paper onto the table. "There, this should solve the problem we have and will allow you to be on your way."

"What is this?" asked Yuri.

"Open it and see."

Mallory reached for the folded paper and opened it up; it was a death certificate for Douglas Quinn, saying he had died the week before.

"That was the main reason you are here isn't it, to find out what happened to Douglas?" said Fritz. "Well now you know. I am very sad to inform you that he passed away. You can take that back to London and it will allow his wife to gain access to his bank accounts and have the house transferred over into her name."

"A heart attack?" said Mallory, failing to hide his scepticism after reading the cause of death that was written on the certificate. "It says here he died of a heart attack."

"Yes," replied Fritz, "he died peacefully in his sleep."

"Strange," said Mallory, "when we saw you in London you said that he was alive."

"Oh, he was, the heart failure was very sudden. One minute he was fine, the next he was gone."

"It's signed by you," Mallory pointed out.

"That's right," replied Fritz, "I am one of the local Doctors."

At that point Anna returned to the table and refilled Mallory and Yuri's empty cups from the strange cylinder. "I'm so sorry to hear about the loss of your friend. My brother here did everything he could, but sadly it was too late."

"Brother?" said Mallory.

Fritz nodded. "Yes, Heidi and Anna are my sisters. I chose medicine and left the running of the family Hotel to them."

With that Anna smiled and headed off to another table.

Mallory placed the death certificate on the table. "I don't believe this for a moment. I know for a fact he didn't have any problems with his heart."

Fritz shrugged. "I don't care what you believe, Douglas is dead. You have the certificate to prove it. That is the end of the matter."

"So where is body?" asked Yuri suddenly. "If he is dead as you claim we will need body so we can return it home for a funeral."

"I'm afraid that won't be possible," replied Fritz. "He was cremated and the ashes have been scattered in the river."

"That does not sound likely," said Mallory.

Fritz shrugged. "I can take you to the spot where the ashes were scattered if that would help."

"That won't prove anything would it?" pointed out Yuri. Fritz smiled.

"But what about the creature?" asked Mallory, trying a different tact. "You said that it killed the Curate, you cannot just leave it at that surely?"

"Oh, I won't, I can assure you that as soon as we capture the creature it will be held accountable for its crime."

"Perhaps we can help you catch creature," followed up Yuri quickly. "This time he will not evade me so easily."

"That will not be required," said Fritz flatly. "This is an internal affair and one that will be dealt with by those here in Karlstad. You are welcome to stay and enjoy our Dumpling festival, but be warned you will be under constant watch and the slightest trouble," his eyes moved to Yuri, "you will all be required to leave immediately. Do you understand?"

Mallory and Yuri nodded.

Fritz then stood, pushed the chair in, before silently turning and leaving.

Mallory looked over the certificate again and shook his head. "This is not right at all!"

"So what do we do?"

"Carry on as planned until the Professor and Jazmine get here," replied Mallory, "and hope there are no more surprises waiting for us!"

CHAPTER 25

After they had finished their breakfast, Mallory and Yuri left the dining room, ready to head out for the day, with Mallory stopping at reception to hand in their room key. However, there was no one there at the desk. He rang the bell on the counter a number of times, but still no one responded.

"You can drop it off in that box to the side," said a voice from behind.

Both men turned to see a young girl, no more than twelve, who was seated in what looked like a low bath chair made out of wood and brass. It had two wheels at the rear, with one at the front attached to a sloping steering column. On the handles of the steering column were two hand cranks which seemingly powered the chair. On the flat back of the bath chair was a small leather bag and attached to that, hanging loose, was a small toy white yeti type creature. "I'm Greta," announced the girl. "My Mother is Heidi, who runs the hotel."

"Pleased to meet you," said Mallory, as he dropped the key off into the box.

"Quite a cart you have there," said Yuri, noting the strange design of the bath chair.

"Yes, it was made for me by the optician, as my legs don't work too well."

"Not the sort of thing I would expect an eye specialist to come up with," said Mallory.

"He does a lot more than make glasses," replied Greta.

"He's an inventor too, and he comes up with all sorts of things. You probably have already seen a lot of them around Karlstad. His shop is amazing, filled with all kinds of inventions."

Mallory and Yuri looked at each other, realising that this was the cover story told to visitors to explain all of the strange technologies.

"What is that thing hanging on the bag you have on the back of your chair?" asked Yuri, pointing to a little white soft toy.

124

"It's a toy of the 'Beast of Karlstad,'" she replied. "It's based on the creatures that were said to roam in the forest and mountains that overlooked the town. Most of the shops sell them to tourists and visitors, as a good luck charm. There is also a picture of him on the Strube wall."

Mallory and Yuri exchanged another quick glance.

"Yes, we saw it last night. Speaking of pictures," said Mallory, taking the opportunity, "do you know what happened to the one on the first floor, of the man with the crystal skull?"

Greta paused for a moment. "Not sure, I think that I heard someone say it was moved to the Penthouse suite."

"The hotel has a penthouse suite?" replied Mallory in surprise.

Greta laughed. "No, it's not an actual penthouse, where people stay; it's the name we give to the loft space above our private quarters on the first floor. Why do you ask?"

"Oh no reason, it was just an interesting picture. I wouldn't mind seeing it again."

"Also," said Yuri, realising that the girl was much more willing to give out information, "we are looking for a friend of ours. His name is Douglas Quinn. I don't suppose you met him. He stayed here at the Post."

"Oh yes, he stayed here before…"

"Greta!" broke in a voice from behind the reception desk.

"What have I told you about annoying hotel guests?"

"Sorry Mother," said the girl sheepishly.

"Oh, she was not bothering us," said Yuri quickly. "In fact she has convinced me to find one of those soft monster toys."

125

"Really?" said Heidi, with a disapproving look. "Greta, don't you have studies to be getting on with?"

"Um, Yes, Mother." And with that the girl took hold of the hand cranks of the bath chair, turned the handles and started to reverse, turn and then disappear down a small corridor.

"Delightful girl," said Yuri, "she is credit to you."

Heidi smiled nervously. "Thank you. Is there anything else I can help with?"

"No, no, that's fine," said Mallory. "We had better be getting on."

With that, Mallory and Yuri headed to the door and out onto the main street of Karlstad. Immediately Yuri noticed a man loitering in the doorway of a shop opposite. He suddenly turned and pretended to be looking in the window. "Looks like Fritz was not joking about us being watched," said the Russian. "So what shall we do now?"

Mallory looked over to the town square and then down the main street. A particular shop sign caught his eye. It showed a brass set of goggles surrounded by cogs and gears. "Over there, the opticians. That must be the one Greta was talking about."

"Now that is worth checking out," replied Yuri.

So the two men made their way over to the Optician's shop, noting that they were being followed the entire time at a discreet distance. At the door they paused and looked round to see their follower momentarily distracted. He was talking to a young woman, clearly a tourist who had seemingly stopped him for directions.

"Lucky break," said Yuri, and he pushed on the door. "We get to lose our friend."

The inside of the shop was not what they had expected, certainly not what a traditional optician looked like. One side of the wall was taken up with different style goggles that the residents of Karlstad seemed to wear, with a large mirror in the middle. In the centre of the shop there was a chair with equipment around it that would be used to look into the eyes, and on the ceiling directly above the chair were four different charts that seemed to be attached to a spinning wheel, so they could be rotated in turn. The rest of the shop looked to be more like an inventor's workroom. On two large work benches were all kinds of strange devices. Most of which were in some state of repair (or creation?). There were tools, brass cogs and gears spread everywhere as well as in one corner a Bunsen burner, surrounded by various vials and test tubes, merrily burning away. Mallory went over to the table and started to examine some of the items that were there. "Look at this stuff, Yuri. I've never seen anything like it before. I wonder what that thing that looks like a typewriter does."

"I'm afraid that is none of your concern," came a slightly annoyed voice.

Mallory and Yuri turned to see a man who had just appeared from the back room and was now standing behind the main counter, presumably the owner of the establishment. He was a balding man in his sixties with shocks of white hair sticking out from the sides of his head. He was wearing a long white coat that had leather pouches attached to the material.

"Um, I was just looking," said Mallory.

"Well don't," said the owner of the shop. "Please can you leave?"

"This is really interesting place," said Yuri, quickly picking up from the work bench a long metal board that had a small wheel about eight inches in diameter attached to either end. "I hear you inventor, and create things like this. What is this by the way? It looks as though you could stand on it."

"You can," replied the optician bluntly, "but I advise you don't. It has a habit of unexpectedly catching fire."

Yuri immediately placed the device back down and before he or Mallory could say anything else, the shop opened and in walked the man who had been following them. "Ah, here you are. I have been looking for you. Come on Mr Mallory, Mr Romanovsky. There are certain places that are off limits to you and this is one of them. I think I will have to show you around the town personally until the shops close today at lunchtime; so you don't wander into anywhere you are not welcome."

"I go where I want!" replied Yuri defiantly.

"Guess again," said the man, as he produced a brass gun that had a glass cartridge on the top that contained sparks of electricity.

Yuri looked at Mallory who shook his head, indicating he was not to try anything. The Russian grunted. "Well, in that case can you show me where to buy bottle peach schnapps and one of those yeti type toys?"

CHAPTER 26

For the next couple of hours Mallory and Yuri were escorted around the main street of Karlstad by the man who had been sent to keep them under observation. He introduced himself as Oskar. Despite the potential threat of being shot and general awkwardness of the situation, Mallory and Yuri could not help find themselves warming to their 'guard' who was polite, witty and even helpful; advising which shops were best.

At noon, as Oskar had told them, the shops began to close and Mallory and Yuri decided to head back to the Hotel Post.

"Are you going to stay with us the rest of the day?" enquired Yuri.

Oskar shook his head. "No, my shift is done, but there will be someone else to look after you." With that he looked over to another man who was standing by the tobacconist on the edge of the town square. "Take my advice, just stay in the hotel, put your feet up and rest. It would save us all a lot of time." With a polite smile he turned and left.

Back inside the hotel, Mallory and Yuri picked up their key from reception and headed up to their room. However, at the top of the stairs to the first floor the Russian stopped, grabbing Mallory by the arm and pointed to a door off to one side marked 'Private'. "Well, what you think?"

Mallory paused, remembering what Greta had said about the mysterious painting that had been moved to the 'penthouse' in the family's private quarters. "We would be taking a tremendous risk."

"If we want to find out truth about painting it is only way," replied Yuri.

"We might be better off leaving it 'til tomorrow, when everyone is busy at the Dumpling Festival," said Mallory.

"True, but why wait?"

"Well, for a start, the family could be there."

129

In response Yuri went up to the door and knocked loudly.

There was no reply.

He knocked again.

Nothing.

With a quick look around to ensure that there was no one else about, Yuri reached for the handle, turned it and pushed. The door creaked open and the Russian tentatively leaned forward into the gap and called out. "Hello. Anybody home?"

There was no response.

He turned to Mallory. "What you think? Might be only chance."

Mallory paused. He knew that this was a bad idea. The very fact that Yuri was exercising caution and not barging in seemed to underline the fact that this was a dangerous venture, but despite that he found himself looking round to double check that there was no one around to see them, before nodding. As soon as the go ahead had been given, Yuri silently stepped inside. Mallory quickly followed and closed the door behind them.

They found themselves in a large sitting room. Directly in front of them were two windows, with a door in between that led out onto the balcony, which was over the main entrance to the hotel. To the far left seemed to be a kitchen/dining room area and on the far right of the sitting room was a small corridor that led through to where they presumed the bedrooms were located. The sitting room itself was filled with heavy looking hand-made wooden furniture. The large rug in front of the door they had entered was decorated with a pattern of interlocking cogs of different sizes. Overhead there was a set of bulb lights fixed directly onto the ceiling by a brass rail. However, it was the wall that was by the door they had come through that caught their main attention. It was covered with framed photos.

"All these photos are in colour," said Yuri in surprise.

"Unbelievable," said Mallory, "I know the process for colour photos is very complex and expensive. I can understand one or two photos in colour yes, but not all of them. There must be at least twenty here, and the colour photos I have seen were never this vibrant."

"Mallory, you remember plan to take photo of creature?"

"Yes."

"Think you have been beaten to it. There."

Mallory looked to the photo Yuri was pointing at. It showed a picture of a creature holding a young Greta in his arms, in front of a large Christmas tree. Both were smiling and laughing.

"Was that the creature we encountered?" asked Mallory.

"You had a better look than I did."

"No, and neither was this one," replied Yuri, pointing to another photo of a different creature. Looking at the photo wall they counted five different ones in total.

"So," mused Mallory, "what we seem to have here are a number of these creatures who know and interact with the owners of the hotel and also," he continued, looking at a particular photo showing one of the creatures who was working on some kind of clock, "this confirms what the Curate told me, without doubt, that it is the creatures that provide the strange technology we keep seeing."

"I wonder if there are creatures based at opticians out back?" mused Yuri.

"Could well be," replied Mallory. "That place was a functioning workshop and they would need to be there to work on the inventions. It also explains why they didn't want us looking around."

"But how is that even possible? Why are creatures so intelligent?"

Mallory shook his head. "I have no idea. Perhaps Professor Montacute or Dr Fredrickson will have the answer to that."

"Or perhaps Douglas had answer and that is why he disappeared?" mused Yuri.

Mallory nodded. "That is what I was thinking too."

"But what of creature we encountered? He was animal. Certainly not docile or able to invent or fix machinery; more likely to destroy it."

Mallory shrugged. "Perhaps not all creatures have the same level of intelligence, or perhaps there are some that are just truly wild, or that some are just bad and want to cause trouble."

"We need to get word to Professor at once," said Yuri. "We may not have found Douglas, but finding out what we have about these creatures, is of vital importance."

"That might prove difficult," observed Mallory. "Everything is shut for the weekend now, including the Post Office, so that rules out sending a letter or telegram, and even if we tried I have a feeling that it would be intercepted and checked. Then when they saw the contents they would stop it."

"What about telephone? We could make direct call?"

Mallory shook his head. "Any phone call would have to go through the local telephone exchange and you can bet if we tried to put the call through, it would be blocked."

132

"So what we do? We need to get this information to London before they leave."

"First thing on Monday morning we visit one of the nearby towns and make the call from there."

"We could take one of the photos here and send it as proof," suggested Yuri, looking at the photo wall in front of them.

"No, they would soon spot it was missing and would come straight to us. We might be able to sneak back in and take a photo of one of these photos later, but then that would be open to questioning, as the quality would not be good."

"If only we could find ally here who would help us."

Mallory shook his head. "I don't think that is likely. Our best chance would have been the Curate, but of course that's not an option now. No, until the Professor and Jazmine arrive we are on our own. Our best bet is to carry on trying to gather as much information as we can."

"Looks like we have work cut out. Let's hope that painting can give us more information."

Mallory nodded with agreement. He had been so taken up with the photos that he had almost forgotten the reason for them being there in the first place. Taking a quick look round they soon found the hatch that led to the storage space which was located just inside the corridor that led through to the bedrooms. On the wall underneath, set into a brass plate was a large switch. Cautiously Mallory threw the switch. There was a pause and then the hatch slid slowly to one side and from above there was a clicking sound and a light automatically turned itself on. Then, with the sound of gears and chains moving, a metal ladder very slowly lowered itself down to the floor.

CHAPTER 27

Carefully Mallory, with Yuri not far behind, started to climb the ladder and entered the storage space. They found themselves in a large room, which was filled with tea-chests, old furniture, boxes, piles of old colour newspapers and all kinds of other items that had been placed here out of the way. Standing at the far end of the room, to one side, was an easel on which there was a large painting, covered by a dust sheet. Quickly they made their way over to it and, without a word, Yuri took hold of the sheet and pulled it off to reveal the picture they had seen hanging on the wall on the first floor.

"We found it!" said Mallory triumphantly.

"Indeed," said Yuri. "Right, let me take a closer look at it. At Royal Palace in Russia I was assigned to work with Tsar's art adviser for a time after unfortunate incident."

"Incident?" asked Mallory.

Yuri looked a bit sheepish. "Let's just say bottle of vodka followed by guard duty with loaded rifle a terrible mix. Anyway for six months to keep me out of trouble I was, as you would call it, 'Art Handler'. I helped move and keep record of paintings at palace as well as do all kinds of other tasks as required by Art Advisor. I learnt lot in that time." Yuri took a step back and expertly began to cast his eye over the painting. "Interesting," he mused, eventually moving closer to focus in on the bottom right corner which showed the table on which there was a green crystal skull and by it a closed book. Seemingly happy, he stood back up. "Title of book has been painted out. Also skull had been repainted. Brush strokes different to those used on rest of painting and slight colour variation."

"Are you sure?" asked Mallory, astounded as he could see no signs of the fact the painting had ever been altered.

"Oh yes," replied Yuri nodding. "Whoever did this did very good job, but there are subtle clues."

"Why would they do that?"

"My initial guess is that original skull looked to be more like skull of creature so repainted to look like a human. As for book, they didn't want people seeing title."

Again, Yuri then moved in closer to the painting, this time focusing on the mountain scene that could be seen through the window above the table. "Interesting; on mountainside there is fortress and what looks like airship flying."

"The fortress of Upper Karlstad," said Mallory. "That's going to be the key to the whole mystery. As soon as the Professor and Jazmine get here, that's where we need to go."

The Russian nodded and then took hold of the painting and turned it round, placing it back on the easel. "You really want to know history of painting," he said with authority, "you need to look at the back. It can tell you so much."

Mallory looked at the back of the canvas. On it there were a couple of labels and official stamps, as well as some dates and numbers that had been written down.

"First," began Yuri, "frame not original, but I don't think that matters here. Also painting has been bought and sold, before ending up here where originally painted. See that label there? It gives description of full painting, placed there by first auction house that sold it, usual practice and would be crossed reference with sale book. It says 'Unknown man at desk in library beside table on which

135

green crystal skull and guide to town of Karlstad.' Dated 1798, by unknown artist."

"So we know what the title of the book is," said Mallory.

Yuri nodded. "Also, there is more." He pointed to Roman numeral number two that had been painted in one corner. "This not the only painting, there is another somewhere. I think that this one practice painting, like draft. Some artists do that. In many cases draft painting is painted over and canvas used again, but this one survived."

"I bet that first painting was the one Douglas saw in Vienna, and it led him straight here," said Mallory.

"Very possible," said Yuri, as he turned the painting back round and then reached for the discarded dust cloth to recover the picture. "I guess that picture had all features that painted out on this one. Although why they paint them out I cannot answer. Come, I think we should go now. Painting holds no more clues for us."

Mallory nodded, he was aware they had spent far too much time in here already. Quickly, he and Yuri descended the ladder back to the sitting room and immediately realised they were being watched. Sitting in the middle of the room, looking at them intently, was the figure of a German Boxer dog.

Mallory and Yuri froze.

The dog stood up and then started to growl.

"That must be Casper," said Mallory, noting the letter C on the collar.

"Where's the other one?" asked Yuri.

"So, one annoyed dog not enough for you?"

Yuri grunted in reply.

"Heidi told us they were docile and harmless," said Mallory hopefully.

136

Yuri shook his head. "But now we in *his* territory, I think we are in big trouble."

"Any suggestions?" asked Mallory. "Please tell me you have experience with dogs."

"Russian sledge dogs yes, but this dog different. Not so cute and fluffy."

As if to emphasise the point Casper growled a little louder.

"I think I have plan," said Yuri, as he took off his jumper and quickly wrapped it around his arm. "It not very good plan, but time is against us. We need to get out of here. Stand back."

Mallory did as he was told. Then Yuri hit the button on the wall which immediately started to retract the loft ladder back into place. The Russian then moved forward, keeping a close eye on Casper. "Come on doggie!" he cried. "Come to Yuri."

Casper growled, barked and lunged forward at the Russian, who in response held up his padded arm in front of him. Casper's teeth closed round it and Yuri yelled out in pain as, despite the protection, the dog's teeth sank into his arm. "Now I have you!" Yuri cried. With his free arm he put it round the dog's body and lifted it up into the air, turning as he did so. In surprise at finding himself suspended in the air Casper yelped, releasing his grip. Then in one awkward move Yuri turned and propelled the dog forward onto the ascending loft ladder. Casper's front paws caught the rungs and with a push from behind from Yuri, added to the fact that there was nowhere else for him to go, the dog scrambled up through the hatch and into the loft. Moments later the hatch closed trapping him up there.

"There," said Yuri triumphantly as he put his jumper back on, "doggie safe and unharmed as are we!"

"But he's trapped in the loft," pointed out Mallory.

Yuri waved his hand dismissively. "He will be fine. He will scratch and bark, will be heard then released."

Immediately there was another sound of growling.

Mallory and Yuri turned to see, standing in the entrance to the kitchen, Felix.

"Any ideas how we handle this one?" asked Mallory.

"Yes," replied Yuri, "we run!"

With that the Russian started forward towards the door that would take them back into the hotel. Following his lead, Mallory ran after him. However, from the kitchen, Felix also sprang into action, and was faster. The dog arrived at the door first, stopping on the rug decorated with cogs and gears, snarling and growling. The reaction of both Mallory and Yuri was instant. In unison they bent down, grabbed hold of the edge of the rug, lifted it up and threw it over the dog, who found himself covered in it and was temporarily disabled. Then Mallory dived for the door, opened it, and without even checking to see if there was anyone beyond he, followed by Yuri, quickly ran back out into the hotel and immediately slammed the door shut behind them.

With great relief, they looked around to see the corridor and staircase empty.

"That was close," said Mallory.

"But worth it," replied Yuri, with a smile.

Mallory nodded. "Agreed, but I wouldn't want to take such a chance like that again."

"With the information we just got, I don't think we need to; Very big pieces of the puzzle now in place."

"Except for the most important," said Mallory glumly. "We still don't know what happened to Douglas."

"Yet," said Yuri with a smile, "yet."

CHAPTER 28

Fritz entered his small office which was located at the back of The Hotel Golden Rose, far away from the bustle of guests that usually filled the building. As the main representative in Lower Karlstad, the room had been set aside to allow him to carry out his duties undisturbed.

Looking over to his desk he could see that the small control panel attached to the large brass typewriter was flashing, indicating that there was a message for him. He went over to the desk, seated himself and looked at the paper that was placed in the typewriter, on which a simple message had been typed.

Fritz, could you contact me at once. Netvor.

Fritz reached to the control panel and turned the large dial to position number twelve and began to type.

Netvor, this is Fritz, are you there?

Fritz sat back and waited, knowing that the words he had just typed would instantly be transmitted to a similar machine that belonged to Netvor, which was located in the creature's study in Upper Karlstad. Of all the technologies that had been developed, this was the one that caught Fritz's imagination the most; the instant communication of words from one machine to another over distances. It was even possible for very basic images and diagrams to be transmitted in this way. Not just the simplistic faces consisting of a semi colon, dash and right bracket, and similar, that was now sometimes added to less formal messages, but actual photos. First a photo would be taken and then the camera with the undeveloped glass plate still inside, would be attached to the typewriter by a special wire. Then the image, using the appropriate letters and symbols, would be typed out and would appear at the other end. It was a laborious process and the image quality was severely reduced. However, it was a great development and it was predicted that over time the concept would improve in speed and clarity.

Suddenly Fritz's typewriter sprang into life. The arms of the machine flicked up of their own accord, hitting the paper, leaving behind letters that would spell out a message.

Yes, I am here. Fritz we have a problem, now Rakasa has fallen ill. He has not been himself of late and has suddenly taken to his bed with a high fever. We think he is suffering from the same illness that struck Zidal.

As he read the words Fritz felt his heart beat faster, knowing the implications of what he was seeing. One creature in this condition was bad enough, but to have two, that was going to cause major problems. Fritz moved to the machine and hurriedly typed.

This is terrible news. How could this happen? What treatment is he getting?

Almost as soon as he had finished typing, the machine sprang into life with Netvor's reply.

He has been taken to the cellars here under 'The Manor' and isolated. We cleared an old storage area and turned it into a medical room for him. We have administered the usual medicines to try and keep his fever under control, with some success. We have also taken one more sinister precaution. The room is guarded day and night by an armed guard. We have allocated one of your kind, a human, to the task. Should the madness take hold and he tries to escape, he has orders to use lethal force.

As he read the message Fritz found himself nodding in agreement. The actions Netvor has spoken about were the ones that he would have instigated had he been in charge of the situation. The cellars of The Manor house had long since been given over exclusively for use by the creatures of Upper Karlstad. It contained meeting and meditation rooms, a library, workshops and recreation areas. It seemed logical that with the current developments he should be kept there. Even better than having him secured in Upper Karlstad's church, St. Magdalena's, which was the only other plausible option. Fritz moved back to the keyboard and started to type.

I think you have handled things as well as you can. But this is the second case. Are we looking at a more widespread illness? Could more of you succumb to this?

As he waited for the reply, he could feel his heart beating in anticipation. What if the creatures that had protected and enriched their town for centuries suddenly posed an actual danger to them, and even the towns and villages beyond? What would they do if it became clear that one after another they were to contract this illness and become uncontrollable monsters?

The typewriter again started to spell out a message.

No, we are not looking at an epidemic here. I am certain of that. If that were the case Zidal would have no doubt infected others and many more of us would be ill by now. We are ....

Suddenly the typewriter's arms stopped and there was a beeping sound from the panel and a small red light began to flash, indicating that the paper was about to run out. Fritz had been so absorbed in the instantaneous messaging that he had not noticed the paper was all but used up. He took out the existing sheet and then replaced it with a blank one from his desk drawer. There was a pause and then the machine continued where it had left off.

.... of course making investigations into possible causes of their condition, but so far we have not been able to find anything of real use, even in the archive. Although, we have managed to rule a few things out for certain.

Fritz moved to the typewriter and immediately started to type.

Have you had any more reported sightings of Zidal?

He sat back and stared at the machine as Netvor's reply appeared in front of him.

No, we have sent out regular patrols but have found no trace of him. I had wondered if he would try to return here to Upper Karlstad, but he hasn't; well so far anyway. All we can do at this stage is keep vigilant and hope. Although I fear it will not be a happy ending. Are there any developments with the English man and the Russian?

Fritz grunted and started to type. The problem of Mallory and Yuri was one that seemed to be constantly evolving and was an unwelcome distraction from everything else that was presently going on.

We are keeping them under continual observation and are restricting their movements as needs be. They are already aware of far too much already and it will only be worse when their friends arrive. I fear that we will have to engage our 'Ultimate plan' to deal with them all. By the way, how are the repairs going following the rockslide?

Two weeks earlier there had been a rock fall on the mountain above the fortress of Upper Karlstad. Certain areas were known to be unstable, due to slight earth movement and on occasion there would be minor rock falls. The creatures regularly undertook survey work to check the mountains stability and had over the years been forced to undertake action such as blasting certain areas and securing others with rods and barriers. For the past two years no action had had to be taken at all. All seemed well, until recently where minor traces of slippage were noticed, followed by a larger slide, which caused some damage and also inconvenience. Then this more major incident occurred.

The hands of the typewriter began to spring up one by one to write Netvor's reply.

Fortunately the fortress wall took the brunt of things. Most of the rocks have been cleared and disposed of now. The damage to the outer wall was more than we expected, but we have set a repair team to fix it. However, as you know, some rocks did make it into the fortress and crashed into Mirka's house. A section of the roof was smashed in and one wall took extensive damage. Fortunately he and the rest of his family were out when it happened; otherwise there could have been serious injuries. They are now staying at Migoi's house while the repairs are being made. Right, I am afraid that I will have to go now. Keep me informed as to any developments.

: -)

With that, the machine stopped. Fritz sat back in his chair. He had asked about the rockslide as an after-thought, but got a sudden chill down his spine when reading Netvor's reply. He hoped that the incident was a one off and not a sign of something more serious to come.

CHAPTER 29

After an evening meal at the Hotel Post, Mallory and Yuri decided to head out to see if they could find some more information about the strange town they found themselves in, and any further clues as to where Douglas could be.

"I want to mix with some of the locals," said Mallory, as he stepped out of the main door of the hotel onto the main street. "Hopefully they may be a bit more forthcoming."

"Sounds good," said Yuri cheerily, "I am happy to spend evening going from tavern to tavern."

"Um, let's try a different tact," said Mallory, fearing the result of what Yuri would treat as a 'pub crawl'. "I think that we should try some of the café's and coffee houses instead."

"You think so?" replied Yuri, sounding disappointed. Mallory nodded. "I don't think that Douglas was much of a drinker for one thing. The café's will be our best bet by far."

"So where do we start? There seems to be a lot of those establishments all over town."

Mallory paused, and then an idea came to him. "I think we should do what any other tourist would do in this situation. We start at the biggest, most noticeable place and then go from there."

"What about our friend?" asked Yuri, pointing to a man standing over the other side of the street who was trying not to look over at them.

Mallory shrugged. "I guess he will follow. As long as he keeps his distance there won't be a problem."

With that, they headed across the main square to a large building on the corner named 'The Karlstad Coffee House.' It had about twenty round tables in front of it; most filled with customers.

Inside, the café was richly decorated with dark wooden panels, red and black ceramic floor boards and a number of expensive looking chandeliers hanging from the ceiling. The left hand side was taken up with the counter area consisting of a number of display cabinets filled with cakes and a variety of chocolates. This gave way to the main ordering area, where you could choose from the seemingly endless list of different types of coffees that were sold. The right hand side of the building was taken up with booths and tables; most of them occupied by people happily chatting away as they ate and drank.

From behind the counter a woman in her twenties smiled over at them. "Are you are here for the duelling?"

"Duelling?" repeated Mallory, clearly confused.

"Yes, Tea Duelling." The girl pointed towards the end of the counter. "Down the stairs there, hurry, they are just about to start."

Their curiosity tweaked, Mallory and Yuri headed to the stairs and followed them down. They found themselves in what had clearly once been the cellar, but had been lavishly decorated and was now used as an additional customer area.

In the middle of the room, standing in front of a round table with two empty chairs, there was an impressive looking man with a waxed moustache wearing a tweed suit. He was calling people to gather round. On the table was a teapot, two cups and a plate on which there were strips of the local Lebkuchen biscuits. "Now," he called out in English, "I am Leopold, the Master-at-arms of our fair sport. I welcome one and all to our session of Tea-duelling."

A cheer went up from the crowd.

"Now who is brave or foolish enough to take up the challenge?"

A number of eager hands shot up.

Leopold looked around and pointed to one man who came out and took one of the seats; and on seeing Yuri pointed at him too. Caught by surprise, the Russian also came forward and took the other empty place, not quite sure what to expect. Leopold leant down to both competitors and asked them their names before addressing the crowd.

"Ladies and Gentlemen, I present to you Hans Joseph Bernhard and Yuri Alexander Romanovsky."

Another excited cheer went up.

"And now," Leopold continued, "I will go over the rules. First, you must choose a Lebkuchen biscuit and then on my command you must dunk it in the tea for the count of five, then you must withdraw it. At that point the battle begins! The person who can keep the Lebkuchen intact for the longest before *successfully* eating it will be declared the winner. Are you clear on the rules?"

Both men nodded.

"Then gentlemen, choose your weapon!"

Both Hans and Yuri picked up a slice of Lebkuchen. Then Leopold instructed the men to dunk and then remove the Lebkuchen after five seconds and hold it up in the air, as he began to count.

Almost straight away Hans' Lebkuchen started to wobble, while Yuri's held firm.

"Six, seven, eight…," counted Leopold.

Hans' Lebkuchen started to fall and he leant down to try to eat it, but it was too late. The biscuit fell and landed on the table in a heap. Seeing Hans fail, Yuri Immediately dipped his head and his mouth closed around the Lebkuchen to seal the win.

147

The crowd cheered and Leopold grabbed Yuri's arm, lifted it into the air and declared him the winner.

Then, as the rules stated, the winner must continue. So Leopold called for another challenger from the audience to take on Yuri. The one who responded happened to be the man who had been following them since they left the hotel. Yuri recognised him instantly and it was clear that this was going to be a grudge match. As before, Leopold instructed the men to pick and dunk their Lebkuchen and then withdraw it. Yuri and the man did as they were instructed, but this time the Russian stared intently at his rival. At the same time both Lebkuchens began to wobble and both men lunged for them. Yuri was faster and caught his, as the other man's fell onto the table, much to the crowds delight.

It seemed that Yuri had a natural talent for the tea duelling. He successfully took on and beat the next six challengers and it soon became clear that he was a favourite with the crowd. However, on his seventh go, Yuri had decided enough was enough and he would deliberately lose. His opponent held the Lebkuchen intact and ate it for the count of nine. All Yuri had to do was eat his own to win, but he decided to wait until it disintegrated.

"Ten, eleven, twelve!" counted Leopold.
Somehow Yuri's Lebkuchen stayed intact.

"Sixteen, Seventeen."

"He's going for the longest hold!" shouted someone.

"Come on Yuri!" called someone else, "hold it for twenty eight seconds and the record is yours!"

That was enough to allow Yuri's competitive streak to kick in and he decided to try for it.

"Twenty, twenty one, twenty two...."

"Come on Yuri!" Mallory found himself shouting.

"Twenty seven, twenty eight, twenty nine, thirty ….." Seeing the Lebkuchen was about to finally fall, Yuri leant down and swiftly ate it.

The loudest cheer yet went up and Yuri stood, taking in the appreciation as the new record holder. He was immediately approached by another man, dressed similarly to Leopold, who was smiling and talking excitedly. Yuri looked over and signalled to Mallory that all was well and he would be over shortly.

Meanwhile Mallory made his way over to the small bar area, and after a chat with the serving girl, bought two drinks before finding a table.

Shortly afterwards he was joined by a still smiling Yuri, who picked up his drink and took a large swig. "Now that is good! What is it?"

Mallory smiled. "It is a local concoction called Funkelwiesen made with apple, grapes, spring water and a mixture of herbs."

Yuri gulped down the rest of the drink in one go. "I like it!" He then caught the attention of a serving girl and ordered another. "What you laughing at Mallory? You know I like a good drink."

"Yes, but that one happens to be non-alcoholic." Yuri paused, visibly shocked.

"Now," continued Mallory, "where did you go off to just then?"

"It seemed I qualified for their wall-of-fame," said Yuri, with a smile. "My name was entered on their board. The name below me was Douglas Quinn! I asked about it. It was added two days ago!"

"So he's alive!" said Mallory, with a smile.

"Yes. I asked where he is, but could not get straight answer. He did mention that Douglas had something to do with burnt house on square, but no more." Yuri looked around. "Wish that girl with the Funkelwiesen would hurry up."

Mallory couldn't help but laugh.

CHAPTER 30

After breakfast, the following morning, Mallory and Yuri headed out, eager to see what the famous Dumpling Festival of Karls tad was all about. Stopping on the hotel's steps they could see that the whole town had been transformed.

Down the main street a number of tables had been set out, placed end to end, stretching for over one hundred feet, covered with a series of matching red checked table cloths. At regular intervals along the street were cooking pots that had been set up, where people were in the process of preparing and making the varieties of dumplings that would be served up throughout the day and late into the night. Another key feature of this event was the numerous beer stalls that were also stationed along the road. The idea seemed to be that you would help yourself to dumplings and beer whenever you wanted and seated yourself at the communal table to eat them. To the right of the hotel, on the very edge of the town square, a platform had been erected, where a small band was located, playing traditional Alpine music. The main town square itself had also been transformed. Around the sides were all kinds of stalls selling various crafted wares and in the very centre of the square a large Maypole had been erected. The top was decorated with a display of Alpine flowers, on which stood a small effigy of a white Yeti type creature.

Although still fairly early, there were a lot of people around. Some were already seated and sampling the various dumplings that were on offer.

Turning left they decided to walk down the main street, and as they did so Yuri made an observation. "Something not right."

"What do you mean?" replied Mallory.

"Strange atmosphere here. This presumably a happy event but I feel the tension in the air."

Mallory looked around, and noticed for the first time that a lot of the people were looking nervous and on edge. These people seemed to be the Karlstad residents, who stood out by their brass goggles and various leather pouches. While other people who were without such paraphernalia, presumably visitors to the festival, were smiling and looking relaxed. Another thing was that a lot of the Karlstad residents seemed to be armed in some way, either with rifles slung over their shoulder, or with discreetly placed daggers and short swords hanging from their belts.

"I think," suggested Yuri, "they might be expecting visit from our angry hairy friend."

Mallory nodded. "I hope not. Can you imagine the devastation he would cause?"

"I dread to think," replied Yuri, thinking back to the raw power of the creature that he had fought.

After a short distance Yuri stopped to examine one of the dumpling stations, which was being seen to by a woman in a bright yellow dress. Inside the large cauldron, which was suspended by a small tripod over a small fire, a

151

number of dumplings were cooking away inside the boiling water.

"Mallory," said Yuri in a whisper, "look behind you, upwards to the Hotel Post's balcony."

Mallory turned and looked where Yuri indicated.

Standing on the first floor balcony staring at them intently were Fritz and Heidi. Yuri looked back at them and waved, but the two remained still and continued to glare at them. "I wonder if they realise we were in their living quarters?"

"More than possible and I think they have doubled the watch on us as well," said Mallory.

Yuri looked round to see two different people, who were clearly Karlstad residents by their clothes, discreetly looking at them from a distance.

"Looks like we have to tread very carefully," said the Russian. "Come, let's go."

The two men continued on their way down the main street, until eventually the long tables ended and beyond it fair ground style stalls took over, such as 'Hook a Duck', 'Coconut Shy' and the like. The stalls held no interest for them and so they continued onwards until the stands thinned out and eventually disappeared.

At the very end of the long street, next to a particularly grand looking hotel signed as The Golden Rose, they came to a level crossing. As they approached the track, a man that was standing by the ornate brass gate moved forward to block their way. He was wearing various leather pouches and an Alpine Hat that had a set of goggles attached to them. The most noticeable thing about him, however, was his false left arm. The entire limb, which was attached to his shoulder by leather straps, was made from brass rods with a large cog mechanism which served as an elbow. Smaller, more delicate, cogs and rods had been crafted to resemble a hand, which looked fully functional.

"You appear to be blocking our way," said Yuri, with a hint of menace in his voice.

"Yes, I am aren't I?" came the reply, with equal hostility.

"Why not just turn around and go back to the festival? There is a lot to see and do there and if you hurry you will catch the main parade."

Yuri nodded past the man. "Because I want to see what is over the train tracks."

"Just a road which leads to the next village, nothing more."

"I like seeing little villages," said Yuri, "reminds me of home."

"Nothing to see in that one," said the man. "Everything is closed. Everyone is here enjoying the festival. Why don't you turn back and join them?"

"Because I want to explore a bit. How about instead I take cable car up to fortress and mountain for look round? I am curious as to what's up there," said Yuri, glancing up and in the distance seeing the moving pods of the cable car that would take people to Upper Karlstad.

"Sadly the cable car is not running today," replied the man flatly.

"Strange," replied Yuri, "it certainly looks to be running."

"Oh I think you are mistaken," replied the man flatly.

"No, perhaps you take a look through those silly goggles of yours?"

A look of annoyance crossed the man's face. "It is *not* running. Anyway, even if it was, there are strict instructions that you are not to board it. Now turn round, go back to the festival, and enjoy yourselves."

"What if I insist?" said Yuri, standing up to his full height and looking as though he was preparing himself for a fight.

The man raised his mechanical arm and curled the fingers into a fist. "Oh, you don't want to do that. I can pack quite a punch with this, enough to put you out for a week."

"So what happened?" asked Mallory quickly before Yuri could respond. "I mean to your arm."

The man paused, almost unsure if he should answer, before replying. "It was an agricultural accident. I got caught in machinery and it got cut off just under the shoulder."

"I used to be a soldier," said Mallory. "I've seen a lot of lost limbs and the pitiful replacements that the men were given as a substitute, but I have never seen anything like that before."

"We have a chap here, an optician. He's also a bit of an inventor…."

"….he makes all kinds of amazing things," broke in Mallory. "Yes, we know."

The man grunted. "Now, please go. I don't want any trouble."

"Come on Yuri," said Mallory, "let's head back."

With a grunt, the Russian nodded and the two men turned and headed towards the town. They continued without stopping until they were back outside the Hotel Post. It was now noticeably busier, with many more people sitting at the tables eating and drinking. The band that was on the corner platform had now changed. In its place was a string quartet consisting of two male violin players, a viola player and a cellist, both female. The instruments seemed to be decorated with various cogs and ornate brass-work, while the musicians were dressed in traditional Austrian 17th century court attire, which was coloured deep red and the outfit was complete with white gloves and wigs. What was almost sinister about them was the fact they each wore a polished brass curved mask, and looked straight outwards towards the audience as they played. The music they made was classical but played to a much faster beat. Mallory and Yuri stood watching the band for several minutes, captivated by the strange almost hypnotic sounds.

CHAPTER 31

"Um, Mallory," said Yuri, after a while, "those musicians, we can't see their faces. You don't think that they could be, you know ……?" He left the sentence hanging, almost embarrassed to finish it.

"Could be what?" replied Mallory, unsure what his friend was driving at.

"No matter. So what we do now?"

Mallory paused, beyond the Maypole the burnt out house caught his eye. "I think we should follow up your lead from the tea duelling and take a closer look at that gutted building."

"Alright, but I have feeling that will not be straight forward to just walk in," Yuri smiled. "I think it's time I

155

got into scuffle. In confusion you can slip away and investigate the house."

"Okay," said Mallory, "but nothing too serious, best just make a scene. I don't want anybody getting hurt. Now, who's your target?"

Yuri pointed across the square to a man who was located between the burnt out building and the strange machine selling Ice-Cream. "Him!"

With that, the two headed across the square and straight to the man that Yuri had decided was his prey; an artist selling his paintings that had been carefully arranged on the roadside. When they reached him, they spent a few moments looking at the pictures. Most of them were watercolours of landscapes and houses, some Yuri instantly recognised as Karlstad. The artist, who was sitting on a small stool, was a man in his mid-twenties, who had dark hair and a neatly trimmed moustache.

Yuri stooped down and picked up one of the canvases, looking it over. "Where is this?"

The man shrugged and shook his head indicating he didn't understand. Yuri repeated his question again, this time in faultless Austrian.

"Ah, that is a scene from the outskirts of Vienna," the artist replied.

Yuri bent down, half dropping the canvas to the floor, before scooping up another one.

"Please be careful, the canvases can easily be damaged." Yuri smiled to himself. That was the opening he needed. "I know how to handle art my friend! I used to work for Tsar of Russia. If I can help catalogue priceless Royal collection, I can deal with these meagre offerings." With that, he again half dropped the painting to the ground making sure that the corner landed first, bumping the edge. In response, the artist jumped to his feet. "What are you doing, you fool?"

A couple of nearby people turned to look at who was shouting and over what.

"Hey, no need to get nasty little man, it was an accident!"

"No, that was deliberate!" cried the artist. "You damaged the painting, so you must buy it!"

"I am not buying that rubbish!" said Yuri, just as loudly. "I would only buy that if I needed to cover a damp patch on my toilet wall!"

Seeing that things were developing, Mallory took a discreet step back. He looked around, noticing that even more people were now starting to look at the developing disagreement.

"That was one of my best paintings!" cried the artist, starting to get more animated. "You will pay for it!"
Yuri stepped forward slightly, his foot catching on the edge of another canvas. This last act sent the artist into a rage. He started to yell uncontrollably, waving his fists at Yuri.

Mallory continued to back away, looking round he could see that most people were now engrossed in the argument that was taking place. Then just as Yuri reached out and pushed the man to the ground, Mallory made his move. Quickly he turned and, using the surrounding people as cover, moved straight over to the burnt out house. The detached building stood three stories high with a roof that sloped towards the square. The large central wooden door, along with the ground and first floor windows, were all boarded up and the rest of the building, up to the second floor, was stained with soot. Realising that he would not be able to gain entry from the front, Mallory quickly ran down the left hand side of the building, leaving the main square, the Dumpling Festival and everything else behind him.

Towards the back, he found his point of entry into the building, a small side door that had not been boarded. He tried the handle which was locked so, bracing himself, he slammed his shoulder against the door.

Once.

Twice.

On the third time there was a sound of splintering and the door flew open. Immediately Mallory went inside, closing the door behind him and hoping that no one had happened to see him break into the building. He paused for a moment and waited as though expecting the door to be kicked open again and find himself grabbed and dragged out by someone and then pulled out and back to the square, but there was nothing. Breathing a sigh of relief he moved towards the front of the building until he found himself in the large main hallway, which was dominated by a large staircase; the middle of which had collapsed. Everything was blackened and covered with soot which still filled the air making it hard to breathe. To the right there was some kind of reception desk and what was left of a number of chairs set out in a row, presumably a waiting area. Looking round, Mallory could not actually work out what the building had been used for.

Unsure what exactly he was looking for, or how much time he had, Mallory moved over to the reception desk in the hope of some clue. On the desk were the remains of some kind of large appointment book which, when Mallory touched it, disintegrated in his hand. Out of pure interest he picked up the blackened telephone receiver. He noted that there was no actual wire attached, although he suspected that, like the 'mobile' phone he had witnessed in London, there never had been. The drawers of the desk opened, but the contents were burnt beyond recognition and would yield no clue. Then on the floor, just by the bottom of the staircase, something glinting caught his eye. Mallory moved over to the base of the staircase, bent down and picked it up. Although badly damaged, it was recognisable as a lapel pin. At the top was a battered crown and underneath was a belt encircling a picture of the globe. Mallory recognised it as the emblem he had seen earlier in London of the Royal Geographic Society. He smiled. The pin could only have belonged to one person – Douglas Quinn.

Mulling this revelation over in his mind, Mallory moved over to the main window. He wanted to check if Yuri was still there. Peering through the gap in the wooden boards out into the square he could not see the Russian anywhere in sight. The pavement outside was now packed and he could instantly see why; for at that very moment a horse drawn cart moved past. On the back of which stood a woman in her early twenties who was smiling and waving to the crowd. She was wearing a long white dress and her long blond hair was tied in a long plait that was decorated top to bottom with wild flowers.

Then a strange noise caught his attention. He moved to the centre of the hall and listened, trying to make out where it was coming from.

Mallory got down on his knees. The noise seemed to be coming from beneath him. It was a low growling, followed by a thump. Unsure what to do in response, he knocked on the floor.

His knock sounded hollow.

From below there came the noise of more movement.

Carefully Mallory started to move his hand over the area where the sound had come from, convinced that there was a trap door there. After a few sweeps his fingers caught the edge of a broken corner of tile. Pulling at it, the entire tile came up to reveal a large brass ring underneath. Mallory took hold of the ring and, taking a deep breath, lifted up the hidden hatch and peered inside.

Two glowing red eyes met his gaze.

Mallory dropped the hatch and instinctively threw himself backwards. However, his reaction was too late as a large hand, followed by a large arm covered with short hair, appeared from the darkness and grabbed him firmly by the foot and started to drag him slowly and deliberately towards the hatch.

CHAPTER 32

With his free leg Mallory kicked out, and he flung his arms out in a vain attempt to stop himself from being pulled down through the hatch. But he knew that it was a futile gesture.

The creature had him.

Then, from behind, there was yelling and Mallory suddenly felt himself being grabbed and pulled in the opposite direction. Someone ran past and dropped to their knees and grabbed at the white fur covered hand to try and remove it from his leg. With surprise Mallory realised it was one of the musicians from the strange looking band, complete with brass covered mask. From below the hatch there came a yell and the hand let go and disappeared, the hatch cover dropping back into place.

"Are you alright?"

Mallory looked behind him to see Fritz, the man they had encountered earlier with the mechanical arm, and a man dressed in a police uniform.

"Um, yes, I think so, thank you." He climbed to his feet. "The creature, it had me!"

"What creature?" replied the man with the mechanical arm.

"The thing that had my leg, you must…." Mallory's voice trailed off, realising what was about to happen. Fritz shook his head. "No idea what you are talking about."

"Now," said the Constable, "what are you doing here? This building is dangerous."

"I'm well aware of that!" said Mallory, glancing back down at the hatch. "I came here to try and find out what happened to Douglas Quinn."

"This again?" said Fritz. "I told you what happened to him. He died. I am sorry for your loss, but you must accept his death."

In response Mallory held up the battered R.G.S. pin which he had managed to keep hold of.

"Oh dear, you have been busy haven't you," said Fritz, as he looked over at the Constable and nodded. In response the Constable stepped forward and took hold of Mallory by the arm. "Consider yourself under arrest."

"What for?"

"You broke in here for a start. You can join that Russian friend of yours in the cells. He's just been arrested for assault."

161

The Constable led Mallory away, with the man with the mechanical arm close behind, leaving Fritz and the musician alone in the abandoned building.

"That was a close one," said Fritz. "Another few seconds and he would have been a goner for sure."

"Indeed," said the Musician, as he started to take off his gloves, mask and then finally his coat, to reveal his white fur covered body. "I do enjoy playing in public, but the disguise does make me so hot!"

"Well, Canavar," said Fritz with a smile, "can you imagine the reviews you would get if you appeared without them?"

Canavar smiled. "Sadly I think that my playing would be the last thing on their mind. I don't even think that they would care that my violin has the playing qualities of a Stradivarius! What will happen to the Englishman and the Russian?"

"The usual plan that is put in place when people know too much," said Fritz. "We will wait for their friends to arrive from London and deal with them all in one fowl swoop."

Canavar nodded. "A pity, I thought they had potential. Perhaps they could all be persuaded to stay and join us?" Fritz shook his head. "I cannot see that can you?"

"No," replied the creature sadly.

"Anyway," continued Fritz, as he produced his gun from his jacket. "We have more pressing matters that need our attention now don't we?"

Canavar nodded, then stooped down and took hold of the hatch ring and pulled up the cover, while Fritz stood ready to fire in case Zidal appeared again. However, the creature did not and the two found themselves staring into a dark void.

"How far does the tunnel network go?" asked Canavar.

"I'm not totally sure," replied Fritz. "The system hasn't extensively been used in decades."

"There must be a plan though?"

Fritz nodded. "Somewhere, yes, in Upper Karlstad. We can check the archive later. Right now I think that our best bet is to try our luck now." Then from his pocket he produced a small torch which he turned on and shone downwards through the hatch. The drop to the floor below was ten feet, and attached to the wall was a metal ladder.

"Let me go first," said Canavar. "I can just drop down and I don't need a torch. Just in case Zidal is waiting for us a little way down the tunnel and hoping for a surprise attack."

Fritz nodded and stood back. Due to the physiology of the creatures, as well as amazing strength, they were also able to make jumps, such as this drop, without any injury. They also had a different range of visual abilities that included being able to see in the dark as though it were day.

Canavar took a breath and then dropped down into the darkness. A moment later Fritz heard a slight thump of him landing, then nothing until Canavar broke the silence by calling that everything was clear. Fritz then climbed down the ladder to join him.

The tunnel itself was made from stone and had a cobbled floor which stretched out into the distance. Carefully Fritz and Canavar advanced, Fritz holding his torch and modified gun that shot an electrical charge in front of him. The hope was that it would be enough to stun Zidal so he could be taken alive. However, if things proved too much, with a flick of the switch the weapon could be set to the kill setting.

Carefully they made their way down the tunnel and after about a minute Canavar suddenly said, "You know, if I was in Zidal's situation, I would most likely think of setting up some kind of booby trap."

Before Fritz could reply, Canavar felt his fur covered shin hit by some sort of wire and then there was a sharp pain in the side of his upper leg. He yelled out and stumbled backwards, but still managed to keep on his feet. Now sticking out of the creature's thigh was a long metal shard that was now surrounded by his dark purple blood.

"That's going to need some attention," said Fritz, who quickly took a look at the wound. Canavar grunted, reached down and in one movement pulled out the protruding piece of metal and threw it away. "There, solved. Luckily my fur and thick skin prevented it from doing too much harm and the bleeding will stop shortly. If it had hit you it would have gone right through your leg without question."

"Do you want to go back? There could be more traps," asked Fritz.

Canavar shook his head. "No, this is the best chance we have to get him. But let me lead, just in case there are any more surprises waiting for us."

With that, the two continued cautiously. Canavar was in front with Fritz a couple of paces behind, his gun held ready. They continued carefully for another five minutes until the tunnel split into two different directions forcing them to stop.

"What do you think?" asked Canavar.

"I think it would be unwise to separate," said Fritz. "Either we just go back or take a gamble. This is the first sighting we have had of him in a while. I say we try our luck while the trail is still fresh."

"Agreed, but which path?"

At that very moment, there was a noise from the right tunnel and something rolled into view towards them. It was the size of a large apple, made from beaten brass sections and making a strange clicking noise. Fritz and Canavar reacted instantly, turning and starting to run. As they did so, the strange brass sphere exploded into a large ball of fire and the pressure wave knocked them forward. A large section of the tunnel collapsed around them and the two found themselves covered with debris.

For a moment there was a deathly silence and then from somewhere beyond there was the sound of deep manic laughing.

"Fritz, where are you?" called Canavar, as he pulled himself from the rubble.

"I'm here," called Fritz, as he slowly rose to his feet and made his way over to his friend and helped him up.

Looking back through the subsiding dust cloud, they could see that the tunnel was now completely blocked.

"Well, it seems Zidal has been busy hasn't he?" said Canavar.

"Indeed," replied Fritz.

"So what do we do next?"

Fritz surveyed the blocked tunnel. "The only thing we can do is get a team down here to clear the rubble and then mount an armed search of the tunnel system and hope that there are not too many more surprises waiting for us."

Canavar nodded. He hated having to give up, but knew that there was no other option.

CHAPTER 33

For just over a week and a half Mallory and Yuri languished in the prison cell in Karlstad Police Station; this was located opposite The Hotel Golden Rose.

The cell they shared, which was located at the back of the building down a narrow corridor, had one bunk bed, a table and a toilet and sink. The walls were made of thick stone bricks painted white and there was a small glassless barred window that let in light as well as the elements. The cell door consisted of nine thick vertical bars with three sets of horizontal bars crossing them, and a large covered lock.

They were not ill-treated in any way, far from it. They were given books, and London newspapers (although they were a few days old as they took so long to get from England) to read and also one of the Chess sets that they had seen played in the Strube on the first night. They were also shown how it was played. Despite his earlier protests, Yuri actually enjoyed this new version of the game, especially the added piece called 'The Jester' which could totally change the dynamics of the game at any time when brought into play. Home cooked food was regularly brought over from The Hotel Post to their cell twice a day, morning and evening, by Heidi. Mallory noted that she was also allowed to supply them with a ration of alcohol. He presumed that this was done in order to keep Yuri pacified and stop him from going into any type of 'withdrawal', which could lead to mood swings and erratic behaviour.

Much to Yuri's delight Heidi also seemed to bring a daily bottle of Funkelwiesen, which he seemed to like more and more.

While they were eating Heidi would stay and chat with them before clearing their trays away. It soon became clear that she was warming to them both, to the point where she actually started giving them information about what was going on in the strange town they had found themselves in. She confirmed their findings that there were indeed a number of creatures that were based in Upper Karlstad and who provided the town with the strange technology and generally looked after the town, working in harmony with the locals; an arrangement that had been in place for hundreds of years. She also told them what she knew about the creature that they had encountered at the church.

The once noble Zidal was suffering from a rare illness that caused him to revert to an almost animal like state; although still at large, steps were being taken that would ensure his capture and punishment. As for Douglas, she was told by Fritz that he had passed away, dying of heart failure and then two members of the Karlstad Council turned up and cleared out his room and also removed the page from the hotel register where he had signed in.

Despite the attentiveness and the generally relaxed nature, their incarceration did have some worrying aspects to it. Mallory noticed that they had not been given any legal representation nor had they been allowed to contact anyone, namely by sending a message to Professor Montacute, to alert him to their plight. It also seemed from the guards that the charges they faced seemed to change day by day and there was no indication of when any kind of court appearance or trial would take place.

Heidi told them that she would try to find out what was happening, but was only able to report that on making enquiries, she was approached by a member of the Council of Karlstad and told in no uncertain terms not to interfere, as the situation was being dealt with.

Then one evening, out of the blue, when she turned up with their nightly meal, she did not come alone.

"Well, well, Mr Mallory and Mr Romanovsky trust you two to get yourselves into a complete mess without me to guide and look after you."

"Professor!" cried Mallory and Yuri, as they jumped off of the bed and ran over to the bars to greet him and Jazmine, who was not far behind. She went straight over to Mallory and tried to hug him through the bars, while the Professor greeted Yuri.

"I don't want to rush you," said Heidi, looking round, "but we don't have much time."

"Indeed," said the Professor, standing back. "The powers that be did not want us to see you. It was only down to Heidi here persuading the guards to let us in that we have this few minutes. Now Mr Mallory, Yuri; Heidi has told us everything that has been going on so we are more than up to speed on what you have been up to."

"Yes," added Jazmine, "it seems you have been very busy."

"We try to make good with our time," replied Yuri, with a smile.

"And look how it ended up," she said, tapping the bars. Yuri smiled sheepishly.

"Anyway," said the Professor, "Heidi has some very disturbing news. It seems that it has been decided that we are all to be killed."

168

"Yes," said Heidi worriedly, "I found out that the Council had met and once Jazmine and the Professor had arrived a plan would be put in place for some kind of accident. It seems they decided that you all pose a threat and must all be dealt with. I'm not prepared to let that happen and so I have devised an escape plan. Once you are free, you must leave Karlstad and never attempt to return. If you do, it will surely end in your deaths."

"That's all very well," said Mallory, "but your brother came to England to steal the crystal skull and notes. What is to stop someone coming after us in London? After all, we would not be that hard to find."

"The main concern is that you will tell everyone about Karlstad," explained Heidi. "If you escape, and it is clear that you will keep quiet about what you have seen here, I'm sure that the Council can be persuaded to leave you alone."

"What if we just promise not to say anything?" asked Yuri.

Heidi shook her head. "I don't think they would believe you. Your only hope is to make a clean getaway and leave the Council to me. But be warned, the slightest hint of a story about our town, or if you were to send someone to investigate us further, then I would not be able to do anything and you would be dead for sure."

"You can count on our discretion," said Professor Montacute. "No one would take us seriously anyway, not without any firm proof, which we don't have. No, as much as I hate to admit it, with the threat of impending death and seemingly an entire town against us, I fear all we can do is just leave."

"But what about Douglas?" asked Mallory. "We know he is alive. He was in the Karlstad Coffee House tea duelling after he was supposed to be dead, and the wall of fame proves that."

"Please no!" interrupted Heidi. "Look, I am putting myself at considerable risk for you. Whatever is happening with Douglas I am afraid that whether he is alive or dead, he is beyond you. I am afraid that is how you must leave it."

There was a pause. Mallory and Yuri looked over at the Professor, who nodded indicating that they would have to go along with the escape plan and leave with so many unanswered questions.

"Alright," said Mallory finally, "we will do it your way. So what happens next?"

Heidi gave a visible sigh of relief. "Right, make sure you and Yuri are awake and ready at dawn. There will only be one guard on duty in the main building. I will arrange a distraction, so he won't be a problem while we break you out. After we get you out of the cell I will take you to a railway station. There is a goods train that is bound for Innsbruck at six o'clock. It will be easy to smuggle you on board unseen in one of the wagons. By the time anyone notices you are missing it will be too late to do anything. From Innsbruck you should easily be able to make your own way back to London."

"Okay," said Mallory, "but you haven't actually said exactly how you are going to get us out of the cell."

Heidi gave a smile. "Just you leave that to me."

CHAPTER 34

At five o'clock in the morning, the face of Professor Montacute appeared outside the small barred window of the prison cell. "Are you two ready?"

"Yes," replied Mallory, while Yuri, who was clearly still half asleep, grunted.

"Good," replied the Professor, who, from outside, started to feed a heavy duty chain through the window into the cell. "Attach this to the bars and stand back. The other end will be tied to a modified tractor which will take half the wall down!"

Mallory did as he was instructed. "What about the guard?"

"All taken care of," said Heidi, appearing at the window. "He's been called away from the station, we won't be disturbed. By the time he returns you will be safely on your way to Innsbruck."

"Right," said the Professor, checking the chain, "stand back!"

Mallory and Yuri moved over to the other side of the cell as they were instructed. The Professor disappeared from sight. After a short while there was the sound of an engine roaring, the spinning of tyres and then the chain was pulled tight on the bars and a moment later the window, as well as a large chunk of the wall below it, was ripped away.

Through the settling dust Mallory and Yuri could see the large hole that had been created, and beyond that the figures of Jazmine and the Professor, as well as Heidi, who was seated upon a large green tractor type vehicle, on the back of which luggage was attached.

"Come on you," ordered the Professor, "we need to get moving."

Quickly the two gathered up their things. Yuri making a point of taking the Chess set that he had been given. Mallory went through the hole first, however, as Yuri was passing through he suddenly stopped, something catching his eye in the dawn light. The Russian suddenly bent down and picked up one of the broken bricks and examined it.

"Yuri, what are you doing?" asked Mallory.

"One moment," replied the Russian, as he stepped back into the cell and started to look at the edges of the hole that had been made.

By now Heidi had turned off the engine of the tractor, uncoupled the chain and had come over to find out what was wrong. "Come on," she urged, "time is of the essence."

Yuri held up the brick and pointed to the wall by the hole. "Different," he said simply, "I once was sentenced to three months hard labour. I know a thing or two about rocks and brick. These different. Not built at the same time."

The Professor stared at the brick and nodded. "My goodness, you are right."

Yuri pointed to the side of the hole that had been made. "I see at least three other type of brick here too."

Heidi shrugged. "So? We don't have time to discuss building techniques."

But Yuri stood firm. It was clear that he was not going anywhere. "This wall has been rebuilt a number of times hasn't it?"

"I have no idea what you are talking about," replied Heidi. "Look, please, we have to go."

172

Yuri shook his head. "No, something not right here. What is going on?"

"Yes, what is …." But the Professor never got to finish his sentence.

From a pocket in her dress, Heidi quickly produced the modified pistol with the glass vial on top that was sparking electricity. "You blasted fools!" she cried, her voice hardening, "We gave you an opportunity to all get out of Karlstad unharmed and now you have ruined everything!"

Then from somewhere behind them there was a loud animal like scream, and a strange mechanical sound, which made everybody turn. The cause of the noise seemed to be coming from the cable car which served as a link to Upper Karlstad. In the early light of the day, it could clearly be seen a short distance away that the cable cars were swinging wildly.

Yuri was the first to react.

His right arm shot out, and in one move, he grabbed Heidi's gun, removing it from her instantly. Her eyes widened and she raised her hands in surrender.

"No!" cried Yuri, "I would never harm unarmed woman!" He pointed to the cable car. "What is happening?"

Heidi shook her head. "I have no idea, but whatever it is it can't be good."

Then, in the distance, another cry went up.

"That sounds familiar," said Mallory.

"It's Zidal," said Heidi, "he must be trying to start the cable car to get to Upper Karlstad. He has to be stopped!" From another pocket she produced the cordless telephone receiver and pressed a button on the side. She tried to speak into it. "Blast, it's not working! I should be able to

173

get a signal. I think the internal electrical charge has died!"

"No matter," said Yuri, quickly stuffing the gun in his belt, "I handle this". Before anyone could stop him, he ran over to the tractor, climbed aboard, started the engine and began to drive off.

"Stop him!" cried the Professor.

Mallory ran after the tractor and, as it turned, he managed to jump on the back, his foot resting on the coupling where trailers and other machinery were attached and his hand grabbed the back of the seat where Yuri was sitting.

"Welcome aboard Mallory! Now hold on!"
Yuri shifted a gear and the tractor shot forward.

"I learn to drive tractor as child in case you were wondering. My parents were farmers."

"You seem to know pretty much everything," said Mallory, reflecting on the man's extensive skill set.

"I not so good at embroidery, but I may yet still learn!"
By now the tractor had turned onto the road and was thundering towards the cable car, leaving the Professor, Jazmine and Heidi far behind. They drove for about a minute, before turning off the road and headed the short distance towards the cable car system itself. As they did so they were greeted by a man running towards them, who was waving frantically. Yuri slammed on the brakes and the tractor skidded to a halt.

"You have to get help!" cried the man, who Mallory and Yuri assumed was the cable car operator. "It's Zidal. He broke into my operation hut and attacked me! He wanted me to start the cable car so he could get up to the fortress, but I refused. He almost killed me, but I managed to get away."

174

Mallory and Yuri looked at the small hut at the base of the cable car system. Through the window they could see the large figure of Zidal, who looked to be trying to operate the controls, by randomly banging and hitting the buttons and levers in the hope of getting it working. He was obviously failing to do so as, although there was a humming sound from the machinery, the cars were stationary, other than wildly rocking back and forth on the spot.

"You have to drive me back to the town. We need help to stop him," said the cable car operator.

"No, it's too late," said Mallory, "look!"

As he spoke, the humming sound changed as the cable cars slowly started to edge there way upwards despite a horrible screeching sound. Zidal let out a triumphant yell and appeared from the hut and started to run across the wooden platform towards one of the moving pods. Yuri slammed his foot down and the tractor shot forward, aiming towards the cable car pod that Zidal was heading for, with Mallory holding on for dear life. The pod in question was now rising into the air and in one small jump Zidal grabbed the side of it, but instead of trying to open the door and climb in he opted to climb up until he stood on top of the roof.

Again Yuri slammed on the breaks of the tractor, bringing it to a halt, and he, with Mallory behind him, jumped off and started to run along the small platform for Zidal's cable car pod which was now about six feet off the ground.

"Mallory we have to jump!" shouted the Russian as he threw himself into the air, his hands catching hold of the wooden lip that ran around the bottom of the cable car. A few moments later Mallory was beside him, having also jumped and caught the rail, and the two were lifted into the air, with the ground dropping away beneath them.

"Hey Mallory!" shouted Yuri. "This better than travelling on the train to Innsbruck eh?"

All Mallory could do in response was grunt and hang on for dear life.

CHAPTER 35

Slowly the cable car rose into the air, but it was clear from the jerky movement of the pod and the strange sound from the gears that it was not operating as it should be. Then Zidal, seemingly deciding he could move faster, jumped and grabbed at the cable above and started to move upwards, hand over hand, towards the next car. With no fear of the creature waiting for them, Mallory and Yuri quickly scaled the side of the cable car and found themselves standing on top of the swaying pod.

"I don't like the look of this," said Mallory, looking over the side to see the trees and bushes far below.

"Ha!" said Yuri, as he reached for the strange weapon he took from Heidi. "Don't worry. This all over soon! Pity I didn't think of this before eh? But then if I did we miss out on riding cable car!" The Russian aimed the gun at Zidal, who had reached the next pod and had climbed on top, and fired. The weapon emitted a single bolt of blue light which streaked its way across the void and hit Zidal in the left shoulder. The creature yelled and crumpled into a heap on top of the pod.

"There," said Yuri casually, "problem of rampaging monster solved. At very least they draw picture of us on

Strube wall as thanks, maybe we even get medal and free accommodation here for life!"

"I hardly think that's likely do you? If we all get out of here with our lives I think we can count ourselves lucky," replied Mallory.

Then, without any kind of warning, there was another strange grinding noise and the whole cable car system stopped. Looking back down, a tendril of dark smoke could be seen rising up from the hut which housed the motors that powered the cable car. It was clear that Zidal's attempts to operate the machine had only destroyed it.

"Now what?" asked Mallory.

Yuri shrugged. "They find some way to get us down, but in meantime we need to check creature truly finished." With that the Russian tucked the gun back in his belt and then took hold of the overhead cable. He started to work his way towards the pod where the fallen Zidal lay and with no other choice Mallory, taking a deep breath, followed.

Yuri dropped down onto the top of Zidal's cable car with a thump and quickly drew the gun and trained it on the motionless creature. A few moments later Mallory reached him, also dropping onto the roof and going over to the hatch that would allow them access to the inside of the pod. He turned the catch and the door opened, dropping downwards.

"So strange," said Yuri, looking the creature over. "They almost human. I wonder if they could eventually evolve like man."

"Maybe," said Mallory, as he moved over to help the Russian with the creature's body, "but that could take thousands of years ...."

Then Zidal struck.

His eyes opened, he let out a sinister growl and brought his feet up, turning, he kicked them hard, hitting Yuri, who stumbled straight into Mallory. With the weight of the big Russian striking him, Mallory was pushed backwards, but instead of his foot landing on the top of the pod, it found the empty air where the open trap door was. With a yell, Mallory fell downwards and as he did so he grabbed out and his fingers grasped around the arm of Yuri, dragging him down as well.

Thud!

The two men landed heavily on the cable car floor. Looking up they could see the angry face of Zidal, framed by the open hatch, peering down at them. With a snarl the creature leant downwards and made a swipe at them. The attack was in no danger of hitting them and it was clear that it was more for show.

In response Yuri, who despite the fall, had managed to keep hold of the gun, raised the weapon and fired. Zidal dodged out of the way and the bolt missed him. Then the Russian sprang to his feet and grabbed the hatch door swinging it upwards, locking it back into place.

"I think your hopes of becoming the town hero are slightly premature," said Mallory, rising to his feet. From above, there was a yell and the metal hatch door buckled inwards.

"Give it moment or two," said Yuri, as he aimed the gun at the hatch and fired. A bolt of thin light shot up through the roof and from above there was an animal-like yell, followed moments later by the view of Zidal's body tumbling past the window.

"I hit him!" cried the Russian triumphantly.

Then there was another noise of creaking metal and straining cable and the pod tipped slightly to the left.

"I don't think that's all you hit," answered Mallory. "I think you hit the mechanism that connects the pod to the cable!"

Yuri stared at his friend, quickly tucking the gun back in his belt, realising what was about to happen.

There was a snapping sound and the cable car started to fall. Inside, Mallory and Yuri grabbed onto the wall rail and braced themselves for the impending impact. Then the cable car seemed to suddenly slow and from below there was a sound of cracking branches as it fell through the large pine tree. The pod continued downwards before crashing with a heavy jolt onto the sloping mountainside, where it immediately tipped forward and started to roll. Mallory and Yuri were thrown around like rag dolls. Through the windows they would first glimpse images of sky followed by hillside and then again sky as they rolled. Over and over the pod tumbled until, without warning, it came crashing to a halt with a large splash as it came to rest on its side in a fast flowing mountainside stream. At once the cable car started to let in the freezing cold water.

Within a few moments it was up to their ankles and continued to rise fast. Mallory, dizzy and dazed, looked round to see that somehow the glass windows of the pod had stayed intact and realised that if they did not do something quickly it would fill up with water and they would drown. Yuri had already grasped the danger of their situation, and was trying to open the roof hatch, now on its side, which would not move. He quickly went for the gun, hoping to blast it open, but the weapon didn't fire; presumably out of charge. He then stood and tried to push at the glass, now located above his head, but that too remained undamaged. Water continued to rush into the pod at alarming speed.

By now the cable car was half filled and the water continued to rise. Mallory moved to Yuri and tried to help him with the glass.

The water continued to get higher and higher.

The glass stayed in place.

"Damn it," cried Yuri, "it just won't budge."

Soon it was at shoulder height, and then a few moments later it was at their necks. Both men took in a large lungful of air and held their breath just as the water rose over their mouths and a few moments later they were fully submerged.

Then above them there was a sudden shadow and movement.

Thump!

Thump!

Mallory looked up and through the water and glass he could see the shape of a figure standing above them.

Thump!

The figure had something in his hand which he was driving downwards onto the glass. It looked like a walking cane.

Thump! Crack!

The figure moved slightly. Mallory focused on it as best he could through the water. The person who was trying to rescue them seemed to be dressed in tweed, and the nimble figure seemed to have white hair and matching beard.

Thump! Crack! Crack!

"Montacute – Professor Charles Montacute," thought Mallory, smiling to himself. He looked round to see Yuri beside him. He wanted to tell him that it was the Professor and they were saved, but of course couldn't.

Thump! Crack! Smash!

A large hole above them suddenly opened up in the glass and both Mallory and Yuri, ignoring the possibility of being cut, drove up to it, broke the surface of the water and gasped the air in, before looking up to thank their saviour.

"Hello Gentlemen," said the man, looking down on them, "I understand that you have been looking for me, and causing a large amount of trouble in the process. My name is Douglas Quinn."

CHAPTER 36

In the backroom of the Hotel Golden Rose, Professor Montacute, Jazmine, Mallory and Yuri sat by the roaring fire, sipping cups of hot coffee. Mallory and Yuri were now dressed in clothes that had been given to them while their wet ones were being dried. The door to the back room opened and in came Fritz and Heidi, who joined them, seating themselves down on the leather sofa.

Fritz smiled nervously. "First, I would like to start by making it clear that at no point were any of your lives in danger. That is not our way, it never has been. On occasion some people do discover the true nature of Karlstad, and in order to protect ourselves from the outside world, we engage our deception, the 'Ultimate plan', the one that you saw through."

The Professor nodded knowingly. "The parties are arrested and placed in the police cells, so they can't find out any more, then they are told it has been decided that they are to be killed, but an escape plan is put into place.

They flee for their lives, with the fear that if they divulge any information, or return, they will be killed."

Fritz nodded. "It is a plan that has worked very well. Of course, as required, we do make variations at times, like in this case waiting till your group was complete and then dealing with you all together. However, I must say, we did not anticipate that anyone would notice that the wall from the prison had been rebuilt a number of times."

"So," said Mallory, "there are people all over the world aware of the secrets of Karlstad, but are too afraid to tell anyone?"

Fritz nodded. "Yes,"

"And just think," said Jazmine, "we were nearly some of them."

"We only employ that plan as a last resort," said Fritz. "However, some people have been invited to stay and have made Karlstad their home."

"Like Douglas?" ventured the Professor.

Fritz sat back. "Douglas is a very unique case. In our history he was the first person ever who actually gained physical proof of the creatures that look after Karlstad and took it to the outside world. As you can imagine we were gripped by total panic after he took the skull and left. However, before a plan could be properly formulated to solve the problem, to our utter surprise he returned and then things took a surprising turn."

"What did you do to him?" asked Mallory.

Fritz smiled. "Nothing. You are of course familiar with the burnt out building in the town square? Well, that was my surgery. A fire broke out, we were able to get everyone out, but then we realised that there was a child trapped in one of the first floor examination rooms. Despite the danger, Douglas ran into the building. He emerged sometime later with the child, and promptly collapsed. Although outwardly unharmed, it seemed that during the rescue he must have inhaled some of the scorching air. The result was that his lungs were severely damaged. It was clear that he would not survive and he was beyond all help. Then Bytost, who is one of the creatures, came up with a desperate plan. With nothing left to lose, it was put into action straight away. Douglas was taken to Upper Karlstad where he was placed in the sacred chamber that allows the remains of the dead to be transformed into green crystal."

"Amazing," said the Professor, "I think I can see where this is leading."

Fritz smiled. "Yes, as Douglas breathed, he took in the crystals that were in the air and they temporarily reformed and repaired his damaged lungs, and he was able to breathe normally."

"Temporarily?" noted Jazmine.

Fritz nodded. "Yes, after a while the crystals begin to breakdown again and he has to return to the chamber so they can be replenished. He has to spend approximately five hours in the chamber to allow three hours of normal breathing. Then he must return to the chamber or risk his lungs deteriorating beyond repair, and death."

"Five hours in the chamber to give three hours of normal life," said Jazmine. "That's not a good ratio."

"Indeed," said Fritz, "but he makes the best of it. He has been given rooms in Upper Karlstad and the three hours do allow him to come down to the town for a short time. You of course just saw him on one of those visits."

"Why not spend longer in chamber to extend the time out of it?" asked Yuri.

"I'm afraid it's not as simple as that," said Heidi. "If he were to spend any longer in the chamber he risks the crystallisation of his other organs, which could mean death."

"Three hours," mused Mallory, "what can a man do in three hours?"

"Not a great deal to be honest," replied Fritz. "But we are looking at ways to extend that time period, but until then, well, he is trying to make the best of things."

"And I can presume this is why you said that he was beyond us," said the Professor.

"At his instructions, yes," said Fritz, nodding. "He can never have any life outside Karlstad now and the life he has here is severely limited. He was doing it to protect his wife. He did not want to be a burden to her with his now limited existence, or force her to move from London. At first he just wanted to disappear, to be presumed dead, but when you showed up he decided the plan could be moved along, and I had him declared dead."

"That was very noble and heroic," said Jazmine, with an icy tone, "but Jane has been in pieces since he went missing, and as for being a burden, well surely that was for her and her alone to decide?"

Heidi looked over at Fritz with a disapproving scowl. "You see? Isn't that exactly what I said?!"

Fritz shrugged. "I was acting on his behalf and Douglas was only doing what he thought best."

Jazmine and Heidi looked over at each other shaking their heads and both inwardly cursing the flawed logic of their male counterparts.

"Um," said Mallory, aware that a quick change of subject was required, "what of the creature Zidal?"

A flicker of sadness passed over Fritz's face. "I am afraid that he did not survive the fall. But please, there is no ill will or reproach to you there. He was beyond even our help and his death was inevitable, if not from the madness it would have been from one of our own."

"I am sorry," said the Professor, "but at least the problem is now resolved."

"Not entirely," said Fritz grimly. "It seems that one other creature is suffering from the same illness, although I can assure you this is being handled more competently."

The Professor was about to ask a question when there was a knock at the door. It opened and in walked a young man, who nervously approached them. "I am very sorry to interrupt you, but it's Douglas; his condition is not good. As you instructed when he arrived, we put him in a room so he could rest, but he is finding breathing difficult and is looking most unwell."

Fritz groaned. "This was what I was afraid of. It seems his excursion in assisting you in the cable car, and the excitement, has reduced his time away from the chamber."

"Then we must get him back up to Upper Karlstad and into the crystallisation chamber at once," said Mallory.

"I'm not sure if that will be possible," said Fritz, shaking his head. "I had a message from the cable car operator. It seems that Zidal's attempt to use it, burnt out the main motor totally. It will take a day to fix."

"But he doesn't have a day!" exclaimed Heidi.

"Is there another way he can get up there?" asked the Professor.

"There is a road of sorts," said Fritz.

"We could use the tractor," suggested Mallory. "If we placed a trailer on the end we could put Douglas in it and take him up that way."

A smile spread across Fritz's face. "I think that we can do better than that, but I think we will need your help."

"Of course, how?" asked the Professor.

Fritz continued with a glint in his eye. "We have another type of beast here in Karlstad and I think it's time I introduced you to it!"

CHAPTER 37

Fritz and Heidi led the small party out of the back of the hotel and took them to a large barn located on the edge of the grounds.

Fritz opened the two big doors and led them inside. In the centre of the barn was a large object which had been covered over with brown sack cloth. He went to one end and carefully undid the ties before rolling back the material. "There!" he cried, as with one final tug he pulled back the last of the sack cloth. "May I present to you what we affectionately call 'The Brachial', which translates into your language as 'The Brute'."

The Professor, Mallory, Yuri and Jazmine stared at 'The Brute', not quite sure how to react.

It was an open top motor car, but not like any of them had ever seen before. It was over fourteen foot long with two wheels at the front and four at the back. Basically box shaped, the rear section of the vehicle had space for four people to sit, including the driver. While the front of the vehicle was taken up with the engine, some of which could be seen by the specially made slits in the bodywork. From

186

each side, running first down to under the car's running boards then to the rear, where they protruded from the back, were two large black exhaust pipes. The vehicle was painted dark green, with areas usually expected to be chrome, such as the front of the radiator and other metalwork, painted black to match the outer exhaust, giving it a sinister look. At the very back of the vehicle there was a small metal cage which served as a luggage rack.

"The Brute was finished last year," said Fritz, seeing that everyone was stunned into silence. "We wanted to create an all-purpose heavy duty vehicle. It is six wheeled drive and the engine was originally from the de-funked Zeppelin LZ1. It has of course been extensively redesigned and altered for its new role. It is twelve cylinders and is able to produce over 1500 RPM. The top speed has been estimated at well over one hundred and thirty miles an hour, although we have never dared to push it to its full potential."

"But the land speed record set a few years ago by Hémery was 125 miles an hour," gasped Mallory.

"I know," said Fritz, tapping the Brachial almost affectionately. "Imagine our frustration of having this vehicle at our disposal, knowing that it could beat that record with ease, but not being able to tell anyone because of the need for secrecy."

"A vehicle of this size looks as though it would get through a lot of fuel," said the Professor. "How many miles do you get from it?"

"Ah," said Fritz, with an even bigger smile. "That is something we are really proud of. It runs on a combustible liquid of our own creation which is essentially a mixture of vegetable oil and alcohol. The concoction also works in traditional vehicles. In fact the tractor that was used in your 'escape' runs on it, as do the other vehicles you see here in Karlstad. The fuel is easy for us to make and has virtually limitless supply, at no cost, and it is also kind to the environment. As for mileage, well, due to the nature of our fuel, we get seventy miles to the gallon."

"Unbelievable!" said the Professor. "How do you drive it? The controls don't look like anything I have ever seen before."

Fritz moved to the front of the vehicle and everyone followed. He then pointed to the driver's side where there were two steering wheels, one inside the other, and an array of buttons and levers on the dashboard. "To start the Brachial, you must press this red button here, and to make the car move forward, you must move the lever by the steering wheels downwards to disengage the static braking system, while pressing down on the pedal to the left. The more you press down, the more fuel goes to the engine and the faster you go. As you will see, it has not one, but two steering wheels. The outer one controls the front wheels while the inner one, which can be engaged at any time, controls the four rear wheels, thus allowing the whole vehicle to turn on a shilling."

"And how do you stop it?" asked the Professor.

"Take your foot away from the pedal completely," replied Fritz, "and then take hold of the lever by your left, sticking out of the floor, and move it backwards and forwards. The faster you move the lever, the sooner you will stop."

The Professor looked over the machine. "This is an impressive accomplishment."

"Thank you," said Fritz, trying to hide his pride. "We are currently drawing up plans for another Brachial, but one that is slightly smaller. Also we are trying to see if it is possible to create a motorised Penny Farthing. But that is more for entertainment value rather than anything else, as you can guess balance is a problem. Now, on a more serious note, with the cable car temporarily not working, this is the only chance we have of getting Douglas to Upper Karlstad. Do you think you can take up the challenge? Your Russian friend seems more than capable, if his skills with a tractor are anything to go by."

A sudden look of horror spread over Yuri's face and he held up his hands. "No, no! With tractor you just put foot down and hold straight; on narrow mountainside totally different!"

"That's alright Yuri," said the Professor quickly. "That won't be a problem. Although Mallory and I have driving experience, I think that this needs a woman's touch. Jazmine?"

She nodded, looking over the vehicle. "The controls look a little heavy, but I'm sure I can cope, after all I managed with the Model T, and that was a real beast to drive."

"Um, I don't think that a woman has ever driven the Brachial before," said Fritz, with a hint of doubt in his voice.

"Have you ever allowed a woman to try?" said Jazmine pointedly, with a dangerous look in her eyes. In the background Heidi stifled a laugh.

"Um er well, er, I mean that the subject has never come up," spluttered Fritz.

"Yes it did," said Heidi innocently. "I asked if I could drive it last week and you refused."

"Um, well ….," said Fritz, looking more and more out of his depth,

"I am sure Jazmine will be up to the challenge," said the Professor quickly. "She has excellent reflexes and visual perception, and is a lot stronger than she looks. Also, the last time I drove we ended up in a ditch. So I don't totally trust myself."

"Well, that was more due to the fact that you were shot through the shoulder at the time, but thank you Father," she said graciously.

"Well, even so," countered the Professor, "I think that you should drive. I want to come with you though."

"I'm coming too," interjected Mallory and Yuri together. "I'm quite happy for you all to go," replied Fritz, "but there are four of you and Douglas makes five and this vehicle seats only four. One of you will have to stay behind, but no matter, whoever does will be well looked after and as soon as the cable car is fixed we will make sure you are sent up straight away to re-join the others."

"Pah!" said Yuri with a grin. "That no problem at all. Professor and Mallory go with Jazmine. I just climb up the side of mountain."

"Are you sure?" asked Fritz.

"Yes," replied Yuri excitedly, "it has been while since I climbed properly and I will enjoy such a challenge. Can you lend me rope and grapnels?"

Fritz nodded. "Of course, that won't be any problem." He turned to The Professor, Mallory and Jazmine. "Time is now of the essence. We must get Douglas up to the fortress and into the Crystallisation Chamber as soon as possible."

"Agreed," answered Jazmine, "but I would need to have a bit of a practice first, just so I can familiarise myself with the way he handles."

A look of hurt indignation passed across Fritz's face. "He? He? 'The Brachial' is most definitely a she!"

Jazmine looked at Heidi and shook her head. "This is why some of my Suffragette friends tie themselves to railings!"

At that Heidi burst out laughing.

CHAPTER 38

As promised, Yuri was provided with climbing equipment. He quickly said his goodbyes to the others before boarding the back of the tractor, where he was to be driven to a suitable starting point, for his ascent to Upper Karlstad, which had been recommended by Fritz.

Meanwhile the Brachial was brought out of the barn. Jazmine set about getting used to it for the perilous journey ahead. When she felt confident enough, the vehicle was made ready for the trip; the fuel was topped up, their luggage was attached to the cage at the back, and Douglas was carefully brought out and loaded into the rear seat of the vehicle. It was clear that he was struggling for breath and was only able to talk in a whisper, which made the task ahead seem even more ominous. The Professor took his place in the back so he could keep an eye on Douglas, while Mallory seated himself beside Jazmine, with Fritz and Heidi watching intently ready to see them off.

"I have called Upper Karlstad to let them know of the situation," said Fritz. "There will be a welcoming party waiting to receive you. Now the mountain road that you will be taking is not in the best condition, and there may be a few hazards, but don't put yourself in any unnecessary danger." He then pointed to a narrow dirt track that ran past the back of The Golden Rose, and stretched off into the distance. "That will take you to the mountain track that will lead you straight to Upper Karlstad.

Fritz smiled and stood back. "Well, I think that is about it, other than to wish you luck and a safe journey."

With the goodbyes said, Jazmine took a firm hold of the outer wheel, started the engine, released the brake by the handle on the steering wheel and pressed down on the pedal. The engine roared in response and the vehicle moved forward.

The dirt track lasted for five miles, and during this first stint of the journey Jazmine used the opportunity to really test the vehicle's power, easily getting up to 70mph before her Father ordered her to slow down. After a short while the track took a sweeping right turn and slowly started to steepen, climbing higher and higher, until it turned into the mountainside road.

The road, which was little more than a badly maintained dirt track, snaked its way up the mountain side at a steep angle. There was no rail or wall to stop them going over the side, but fortunately the path was wide enough to accommodate the car without putting them too close to the edge. Every so often on the climb, the track would turn back on itself in what at first looked like an impossible U-turn. However, Jazmine found that by engaging the inner steering wheel as well, they were able to make the turn with ease. Initially they travelled well, making their way up the huge mountainside without incident, but then, without warning, the dirt path stopped and was replaced with a forty foot section of tightly placed, unsupported, metal girders that had been fixed directly into the side of the mountain to form a new section of road with a sixty foot drop below.

Jazmine, The Professor and Mallory climbed out of the Brachial to inspect the new path that lay ahead of them.

"I have never seen anything like it before," said the Professor, "but bearing in mind what we have already witnessed in the realms of Karlstad, I am not totally surprised. I am presuming that it will support the vehicle, otherwise Fritz would have said something, but just to be on the safe side Mr Mallory, please will you check it out?"

"What?"

"Go on," said Jazmine.

"But, why me?....oh for goodness sake!" and realising that arguing would not do any good, he moved to the edge of the strange new path and tentatively put his foot on one of the beams and pressed down on it.

It seemed stable, certainly enough to hold his weight.

Then, carefully he stepped out onto the metal bridge.

It held firm.

"I think it's alright," he said, and to emphasise the point stamped down. "But the beams seem slightly slippery underfoot."

"I'm guessing that might be the result of rain or the morning dew," said Jazmine. "Go and check the rest of it. I don't want to take any chances."

Mallory nodded, turned and walked away across the girders, stopping occasionally to test their strength or to examine how securely they were fixed into the mountain. All was fine up until the end where the beams finished and the dirt track road restarted. There was an open gap of about five foot where the mountain road had crumbled away. Mallory jumped over the gap to inspect the other side and it was soon clear that the start of the road was still fragile before giving way to much firmer ground. Glumly Mallory returned to the Professor and Jazmine to report his findings.

"Mmm," said the Professor thoughtfully, as he scratched his beard. "Presumably that's why there is a new section of road here. The old part just disintegrated away. Do you think we will be able to make it across safely?"

"I think so," replied Mallory, "with enough speed."

"Well, there is only one way to find out," said Jazmine. "Going back is not an option!"

With that they all returned to the Brachial and took their places. Jazmine carefully reversed the vehicle down the track, which would allow her to build up enough speed on the approach so they would pass over the gap at the end. Then checking that everyone, especially Douglas, was ready, she put the vehicle into forward gear and pressed down hard on the accelerator. The wheels of the Brachial spun for a few seconds before they found their grip and launched forward.

"Brace yourselves everybody!" called out Jazmine.

The Brachial's front wheels hit the metal girders and the whole vehicle started to judder, a situation that was amplified when the rear wheels left the dirt track and the entire car was on the metal shafts.

"Ja – z – mi –ne !!!" yelled Mallory in alarm, as the vehicle started to skid. In response Jazmine yanked at the wheel to correct the slide, resulting in the Brachial slamming into the mountain wall. There was a terrible screeching sound as the side of the vehicle scraped along the exposed rocks. The force of the impact dislodged some loose debris, which showered the occupants of the vehicle. One rock hit the Professor on the head as he tried to protect Douglas, making him yell out. In the front Jazmine struggled with the wheel, managing to separate them from the mountain and straighten the Brachial up so she was in the centre of the metal track.

"Hold on everyone!" she yelled, as they approached the gap at the end of the metal beams.

The front wheels of the Brachial left the last metal girder, and for a second or so they were suspended in mid-air. The momentum of the vehicle propelled them forward before the front tyres hit the start of the dirt road with a jolt. Immediately, due to the force of the spinning wheels, the edge of the track rapidly started to crumble away. Jazmine gripped the steering wheel even tighter and turned it side to side, hoping the wheels would find a more solid surface, but the path continued to disintegrate as they powered forward. Then the juddering stopped as the back wheels left the last metal girder and they were in mid-air. For a second the vehicle remained level before the weight of the rear end and the lack of purchase on the front resulted in the Brachial starting to tip upwards. As it did so Jazmine took her foot off of the accelerator and the roar of the engine stopped.

"We're not going to make it!" cried out Mallory.

The Professor and Jazmine simultaneously shouted out separate expletives as the vehicle continued to slip. There was a grinding sound and a heavy jolt and the vehicle suddenly stopped, having found its natural balancing point. The underside of the vehicle dug into the very edge of the crumbling road. The front wheels rose up in the air ahead of them, while the rear wheels were suspended over the drop below them.

CHAPTER 39

For a few moments the only thing that broke the silence was the desperate wheezing and gasping of Douglas Quinn as he struggled for air, and the sound of the Brachial's wheels spinning in mid-air. It was the Professor who eventually spoke. "Mallory, you are going to have to get us out of this. You will have to carefully climb onto the bonnet of the car. Your weight should be enough to tip us forward and onto solid ground, then Jazmine can power forward."

"I was afraid you were going to say that," said Mallory.

"No other option I'm afraid," replied the Professor. "Douglas and I can't move and Jazmine is driving. I think you had better make your move soon." As if to emphasise the point, a small piece of the ground they were balanced on broke off and sent debris slipping downwards.

Mallory shook his head, but realising that he was the only one who could get them out of their current situation, he carefully started to ease himself up out of his seat. As he did so the car started to rock. To counter-act this, he leant forward, putting his hands and upper parts of his body over the small windscreen and onto the bonnet. After a moment the car settled. Jazmine also shifted herself forward in her seat.

Then very slowly, Mallory lifted his right foot onto the seat and was about to move forward when the Brachial started again to tip backwards.

He froze.

The entire car shifted side wards, as more of the ground supporting them gave way. By some miracle they remained balanced on the edge.

Then carefully Mallory moved his hands and body as far forward as he could.

"Well done!" cried the Professor. "Now for the last push, Jazmine are you ready?"

She nodded, placing her foot on the accelerator making the engine roar.

Mallory extended himself further, and took a deep breath. To get himself over the windscreen and onto the bonnet of the car he would have no option but to push forward with his right foot, but the force he exerted doing this could easily make the vehicle overbalance and fall.

"Don't worry," said Jazmine, as though reading his mind. "Even if we start to slide, your weight should be enough to bring the front wheels down straight away onto solid ground. As soon as that happens we are away!"

Mallory nodded, pausing before making his move. The Brachial started to tip again, but this time much more fiercely. Fearing it was going to fall, Mallory desperately scrambled forward, landing completely on the bonnet. With the extra weight, the front of the vehicle tipped down, and the wheels connected with the mountain path. As soon as Jazmine felt the contact she pressed down firmly on the accelerator. The front wheels spun and then dug in and the Brachial shot forward, with Mallory hanging on for dear life. Moments later both sets of rear wheels found the solid ground of the mountain track. When they were a safe distance away from the collapsing road Jazmine brought the vehicle to a halt.

"That was a close one," said Mallory, as he climbed off of the bonnet of the car. "How is Douglas after that little misadventure?"

"Still not good, but alive," replied the Professor. He turned his attention to Mallory. "You alright?"

Mallory nodded.

"Good, then we better get going."

With that, Mallory climbed back into the Brachial and they resumed their journey. The mountain road continued upwards and they carried on without any incident. After a few minutes they noticed the track visibly starting to steepen until suddenly they were confronted with a near fifty foot vertical climb, which seemed to sharply level off at the top. Jazmine gently brought the Brachial to a halt.

"I think I want to have a little chat with Fritz regarding his definition of 'a few hazards,'" said the Professor, with more than a hint of annoyance in his voice. "What do you think Jazmine?"

She looked at the ascent. "If I have enough speed we should be fine. However, should we slide backwards; I doubt that I will be able to stop it. We could easily end up turning and then rolling and that won't be nice – for any of us. If anyone wants to get out, now is the time to do so."

The Professor and Mallory stayed where they were. Then without another word Jazmine pressed down hard on the accelerator. All six wheels span wildly and then the vehicle was propelled forward. The Brachial reached the bottom of the slope, and then started to climb upwards. Initially they bounced, before the wheels found their grip and allowed Jazmine to apply the proper power needed to get them to the top. The occupants of the vehicle found themselves thrown backwards in their seats due to the steep

198

angle, giving them a view of the impossible gradient in front of them. The engine roared and strained, but the Brachial continued to climb steadily. Then, about halfway up the slope, without warning, the rear wheels started to lose their grip and began to spin on the spot. In response Jazmine turned the steering wheel from left to right, and after a few moments the wheels regained their purchase and the car struggled upwards.

"I think we are going to make it!" cried Mallory, seeing the crest of the bank ahead of them. Then there was a spluttering, followed by an ominous hissing sound and then a wisp of white smoke started to appear from the engine. The fleeting loss of power was soon felt; as gravity started to tentatively pull them backwards. "No you don't!" cried Jazmine, as she grabbed hold of the brake stick and moved it forward and back. The Brachial came to a stop and immediately Jazmine engaged the accelerator pedal. All the wheels spun round on the spot and there was a terrible roar and whine from the engine. The vehicle began once again to climb, but this time at an alarming speed.

"We are nearly there!" cried Mallory, seeing the edge of the hilltop a few feet away. "Brace yourselves!"

The Brachial passed over the apex of the rise, but due to its angle and increased speed continued straight upwards. For a moment the vehicle hung suspended almost vertically in the air, before starting its descent. Its rear right wheels making contact with the flat mountain road, before the rest of the car slammed down hard.

"Is everyone alright?" Jazmine asked.

The Professor and Mallory nodded, as did Douglas. But it was clear that the Brachial had not gotten off so easily.

Smoke continued to rise from the engine and the right side wheels were bent inwards slightly. After a few minutes rest, to allow the engine to cool, they set off again; this time at a reduced speed due to the now buckled wheels. For the remainder of the journey the mountain road mercifully held no more dangers or excitement for them as they slowly limped along. As they climbed, the temperature began to drop and they began to see traces of snow, with a thin layer covering the road in front of them, before large flakes started to gently shower down on them from above. Then after about twenty minutes the track made a sudden turn to the right and carried on straight up the side of the mountain, this time at a gentle angle. After a few moments a large snow covered brick perimeter wall, about thirty feet tall, came into view, and then they found themselves looking at a large gatehouse sticking out of the wall.

"This must be it," said Jazmine, with more than a hint of relief in her voice, as she aimed the car towards the entrance. When they were within a few feet of the gate she brought the vehicle to a gentle halt.

Then carefully she, along with Mallory and the Professor, climbed out of the Brachial. As they did so, the two large wooden doors opened inwards and a large creature covered in white hair, wearing a sash covered with pouches, and a brown top hat complete with goggles walked slowly out to meet them. "Good morning. My name is Netvor and I am the main representative here in Upper Karlstad. On behalf of myself and those who live here, may I wish you a warm welcome."

CHAPTER 40

Professor Montacute, Jazmine and Mallory found themselves stunned into silence as they each looked the serene and smiling Netvor up and down. Mallory had of course seen a creature like this before in the shape of Zidal, but that was a creature gripped by primal madness who was trying to kill them. So encountering a creature like this calmly walking, talking and in control of their faculties was a shock. For the Professor and Jazmine the amazement was amplified tenfold, as this was the first time they had encountered such a creature.

Then suddenly, from behind Netvor, two other creatures appeared carrying an empty stretcher between them. They went immediately over to the Brachial where they began to attend to Douglas who by now was desperately gasping for air. Quickly and carefully the creatures took him from the vehicle and placed him on the empty stretcher, before taking him through the main gates of Upper Karlstad.

"Please do not worry," Netvor reassured them. "We have seen him in a far worse condition than he is now. A few hours rest in the crystallisation chamber and his lungs will be restored. By tonight he will be fine and I expect that he will be able to join us for dinner."

"Do you really think so?" asked the Professor.

"Oh, yes, for certain. But make no mistake; your actions have certainly saved his life." Netvor paused to look over at the battered and dented Brachial. "I would ask how your journey was, but I can see that it was quite eventful."

"Um, slightly," said the Professor with a smile. "I apologise for the damage to the vehicle."

"That is no problem at all. I'm sure that it can easily be repaired."

"Oh, I almost forgot," said the Professor, "our friend Yuri, the Russian, shall be joining us at some point."

"Ah yes, he arrived a short while ago," replied Netvor with a smile.

"What?!" cried out the Professor, Mallory and Jazmine in unison.

Netvor smiled. "Yes, we were surprised as well. To make such a climb in the time he did is unheard of, not that we encourage it of course. Please come with me. I am sure that you would like to freshen up and have some food. All in all it has been quite an eventful morning for you. I shall arrange for your bags to be brought up to my house, The Manor. During your time here you will be my guests. I am sure you will find Upper Karlstad more than interesting. Please follow me." With that, Netvor turned. The Professor, Jazmine and Mallory followed him through the gatehouse which opened out into a small bustling village, but this was a village like none they had ever seen before.

Directly in front of them was a small open cobbled square that sloped gently upwards due to the gradient of the mountain side. Towards the back of the square was a walled pond; in the middle of which, on a small island, stood an iron pillar. On the top was mounted a large clock. On the left was a large Gothic style church, the front doors opened out onto the square. Along the side of the church and disappearing round the back of it was a row of stone built houses that resembled the British Tudor style, but instead of visible timber beams they seemed to have brass coloured metal ones. The wooden doors also had brass-style finishes on them and the windows were latticed with a similar metal. On each roof was a large flat square panel which appeared to be made up from a clear crystal that seemed to catch the sun's rays.

Directly to the right of the square were two more rows of Tudor style houses, and overlooking these were a terrace on which more buildings were located. Due to the signage outside some of them you could surmise them to be shops and businesses, which would serve the residents of Upper Karlstad.

On a second terrace overlooking this small business district was a large two storey house, again built in the Tudor Style, but looking much grander. Directly in front of this building, parked on the large lawn, was a small cigar shaped airship that had a ridged brass coloured canvas.

All around the snow covered village, creatures, as well as the few humans that called Upper Karlstad home, were casually going about their daily business. All happily interacting with each other, in what was for them a perfectly normal situation. Like lower Karlstad, everybody, be they man, woman or creature seemed to be adorned with leather accessories, as well as hats, goggles and long coats.

"Remarkable," said the Professor, "quite, quite remarkable. In all my years I have never encountered anything like this."

"Thank you," said Netvor modestly. "It is a place where humans and my kind can live freely together. Also, up here, without the prying eyes of others, we were fully able to create a place where our technologies can be used and are visible at all times." To emphasise this he nodded over to a female creature that was walking alongside a motorised pram that seemed to move unaided.

"To be fair," said Mallory, "we did spot a number of your inventions back down in Lower Karlstad."

"Yes, well," said Netvor, with a hint of annoyance, "it seems that we have been a bit careless, and our idea of 'seamlessly' blending our technology with what is already there needs to be urgently revised."

"Ah, Professor, Mallory, Jazmine!" called out a voice in an unmissable Russian accent, "you make it up here in one piece!"

Everyone turned to where the voice was coming from, to see Yuri striding towards them. However, the Russian was now dressed in full Upper Karlstad attire. Under the long brown leather coat, which went down to his ankles, he wore long brown boots, britches and a white grandad style shirt. Around his waist was an over-belt from which various leather pouches hung, including a gun holster. On his head he wore a black top hat on which was placed a set of goggles.

"My goodness," said Mallory, "you seem to have gone 'native'!"

"Ha! Yes, I like this style very much!" he replied, as he greeted them in turn. "The hat really adds something to outfit and pouches on belt are very useful. There is even a pouch that takes a small bottle of vodka or Funkelwiesen."

"Really?" said the Professor with surprise. "Are you thinking of changing your tipple?"

Yuri shrugged. "I like the taste of the stuff. Not as big a kick as vodka, but still good. I was hoping that ………." His voice trailed off as something caught his attention.

"Yuri?" asked Mallory "are you alright?"

"Yes," replied the Russian. "Netvor, what is that?"

"Um, that's our church, St Magdalena's," replied Netvor, slightly confused.

"No, not the church itself, the small creature above door," said Yuri, pointing towards the front of the Gothic church.

Everyone turned to where Yuri had indicated, and there, crouching above the main church door on a small ledge, was a small grey goblin like creature, standing ten inches high with tiny wings and red glowing eyes. On seeing that it had been spotted, the creature stood up, snarled and clawed at the air in their direction.

"My goodness," said the Professor, "he's an ugly looking thing. Netvor, what on earth is it?"

But Netvor wasn't able to answer. Instead he seemed to be scanning the church, trying to see the creature that had been spotted.

"It is directly above the main door, slightly to the right," said Mallory, seeing him struggling.

"But there is nothing there," said Netvor, slightly confused.

"You don't see it?" asked Jazmine.

"Um, no," replied the creature, almost apologetically.

Then the church door opened and out of it came another one of the creatures. This one was slightly taller than Netvor. On seeing the newcomer below, the goblin seemed to smile and then jump down, landing on the creature's shoulder, sinking its teeth into him. The creature itself seemed totally oblivious to the attack and carried on walking with the goblin now firmly attached to him.

"My goodness!" cried the Professor in alarm, "the goblin has got him!"

"Not another vampire!" groaned Jazmine, thinking of the events of Highgate, and inadvertently touching her now healed neck wound.

With that they all launched themselves forward towards the church.

CHAPTER 41

Although the creature was blissfully unaware of the goblin that was feeding upon him, he certainly wasn't oblivious of the strangers thundering towards him. On seeing them, his eyes widened in fear and he turned and tried to dive back into the church, but Yuri got to him first, reached out his hand and placed it on the door, slamming it shut before the creature could escape.

"Don't hurt me please!" begged the creature.

"I don't want to!" cried Yuri. "You have goblin on your shoulder."

"What?"

By now the Professor, Mallory, Jazmine and also Netvor had reached him.

"It's all right Padaras," called out Netvor. "I don't know what's going on but they can be trusted!"

The goblin lifted his head, turned, looked at the newcomers and spat at them. A globule of dark green mucus landed on Jazmine's blouse.

"It has a nasty disposition doesn't it?" she said as she reached for a handkerchief to wipe it off.

But Netvor shook his head. "I don't understand. I can't see anything apart from a strange shadow."

"Well, it's certainly there," said the Professor. "We can worry about why you can't see it later. Our first priority is to detach the thing." He reached forward and grasped the goblin and tried to pull it away from Padaras, but it stayed firmly attached, digging in its claws on the creature's fur.

"It's not working," said Mallory.

In response, the Professor let go of the creature and took hold of the top of his walking cane and in one move pulled at the handle and withdrew the long thin blade that was hidden within. "I think this will need a more direct approach!"

"No!" cried Padaras in alarm. "Netvor, do something!"

"Please," implored Netvor, "there must be some other way!"

"I have it," said Yuri, as he reached to the holster on his belt and produced the gun that he had taken from Heidi at the prison. "Power cell would have recharged itself slightly by now and I have been shown how this thing works now." With that he turned a dial on the side. "There, close range stun … I think - stay still!"

"Netvor!" shouted Padaras again, but it was too late. Yuri pointed and fired directly at the goblin. For a moment the creature was bathed in a blue electrical light before letting go of Padaras and falling to the ground twitching. Yuri then quickly stepped forward and with his boot, kicked the goblin to one side, away from the still stunned and trembling Padaras. Just to be sure, Yuri aimed his gun again at the imp, and pulled the trigger, but nothing happened. "Must have used up its charge again. Still, no matter, do you have bag that I can put strange goblin in?"

"Er, no," said the slightly bemused Netvor, who could clearly still not see the imp.

Yuri shrugged, put the gun back in his holster and then took off his coat. "No problems, I'll use this." With that, the Russian walked over to where the goblin lay and casually dropped the jacket down.

However, the imp had other ideas and as the coat was falling, it rolled to one side and managed to scamper away before being smothered.

"Hey, come back!" called Yuri, but the goblin ignored him and, running on all fours, headed down the pathway between the left hand side of the church and the houses that were opposite.

Yuri swore and, choosing to abandon the jacket, started to pursue, sprinting after the goblin, who had already put some distance between himself and the Russian, before then disappearing from view as the path rounded the back of the church. Convinced that the imp had eluded him Yuri rounded the corner, to be confronted with a large house directly in front of him that was covered in scaffolding and was clearly being repaired after some kind of damage. There, sitting on one of the metal scaffolding poles surrounding the first floor, was the goblin, which smiled and waved.

"Ha! Too late to try and make friends," said Yuri. He stooped down to pick up a large stone that was on the floor, sized it up then threw it hard at the little creature. The goblin watched the rock sail towards him before shifting to the left allowing the missile to fly harmlessly past. It then stood up on the pole, turned round and stuck its backside out and waved it rudely as an insult, before jumping inside the temporary structure, onto the running boards that had been placed there to allow the workmen to carry out their job.

"Why you little rascal!" exclaimed Yuri, adding a Russian expletive. He then ran to the house and started to climb up the side of the scaffolding to the first floor where he then moved inside, landing lightly on the wooden planks. Immediately he was forced to duck as a pot of paint was hurled at him. He turned to his right, about twelve feet in front of him was the goblin sitting by a pile of pots that were stacked by the scaffolding's outer rail. The imp jumped up and down on the spot excitedly and then reached for another paint pot. However, Yuri had other ideas. The Russian stooped down and took hold of the end of the plank of wood that the goblin was standing on, lifting and tipping it up and over. The paint pots along with the goblin went tumbling through the open side of the scaffolding. The paint pots landed on the ground with a crash, the lids coming off, spilling their magnolia coloured contents everywhere. Moments later the goblin landed in the puddle of paint. He tried to stand up, but his foot slipped and he landed unceremoniously on his backside, letting out a squeal. The now paint covered goblin tried to stand again, but this time inadvertently put his foot on one of the stray paint pot lids which slid out from under him, sending him back to the ground with a thump.

Laughing out loud at the goblin's comedic predicament, Yuri by now had climbed down from the scaffolding and had made his way over to the struggling creature.

"Last time I see something that funny was in film 'Bangville Police'," said the Russian, wiping a tear of laughter from his eye. "Perhaps I get little 'Keystone Cop' uniform made for you and you can be their mascot?"

The goblin made an insulting sounding noise, making Yuri laugh even harder.

By now the Professor and the others, including Padaras, had made their way over to the scene.

"My goodness!" cried Netvor, who due to the paint was able to see the Goblin for the first time.

"That thing was on me?" exclaimed Padaras. "What on earth is it?"

"Ill-mannered, angry and about to be caught!" said Yuri as he reached down for the imp, who was still trying to scramble away. "Ha!" the Russian cried as he took hold of the Goblin by the foot and held his prize high in the air. "Got you, you little swine! I think that it should be put in cage and studied."

However, the imp had other ideas. Struggling, it managed to reach out and claw the Russian on the forearm, making Yuri yell out and instantly let go. The goblin landed on the floor, and seeing its chance of escape, bolted, dodging the final attempts by Mallory and Jazmine to grab at it. It scampered on all fours over to the walled pond, where it launched itself upwards and landed on the top of the clock in the middle of the island. It then turned, seemed to throw a dirty look at them and then dived into the water with a small splash. Yuri, followed by the Professor, Mallory, Jazmine, Netvor and Padaras, ran over to the pond and stared into the water, where the goblin could be seen swimming downwards until it eventually disappeared from view.

"Ha!" cried Yuri, "good riddance! Hope you drown!"

"I'm not sure he will," replied Netvor. "The pond leads into a cave system."

"Well," said the Professor, "it looks as though you have a vampire goblin on the loose. I think you need our help. We have extensive experience in dealing with supernatural occurrences."

Netvor nodded gratefully, before looking over at the wounded Padaras, a terrible thought occurring to him. "I think we need to start with an urgent visit to our archive."

CHAPTER 42

Netvor called for assistance; the wounded Padaras was then taken off for treatment. He then led the Professor, Jazmine, Mallory and Yuri to a set of stone stairs by the terrace, which took them directly up to the large Tudor Manor House that overlooked Upper Karlstad. He opened the large wooden door and led the small party inside.

"As the main representative here in Upper Karlstad, I am based here," explained Netvor. "It is also where Douglas has set up home. The house has a number of functions and the cellars have been converted into a more general space for our kind. Among other things it contains our archive. If there is any record of that strange goblin creature, it will be here." He led them to a large wooden door off to one side of the hall, which he opened to reveal a staircase leading downwards.

Netvor went down first and the others followed until they found themselves in a large cellar space. Netvor led them over to a large wooden door before stopping outside. "One thing I must warn you about, the keeper of the archive, Izaki, he is not the most social of our kind. In your eyes he could even be classed as rude and obnoxious."

"He can't be any worse than the Head Librarian at our University," said Jazmine.

"Or the woman who is in charge of the archive at the Tsar's Palace," added Yuri. "She was total monster, um, er, no offence."

Netvor smiled. "None taken."

With that, he opened the door and entered. The others followed close behind. Inside, the walls of the room were lined with shelves that were filled to overflowing with a combination of leather bound books and tightly packed scrolls; some parchment and others on what looked to be animal hide.

At the far end of the room was a large fireplace, over which hung a large painting of a scene of a futuristic city that seemed almost to be three dimensional. In front of the fire were carefully placed two leather chairs facing each other, with a small table in the middle. On the table was a chess board, with a game of the Karlstad version clearly underway. Off to the right was a large antique globe, about two foot in diamater, which rested in an elaborate brass cradle. In the centre of the room were two large tables placed together, covered in books, scrolls and maps, and sitting at the far end, clearly at work, was a small figure of one of the creatures who looked up, and noted the newcomers.

"Netvor, why have you decided to disturb me at such a crutial time in my studies?" the creature barked.

"I'm sorry Izaki, " said Netvor apologetically, "but we need your help."

"And who are these people?" he queried, scowling. "I wasn't aware we were allowing total strangers into Upper Karlstad now and giving them guided tours."

"We're not," replied Netvor. "This is an exception. These people are friends of Douglas. They helped save his life."

Izaki nodded, almost approvingly, before he pushed his chair back, stood up, grabbed his cane and walked over to them. "Right, lets see what you have brought me."

It was clear that Izaki was very old. His fur was more silvery grey than white. He was slightly bent over and was using a strange looking walking stick, which he leant on heavily. The main shaft of the walking stick was wood, but the small horizontal handle at the top seemed to be a miniature metal telescope. One by one he looked the Professor, Mallory and Jazmine up and down, tutting in disapproval. When he came to Yuri, he looked particularly offended. "This one smells exceptionally bad!"

"Unfair!" said Yuri, taking the bate. "I bathed in steam this morning!"

"Yes, I heard about that. You were the one that shot and killed Zidal."

"Not totally true. I did shoot him, but was fall that killed him."

Izaki stared at Yuri for a moment before a big smile crossed his face. "Oh I like this one! And for the record I was never that keen on Zidal anyway. He may have been a fellow scholar, but his observations about the fourth planet always irritated me *and* he refused to let me use the telescope to see 'The Great Meteor Procession' back in February! Right Netvor, what do you need?"

Netvor proceeded to explain about what had just happened in the town square and gave as many details as he could about the strange goblin type creature.

"Mmmm, that creature does sound familiar. I wonder...," said Izaki, before turning and going over to one of the bookcases. From one of the lower shelves he selected a large volume and brought it over to the table where he placed it down, opened it and started flicking through the pages. Occasionally he would pause and lift up his walking stick, placing one end of the mini telescope to his eye to look at the text, before moving onto the next page.

After a short while, Izaki stabbed at the pages with a triumphant grunt. "There! I think you are looking at a creature called a Trasgo, or *not* looking at it in our case. Because our eyes function differently to humans, it is almost impossible for us to see them. At best we can make out a shadow, and even then we have to look hard for it. Also, they are extinct. The last one died out about two hundred years ago, well according to this text anyway."

"Well, this one certainly was not dead," said Yuri.

"Now," said Izaki, turning to address Netvor, "you say it bit Padras?"

Netvor nodded.

"Then I am afraid that he is as good as lost."

"What?" cried Netvor in alarm.

"As a Trasgo feeds, it poisons the blood irreversibly. This causes fever, madness and violent behaviour, and eventual death," explained Izaki.

"Well at least we know for certain the cause of Zidal and Rakasa's illness," said Netvor, which was what he had suspected after seeing the goblin's attack.

"What?" cried Izaki. "Rakasa? He was bitten too?"

Netvor almost looked surprised. "Yes, don't you remember? We sent Dabba here to the archive to see if there was any mention of the illness after it happened."

"Dabba?" replied Izaki, with a hint of disgust. "That annoying little waste of space? He just told me he was doing general research. He didn't tell me the specifics. Not that he spent much time doing that anyway. He seemed to spend most of the time reading short fictions."

Netvor sighed. He would have to have a word with Dabba later. "But why is this happening now?"

Izaki shrugged. "Now that, I can't answer; Trasgos tend to live an isolated existence. Perhaps your little friend has only just discovered a route into Upper Karlstad, via the village pond, or it could be something has happened that has caused him to leave his own environment."

"But what of Rakasa and Padaras?" asked Netvor, worriedly.

Izaki looked thoughtful for a moment. "If we could get hold of a live specimen of the creature and take a sample of its blood, it could be possible for us to engineer a cure. We could also develop a vaccine, so if any of us were bitten in the future we would not fall ill."

"A live specimen," said Netvor, "but how?"

"Ha!" cried Izaki. "I thought that would have been obvious, even to you. The Trasgo dived into the well and presumably into the underground water and cave system beyond, right?"

Netvor nodded.

"Then you need to send divers down after it! I have been saying for centuries that those tunnels need exploring properly."

"Couldn't we just wait and hope it appears again?" suggested Netvor.

"You could be waiting a very long time," answered Izaki. "Besides, that pond needs to be boarded up immediately. We can't risk the Trasgo paying us another visit. No, exploration is the only way."

"But our kind can't even see the creature," pointed out Netvor.

"The little goblin did end up covered in paint. That may allow you to spot him," said Yuri.

But Netvor shook his head. "Maybe, but the pond water may have washed him clean. How can we search for something we cannot even see?"

"Netvor, I worry about you sometimes," said Izaki. "Our kind doesn't go, we send in humans for the task." He looked over at the Professor, Jazmine, Mallory and Yuri. "And I think I know the very volunteers!"

CHAPTER 43

After it was decided that the Professor and his companions were to venture into the pond and the flooded chambers beyond, they were kitted out with specially made diving suits. Then they were taken outside the fortress to a nearby pool and given instructions on how to use them. None of them had ever dived before, but soon were reasonably confident and competent in using the strange equipment they had been issued with.

After the training session, which lasted the rest of the day and into early evening, was finished they headed for the Manor where they were to attend an informal reception that had been laid on for them by Netvor. The gathering was being held in the main dining room and was attended by various Upper Karlstad residents. Along one wall two long tables had been placed and a variety of drinks and food had been set out for everyone to help themselves. The Professor and Jazmine were particularly pleased to see a variety of special dumplings were there; as both had been particularly disgruntled at missing the Dumpling Festival. At the far end of the room was a strange looking musical instrument. Behind a waist high wooden console stood one of the creatures, who was busy pressing unseen buttons. The result was narrow brass rods momentarily rising out of the top of the console at different heights, which produced a sound similar to strings being plucked, before retracting down again. This gave the most amazing and haunting tune that filled the background as people talked and mingled. As to be expected, the Professor, Jazmine, Mallory and Yuri were the centre of attention, with everyone wanting to know all about them and their various adventures.

"I must say," said the Professor, as he finally managed to work his way over to Netvor, who was with Mallory, Yuri and Izaki, "it is very kind of you to lay all this on for us, and thank you again for kitting us all out in 'Karlstad attire'!" With a smile he politely tipped the brown bowler hat that had a set of goggles attached to them, which he had been wearing all evening. Both the Professor and Mallory were now dressed in long boots, light trousers, collarless shirts and richly decorated waistcoats. They had also been issued with a leather sash, on which hung various leather pouches. Yuri was wearing the clothes he had originally been given when he arrived at Upper Karlstad, with the addition of a few more belt pouches.

"So," continued the Professor, "where exactly did the style come from? It is like nothing we have ever encountered before."

Netvor smiled. "Well, being covered with fur, clothes were not really needed. As we became more advanced, there became a need to carry objects around with us, so we made the various leather pouches which we put on belts and bandoliers. The people of Lower Karlstad took that concept and started to wear them themselves. Then they just seemed to add things in to fit in with the style: long coats, boots etc etc."

"And the goggles?" asked Mallory.

"Being based high up here on the fortress, surrounded by the glare of snow, they were developed to help protect our eyes. Again, the people decided to adopt them and use them for their own." Netvor paused. "Although I have to admit, over the centuries, my kind's eyes have adapted and we don't really need them. They are more for decoration."

"Ah, speaking of which," said the Professor, "that is something that I am dying to find out. How long have your kind been here and how did you get here in the first place?"

"Well I'm most qualified to answer that," said Izaki, stepping forward and leaning on his walking stick. "It seems that a few of our ancestors moved into this abandoned fortress during the 1200's and quietly lived here undisturbed until we were discovered by the villagers in the following century, when they ventured up here in an attempt to escape the plague. Luckily our ancestors had already found a cure and shared it, which saved the entire town. From then on an alliance was formed between us and we have been living together in harmony ever since. Ah, Douglas. How are you feeling?"

"Most well," said Douglas, as he approached along with Jazmine who was now wearing a long green dress and a brown leather corset. On her head she wore a small brown top hat that was adorned with a set of goggles. "Although," he continued, "I did have to spend a little longer in the crystallisation chamber than I usually do."

"A small price to pay," said Netvor.

"Indeed," continued Douglas.

"And thank you again," said Mallory. "If you had not come along when you did Yuri and I would have drowned!"

Douglas shrugged. "Glad to be of some use."

"You know," said the Professor, with concern, "I still think that you need to contact Jane. She is devastated!"

A look of sadness crossed Douglas's face before he shook his head. "No, today has just emphasised how fragile my condition is. I can't put her through that. No, when you return to London, you must tell her that I am dead. I am afraid that my mind is made up, and as my friends you must honour my wishes. No matter how much you disagree." There was an awkward silence before Douglas spoke again, quickly changing the subject. "So, what do you think the chances are of actually catching this Trasgo creature?"

"Ha!" cut in Izaki, before anyone else could answer. "Slim to none I would say! That little monster could be anywhere in the cave system. You are hunting for a needle in a haystack!"

"Maybe," replied the Professor, "but it is worth a try, especially as it is the only chance to undo the trouble it has caused and save those who have already been bitten."

"Indeed," said Netvor, "their condition is stable at the moment, but will surely worsen. I hope that you are able to find it, but more importantly, without putting yourselves at too much risk!"

"I am sure we will be fine," replied the Professor, with a smile. "By the way, Netvor, I see you have a small airship outside The Manor here. I'm interested to know more, does it fly? Would it be possible to have a trip at some point? I would imagine the views would be amazing."

"That monstrosity," said Izaki, with a grunt, "is proof that Netvor's skills lie in leading rather than inventing. That thing is a flightless Dodo!"

"That's harsh!" replied Netvor, looking hurt. "It does fly."

"When you tested it, it barely got off of the ground and then crashed. That does not count!" said Izaki.

"I'm working on a new type of gas and the ship's design is like no other," protested Netvor. "It is a long term working project."

"Or to put it simply," said Izaki, "for the past sixty years it's been sitting on the front lawn as an ornament."

"But I have been very busy," said Netvor.

"Maybe," said Izaki, "but you seem to have enough time to play with the smaller version you remotely control with strings."

"That drone is a working model, built after my initial 'problems' with the full size one," protested Netvor. "I get that working properly, then I just translate my findings to the larger ship, which I will get round to soon."

"Yes," said Jazmine, unconvinced, "Father has a number of projects like that."

"Now that is unfair," retorted the Professor. "You know what my university workload is like, as well as all my other activities."

Netvor looked over at the Professor knowingly and everyone burst out laughing.

"Well," said Douglas, putting his glass down, "I think I had better head off to bed now. I want to grab a couple of hours sleep before I have to return to the crystallisation chamber for my next treatment."

"Yes," said the Professor, nodding at Mallory, Yuri and Jazmine, "I think it would be wise if we all headed off ourselves. After all, we do have a very early start tomorrow."

"Most wise," said Netvor, in agreement. "Again, I must apologise for the need for you to share rooms. I am afraid that a lot of our 'spare bedrooms' here at The Manor have been taken over with storage and other projects."

"That's no problem," said Mallory, with a smile. "I'm almost getting used to Yuri's snoring!"

Now it was Yuri's turn to look hurt.

CHAPTER 44

Knock! Knock!

Mallory slowly opened his eyes.

Knock! Knock!

"Mr Mallory, Mr Romanovsky, wake up," called the voice of the Professor.

"Mallory, it's for you," said Yuri, as he turned over in his bed and pulled the sheet over his head.

"Mr Mallory! Are you there?"

"Yes! I'm here!" he called in reply. Then, groaning, he stumbled out of bed and made his way over to the door, which he opened slightly, to find the Professor and Jazmine looking in worriedly.

"Professor, your face, what happened?"

The Professor touched the three fresh scratches that ran along his left cheek. "One of the creatures attacked us."

"What?"

"It broke into our room and went for us. Luckily I was able to get to my sword stick in time. Otherwise I would have been a goner. "

"Why did he attack you?" said Yuri, who by now had gotten out of bed and made his way over to the door.

"No idea," said the Professor, "I presume we can find out for ourselves when we catch him."

"Catch him?" queried Mallory.

The Professor held up his sword stick, the end of which was dripping a strange purple substance. "Yes, I made sure he left a trail for us to follow."

"My goodness," said Mallory. "That's its blood? The creatures have purple blood?"

"So it would seem," said the Professor. "It's an interesting concept that they have a different colour blood to ours. I think that this could be a result of ..."

"Father!" broke in Jazmine, "we can discuss its biology later. It's just started to snow again. He's bound to have gone outside and if we don't hurry up any trail he has left will be covered over and we will lose him for sure."

"Alright, give us a moment," said Mallory, as he closed the door. A short while later the door opened again and he and Yuri appeared fully dressed and ready for the chase.

The Professor led them across the landing and to the main staircase, down the centre of which could be seen a trail of the purple blood.

"Shouldn't we tell Netvor and the other's what happened?" asked Mallory.

"No," replied the Professor, as be bounded down the stairs. "We can handle this ourselves. Yuri, did you bring that electronic gun of yours?"

"Yes," replied the Russian, pulling it from the holster. "It fully charged and ready."

"Good, I have a feeling that it will come in very handy!"

At the bottom of the staircase the blood trail led them to the big double doors of the Manor House. The Professor opened them and they were greeted by an icy cold wind and a small flurry of snow. "We need to hurry," said Jazmine, looking down at the ground and seeing that flakes of snow were already starting to cover the trail. Treading carefully to ensure they did not slip over, the Professor, Mallory, Jazmine and Yuri followed the drips of blood and the fading footprints of the creature towards the terrace and down to the village square, where the trail abruptly stopped.

"Where did it go?" asked Mallory, looking around.

"You leave this to me," said Yuri, stepping forward. "I once tracked brown bear for day and a half."

"And caught it?" asked Mallory.

Yuri shrugged. "No, bear got away in end, but I still followed it for day and a half!" He then started to look at the ground. "Don't worry, this won't take long, there will always be clue and then we…"

"He went into St Magdalena's church," broke in Jazmine.

223

"What makes you say that?" said the Russian.

She pointed over at the Gothic building. "The door's been left open."

Everyone looked and they could clearly see that the door to the church was ajar, allowing a shaft of light through. As they got closer they could see a smear of purple blood on the door's handle and frame.

"You had better go first," said the Professor.

Yuri nodded, checked the setting on his gun, then kicked open the door and launched himself inside, half expecting to be attacked straight away, but instead he was greeted with an empty, silent church. "Tis clear," he called and then the Professor, Mallory and Jazmine entered the building to join him.

The interior of the church looked very much like the church at Lower Karlstad, only on a much smaller scale. The pews faced a richly decorated alter and along the side of the walls were pictures depicting the story of the crucifixion.

Looking around they quickly spotted the trail of purple blood running down the central aisle.

"Come on," said the Professor, as he followed the drips which, as the pews ended, veered right to a small wooden spiral staircase that led downwards. Carefully the small party descended the stairs until they found themselves in what looked like another chapel. However it was clear that this one was not devoted to a Christian religion.

The walls of this sacred space were lined with heavy wooden panelling, but devoid of any decoration. Overhead there was a lamp which gave off a dim light. On the left hand side there was an open wooden archway, from which radiated a strange green glow. At the far end of the sanctuary was what looked to be a small wooden altar; the wall behind resembled a honeycomb with small alcoves having been carved into the rock. Many of the recesses held crystallised skulls that clearly belonged to long dead creatures, while others remained vacant waiting to be filled.

"Amazing," said the Professor, looking at the skulls that seemed to be staring back at him.

"Father, we can look at them later," said Jazmine. "We have other things to attend to. Look, the blood goes into that archway."

The Professor nodded. "Alright, Yuri you go first, and be careful. This smells of a trap."

The Russian smiled. "I hope so!" With that he carefully moved over to the archway and cautiously peered inside.

"What can you see?" asked Mallory.

"Nothing, just long tunnel, but it all made from green crystal. Come on." With that he disappeared inside and the others followed.

Carefully they made their way along the tunnel, still following the blood trail which stood out against the green crystal floor. After a short while the passageway turned right and then continued for twenty feet before opening out into a large chamber. The walls inside of which were covered with green crystals.

"That must be the crystallisation chamber where the creatures lay out their dead and Douglas goes for his treatments," said Mallory.

"Hold on!" said Jazmine. "Do you hear that?"

Everyone strained to listen; from the chamber came a strange cry.

"That sounded human," said Yuri.

"That's Douglas," cried the Professor. "He's in trouble. No Yuri, wait!"

But it was too late.

The Russian bounded forward and Mallory set after him. With no other option, the Professor and Jazmine followed.

Yuri entered the chamber to be confronted with Douglas Quinn lying on the floor. The Russian started to head over to him, but was immediately set upon. The creature launched himself from the shadows, grabbed hold of Yuri, and slammed him against the crystal wall. While at the same time ripping the gun from his hand, and then using the butt of the weapon, began to pound at him.

"Yuri!" cried Mallory.

By now, he, the Professor and Jazmine had also entered the crystal chamber and the creature, still holding Yuri, turned to look at them, and roared, bearing its fangs.

The Professor held out his sword stick. "You put him down, this instant!"

The creature turned and, as he did so, lifted Yuri off the ground and hurled him directly towards the Professor, Mallory and Jazmine. The Russian landed on the Professor who, dropping his sword stick, fell back, knocking over Mallory and then Jazmine like dominoes.

The creature roared again and taking hold of Yuri's gun properly, he aimed and fired the weapon.

The concentrated beam of electricity found its mark, hitting the side of the wall by the open doorway where there looked to be some kind of control box. Sparks flew and at the entrance to the chamber a green crystal door quickly started to descend. The creature dived for the closing gap and disappeared under the door, moments before it came crashing down to the floor.

CHAPTER 45

Slowly, the Professor picked himself up off the floor and then helped Jazmine to her feet. "Go check on Douglas," he ordered. She nodded and then went over to where Douglas was trying to get up. "Mr Mallory, how is Yuri?"

"Out for the count I'm afraid," replied Mallory, who was checking on the Russian. "When he wakes up he will have a heck of a headache."

"Well he's used to that!" replied the Professor, stooping down to retrieve his sword stick before standing up again to take stock of their new surroundings. The chamber itself was a large natural cave. The walls were covered in green crystals that gave off a green thick mist that seemed to hang in the air. In the middle of the room were two plinths. On one of these a creature was laid out with a layer of green crystals slowly forming over it. At the far end of the chamber was a much larger plinth, almost waist high, on which a number of skulls were lined up, in various stages of crystallisation. "So this is the famous crystallisation chamber," commented the Professor.

"Yes," said Douglas, who by now was on his feet and rubbing his bruised head. "The bodies are laid out for about three months before the head and brain are removed. Then after a further six months the skulls, reunited with their brains, are placed in the alcoves you no doubt saw in the chapel outside."

"Not the most pleasant of burial rituals," said the Professor, shrugging, "but I have seen far worse." He then turned his attention to the door, particularly the spot where the creature had fired the gun.

"I presume that we are now locked in," said Mallory, joining him.

The Professor nodded. "Yes, it very much looks that way. The control panel is totally destroyed." He then started to examine the door, before kneeling down and sliding the sword stick under the bottom and attempting to use it as a lever to lift it upwards, but with no success. "No, that's not going to budge I'm afraid," he said, finally getting to his feet. "It looks like we are in here for the duration!"

"But we need to get out of here!" said Douglas. "If we don't, we will all end up crystallised from the inside out!"

"How long do you think we have?" asked the Professor.

"I have already been in here for two hours," Douglas replied. "I have another three hours before I reach my maximum capacity. However for you, bearing in mind you are breathing normally, I would say four hours before you are beyond help."

"But surely the creatures will realise we are missing and will come looking for us?" ventured Mallory, hopefully.

"I doubt that," replied Jazmine. "Remember, we didn't tell anyone about the attack. No one knows we are here."

"And I'm afraid that I won't be missed until it's too late," added Douglas glumly. "Because of the nature of my condition I frequently disappear off at odd times for my treatments."

"We need to do something," implored Mallory, "or we will end up like him." He pointed to the creature that was laid out on the plinth. "Or worse, those skulls over there!"

"You know," said Jazmine, looking at the plinth thoughtfully, "I'm not convinced that is just an ordinary platform. It looks to me more like a sarcophagus."

"I think that you might be right," agreed the Professor, moving over to the plinth where the skulls were lined up and proceeded to walk round it, carefully examining the sides and the top.

"What do you think?" asked Mallory.

The Professor nodded. "I believe Jazmine's right. This is actually a sarcophagus made to look like an ordinary slab of stone."

"Will that help us at all in our present situation?" asked Douglas.

The Professor nodded. "I hope so. If we can remove the lid, it is possible to use it as a battering ram to knock the door down. Or if we are in real luck there may be a hidden passageway below."

"Does that kind of thing actually happen?" asked Douglas.

"More times than you would expect," said Jazmine, with a wry smile.

"Right then," said the Professor, as he started to roll his sleeves up, "Jazmine, if you could carefully remove the skulls, and Mr Mallory I will need a hand."
Jazmine carefully took each skull in turn and placed them on the empty stone plinth before standing back.

Then Mallory and the Professor took their places at each end of the stone coffin and carefully tried to find a finger hold on the edge of the lid. Then on the Professor's signal they started to try to move the stone cover.

"It's not budging!" said Mallory, after a minute of struggling.

"Keep going!" replied the Professor.

"But this activity is making me breathe harder. I can actually feel the crystals as I breathe them in."

229

"Can't be helped Mr Mallory! Keep going! Wait, there, I think it moved!"

"Yes," agreed Mallory, adjusting his grip. "I felt it too!"

"On three, Mr Mallory! One, two, three!"

The two men put all their strength into moving the lid. There was a scraping sound as the two surfaces that had been together for possibly hundreds of years shifted, and then with another supreme effort they slid it clear and the lid crashed to the floor. Then the Professor, Mallory, Jazmine and Douglas gathered round to look into the open coffin.

Lying inside was one of the creatures, untouched by the green crystals or decay, in its hands it held a large double edged war axe.

"My goodness," said Douglas. "This creature can only be the one they call 'Kaitiaki the Protector'. He is legendary in the creature's folk law. He was said to have died over four hundred years ago, and his body buried in secret."

"I have seen this creature before," said Mallory. "There is a picture of him painted on the wall of the Strube in the Hotel Post. I remember seeing it when Yuri and I first arrived."

"The axe," said Jazmine. "Do you think that it could cut through the door?"

"Only one way to find out," said Mallory, as he carefully and reverently reached inside the stone coffin and removed it from the hands of the dead creature, and held it up.

"Magnificent!" said the Professor.

"Yes, but very heavy!" replied Mallory, who was clearly struggling under the weight of the weapon, before he was forced to place it down. "I'm not going to be able to use that. We need Yuri."

"Agreed," said the Professor, "but first let's replace the coffin lid. If we get out of this I don't want to have to explain to Netvor that we found one of their lost heroes, but then allowed him to be exposed to the processes of this chamber."

Carefully he and Mallory lifted the lid and replaced it back on the coffin. As they did so, both became aware that their breathing was changing. Also they found themselves blinking more as crystals started to form in their eyes. Then they turned their attention to the fallen Russian.

"Yuri, Yuri!" said the Professor, as he gently slapped him on the cheeks. "Time to wake up. Come on, wakey wakey!"

The Russian gave a groan, and then his eyes flicked open. "What happened?" he said groggily, as he tried to sit up. "I feel I was hit by tram."

"Do you remember where you are?" asked the Professor.

"Um, er, not totally sure, somewhere in Austria-Hungary?"

"Good, that's close enough," said the Professor, practically pulling the Russian to his feet. "Mallory, the axe."

Mallory, with difficulty, handed Yuri the axe. The Russian, who was still clearly dazed, took it, lifting it up with ease. "Good weight, nicely balanced."

"Marvellous," said the Professor dismissively, and taking Yuri by the shoulder, hastily directed him to the door. "Now we need your strength. You must break through that door, with the axe, assuming that it won't

231

shatter on the first blow. You also need to hurry, as we are slowly dying in here due to the mist we are breathing in. But when I say 'hurry,' not too fast as the harder you breathe, the faster you will die. Have you got that?"

Yuri nodded. "I think so. My head hurts. I wish I was still asleep."

"Well if you don't hurry you will be, permanently!" barked the Professor urgently. "Now get to work!"

CHAPTER 46

Still groggy, with his head pounding, Yuri squared up in front of the door. "Best stand back," he warned. "Ancient weapons can shatter badly. I broke two hundred year old sword from Russian Armoury when I tried using it. I got in big trouble."

Everyone retired to a safe distance and Yuri lifted the axe back, and then swung it forward at the door.

Crash!

Sparks flew from the impact and the axe remained intact. Yuri gave out a sigh of relief. Had it shattered he would no doubt have been hit by the flying fragments and injured. Also with no other way to break the door down their fate would have been sealed.

"Again," ordered the Professor.

Yuri nodded, altered his stance, and then swung the axe back. This time, knowing the weapon would not break, putting his entire weight behind it.

Crash!
Crash!
Crash!

"Stand back Yuri. I want to see how you are doing."

The Russian did as he was told and the Professor moved in to examine the door where the axe had hit. He swore under his breath. "A slight chip, nothing more."

"Not fault of axe," said Yuri, testing the blade with his thumb. "It razor sharp."

"It's the door then," said the Professor, running his hand over it. "It is totally coated with the green crystals, which is forming an impossible barrier."

"So what do we do?" asked Mallory.

Yuri shrugged. "I just keep going! No other option."

"I can try and take a turn if it helps," offered Mallory. "The more you exert yourself the more the crystallisation will affect you."

"No offence Mallory, but you could barely lift axe. This is a job only Yuri can carry out. Hopefully my strength will combat it. Now stand back!"

For the next hour Yuri attacked the door with the axe, and slowly but surely it started to cut its way through. However, as he worked, the effects of the chamber on those inside was soon becoming apparent to everyone. They found their breathing harder and even started to cough up green crystalized phlegm, and the corners of their eyes also started to become clogged with traces of the crystals that had to be blinked or wiped away. Also the temperature of the chamber seemed to become hotter, resulting in crystals forming as they began to sweat.

After a short break, Yuri returned to the door and resumed his assault on it, but it was noticeable that his efforts were now becoming more and more laboured. He was encouraged by the fact that he was now making visible progress with a large gash in the crystal which got slightly deeper with every swing. "I can't keep this up for too much more," the Russian confessed, as he again lifted the axe into the air. "I think that we are not going to make it out of this one! I'm sorry. It seems Yuri has failed you!"

Then without any warning, there was a rumble and the entire door slowly started to move upwards. Standing on the other side was Izaki, staring in at them. "What's going on here?" he barked, eyeing the occupants of the chamber.

"Oh thank goodness," said the Professor, visibly relieved. "One of your kind tried to attack me and Jazmine at the Manor. We fetched Mallory and Yuri, then followed him here to the crystallisation chamber where he attacked Douglas and then locked us all in."

Izaki paused, looking at them for a moment, and noting how they were breathing and the traces of crystals forming on them. He stood to one side. "Then you had better come out, and quickly. This chamber is no place for the living to spend long periods of time."

Gratefully they passed through the door and into the tunnel. Immediately they began to notice the difference in the air and began to suck in the clean oxygen which made them all start to cough and bring up large globules of the green crystallised phlegm, which they were forced to spit out onto the floor.

"How long have you been here?" asked Izaki after a few moments, when they seemed to start recovering. "I see that the chamber has well and truly started its work on you."

"A couple of hours," replied Mallory, coughing and wiping his mouth. "How did you open the door? The mechanism was destroyed. The creature fired at it with Yuri's gun."

"The control on the outside is on the opposite side from the internal one. Both operate independently," replied Izaki.

"But how did you know to look for us?" asked Jazmine, clearing her throat.

"I didn't," Izaki replied bluntly. "You have been saved by chance. I came down to the chapel for some silent prayer and noticed the blood on the floor and followed it to the chamber." He then eyed the axe that Yuri was still holding. "That looks like the axe of 'Kaitiaki the Protector. I recognise it from the scrolls in my archive."

"Um, yes," said the Professor. "It turns out the plinth where the skulls are placed was actually a tomb."

"Ha!" cried Izaki, in triumph. "I knew it! I always suspected that was the case, but was never allowed to take a proper look at it. You have done me a big favour. Is his body there as well?"

"Yes, fully preserved without crystallisation," replied the Professor. "We even replaced the lid to protect it."

"Good," said Izaki, with a smile. "Studying them will keep me occupied for…"

"Vile, wicked human creatures!" suddenly came a voice from behind them. Everyone swung round and there, standing in the tunnel, was the creature that had attacked them, with purple blood still dripping from its wounds and a look of insane anger in its eyes.

"Istota, I might have known you would be responsible for this!" said Izaki.

"Out of my way wise-one! These abhorrent and disgusting humans must be punished for what they have done. They have killed one of our kind and yet are allowed to roam free amongst us, and from the look of things have desecrated the grave of one of our own and taken the sacred axe!"

"If anyone is going to be punished Istota," replied Izaki, stepping forward, "it will be you. Violence against the humans in any form is forbidden! The situation was explained to you. You will surrender yourself to me immediately and you will be tried for your actions!"

"I don't think you can reason with him," said Mallory, who was on edge, ready to launch himself forward for the fight that was bound to follow. "It seems that the Trasgo has gotten to him too, and the madness has taken hold!"

"Oh, not in this case, I'm afraid," said Izaki. "You see, Istota's brother is Zidal, this is not madness; it is a case of hate and vengeance!"

"You killed my brother!" spat Istota, looking straight at Yuri. "I will have your life! I will have all of your puny human lives. We should not hide and serve when we have the power to rule! What would this town be without us? They would be in the Dark Ages!"

"Nice speech," said the Russian, who had moved forward slightly, axe at the ready, "but now I am armed with mythical axe; this going to end badly for you."

Istota let out a roar and started to launch himself forward, but before Yuri could do anything Izaki raised his walking stick and pointed the end of it at the attacking creature. There was a bang, a small puff of black smoke and Istota fell backwards, dead before he hit the floor.

Izaki held up the walking cane. "A little device I had made for me in case of emergencies." He then looked specifically at the Professor. "You know how dangerous being an academic can be!"

The Professor nodded, appreciating the joke, and then looked down at the body of Istota. "I'm so sorry that you had to kill one of your kind."

Izaki shrugged. "I don't think it could be helped. Now, I suggest that you head back to your rooms and get some sleep while you can. Douglas, you look shattered, and as for the rest of you, well it will be dawn soon and you have a very important mission ahead of you to capture the Trasgo. I would rather you did not fall asleep during the task!" He then looked down sadly at the body of Istota. "I'll finish up here."

CHAPTER 47

With just a few more hours sleep behind them the Professor, Jazmine, Mallory and Yuri were woken and given a light breakfast of ham, scrambled eggs and coffee. After a final briefing from Netvor, they all, along with two helpers and Douglas, left the Manor house and headed to the St Magdalena's church. In a side room they put on their diving suits directly over their own clothing.

The all in one waterproof suits were made from light tanned leather and at the neck there was a metal ring on which the helmet would be added. The diving helmet itself, which would not be attached until just before they entered the water, was essentially a glass dome which had a small speaking box attached to the front by the mouth allowing them to talk freely to each other at short distances. At the wrists and ankles the material was gathered in tightly with elastic, ready for gloves and the specially made boots. On their back, held on by straps, was a large oval metal canister which contained their vital supply of air. From the pack there was a hose which connected directly into the helmet and attached to the arm of each suit. There was a small gauge which showed them the status of the air supply. In addition everyone was issued with a utility belt worn over the diving suit that held a coil of rope, a large knife, a small lamp that could be detached and used if required, and a brass coloured gun. The weapon fired, at high speed, a Bakelite type dart which was about five inches long and rounded at the end. Netvor explained this non-lethal handgun would be ideal to use against the Trasgo in order to capture it alive. Another key advantage of this weapon was that unlike the electrical gun they had seen before, it could be used underwater. Also Yuri and Mallory were each given a small clear watertight Bakelite carrying cage that had its own small oxygen canister attached, in which it was hoped they could put the Trasgo.

They all emerged from St Magdalena's to find a small crowd of creatures and humans who had gathered to witness the proceedings. Even Izaki had come and seen their departure. The pond had now been boarded up, to stop the Trasgo paying them another visit. However, one panel had been removed to allow the divers access into the water. This same panel would then be replaced, but could be removed from the inside when the Professor and the others returned.

Moving over to the pond, the suits were then double checked for leaks. Final instructions were given on how everything worked and what to do in case of emergency, before the glass dome helmets were added and locked into place.

Then one by one the Professor, Jazmine, Mallory and Yuri, seated themselves on the small wall of the pond, lifted their legs up and swung them round and dropped them into the water.

"Are you alright?" said Netvor, suddenly noting the distant look on Jazmine's face.

"Yes," she replied thoughtfully, her voice sounding distorted through the voice box. "I've just had an idea. In the crystallisation chamber the crystals give off a light mist, the stuff that Douglas breathes in to repair his lungs; and which almost killed us."

"Yes," said Netvor, "that's correct."

"Well, could it be possible to take some of the crystals and put them into one of these air canisters and make it so that it releases its mist at a constant rate? That would mean Douglas's lungs could be repaired away from the chamber. It will by no means be a cure, but he would have a lot more freedom."

"Yes," said Netvor, thinking for a moment, "I think something like that could be engineered. He would still be tied to Karlstad, as this is the only place the crystals are found, but it will certainly allow him a better quality of life."

"Do you really think it could be done?" asked Douglas, excitedly.

Netvor nodded slowly. "I will instruct an investigation into the concept straight away." He then turned to the others. "Well, this is it, if you could all please turn on your air supply."

Each did as they were asked and confirmed that they were working.

Then one by one the Professor, Jazmine, Mallory and Yuri pushed themselves off of the edge of the wall of the pond and entered the water with a splash before they started to head downwards where they found themselves in a rock lined shaft.

"Looks like we have no option but to go straight down," said the Professor, his voice coming through the speaking device almost slightly robotically. "Is everyone alright?" Mallory and Jazmine nodded, but Yuri was not happy. "The suit seems tighter than yesterday. Something does not feel right."

"We should go back then," said Mallory.

But the Russian shook his head. "No, most likely just me; probably me feeling stiff from last night. I'm fine to go on."

"Alright," said the Professor, "but if it gets any worse you must tell us at once."

The Russian nodded, and with that they all continued downwards, the Professor leading the way. After about twenty more feet they came to the bottom of the shaft where a water filled tunnel stretched out in front of them. It had an eerie blue glow to it, allowing them to see clearly through the water.

"I would have thought that it would be pitch black down here," commented Mallory, as he swam forward into the new section of tunnel.

"I think the light, for want of a better word," said the Professor, "is being caused by some kind of algae. Yuri, are you sure you are alright?"

The Russian nodded, rubbing his chest. "Fine, just still uncomfortable. One question: How did Goblin manage to swim through here? We have breathing equipment, he does not. Surely little monster not able to hold his breath for long time?"

"I think I know," said Jazmine, pointing upwards to the tunnel roof. "There, can you see them? It looks like there are regular small air pockets."

"Resourceful little chap isn't he?" said Yuri. "I'm looking forward to catching up with him. I have score to settle!"

"Well, as long as he's captured alive," pointed out the Professor, as he swam along the tunnel. "He will be no good to anyone if he's dead!"

The four continued following the passageway. As they did so it became more and more noticeable that something was wrong with Yuri. He looked more and more uneasy and his movements became slower and more awkward.

"Yuri," called the Professor, swimming alongside him, "something is clearly amiss. What is it?"

The Russian shrugged. "There is minor problem with my suit; tiny leak."

"Where?" enquired the Professor, with concern.

"Somewhere around right foot. I check but cannot find it. It seems to be letting in bit of water."

"How much?"

"Tis nothing. Up to right knee in suit."

"What!" cried the Professor "Why didn't you say anything before?"

Yuri shrugged. "I not want to make fuss."

"You'll have to go back," said Mallory. "Your whole suit will fill up and you will drown."

"I'll be fine," replied Yuri. "We should be near cave soon. It not a problem. I'm not going to miss out on this trip."

"Yuri, your stubbornness is going to get you killed," said Jazmine.

"No it won't," said the Russian firmly.

Jazmine stared at him and shook her head. "I bet you don't even see the irony in what you just said do you?"

"In what?"

The Professor grinned. "Alright, I can't see Yuri heading back, so we need to hurry ourselves up. Jazmine, Mr Mallory, are your suits alright?"

Quickly the two made a check and confirmed that there were no problems. The Professor did the same with his and then, satisfied they were all alright, they continued down the subterranean passageway, only at a much faster pace.

After a few minutes the tunnel seemed to widen slightly and more and more strange underwater corals and plants seemed to appear below them, in addition to the increasing number of small fish and other strange creatures. It also became more noticeable that the blue light that seemed to guide them was getting brighter.

"Stop a moment everyone," called the Professor to his companions, who immediately followed his instruction.

"What's wrong?" asked Jazmine.

"There's a lot of movement below us," he replied. "I think that there is something down there."

Looking down they could see amongst the strange coloured plants certain areas were moving and shifting. Then, without warning, about twenty large blue eel type creatures rose up from their resting place on the tunnel floor and started to swim around them at a discreet distance.

CHAPTER 48

"Stay still everyone!" cried the Professor, as the eels swam around them. "I'm sure that they are just curious!"

Each eel was about three foot long and was coloured light blue, but was surrounded by a strange blue glow. Their heads were flat and from the mouth protruded a set of sharp looking teeth. As they continued to circle, one suddenly moved in close towards them and Mallory, who was nearest to it, reached out his hand to push it away. As he did so there was a spark of electricity causing Mallory to yell out as the eel turned and disappeared off.

"Electric eels," said the Professor. "Are you alright Mr Mallory?"

"I think so," he replied. "That was quite a jolt though!"

"Father," said Jazmine, "they seem to be getting nearer."

"You're right," said the Professor, noting that a number of the eels were now venturing closer towards them. From his holster Yuri produced the gun that had been given to them by the creatures, and released the safety catch. "I think it's time we tested out this weapon." As he spoke, one of the eels suddenly changed course and headed towards him. The Russian aimed and fired. The Bakelite dart shot out of the muzzle of the weapon and headed straight for the eel, leaving a small wake in its path. Seeing the projectile coming towards it, the eel tried to dodge out of the way but couldn't. It was hit on the side of its body and as it turned, it let out a strange yelping sound and for a moment there was a flash of light and pins of electricity shot out, arching into the water as it retreated.

"Wow," remarked Mallory, "considering these creatures claim to be peace loving they are very good at inventing weapons!"

"Oddities like that can happen," replied the Professor, eyeing the eels as they seemed to move near him. "Look at the Shaolin Monks, and I have a Quaker friend who is a master swordsman!"

Another one of the eels turned in and swam at them. This time it was Jazmine who fired. Again the dart hit the target, sending the eel away in a shower of blue electrical sparks. Then it was Mallory who was forced to discharge his gun. The dart hit one eel, which then was pushed into another and both seemingly exploded into an electrical eruption.

"How is your suit doing, Yuri?" asked Mallory, noticing it seemed to be bulging up even more and the Russian's movements seemed slower and more restricted.

"Filling up nicely!" replied Yuri, as he reloaded another dart into the gun. He then quickly fired it off again at another eel, which retreated in a pool of sparks when it was hit.

Another two eels swam in, their teeth bared, but they too were repelled in a shower of sparks.

"I wish they would get the message!" cried Jazmine. "How is everyone doing for ammunition?"

"Oh, that won't be a problem!" cried Mallory, as he reached out to recover a spent Bakelite dart which was floating by. "Aside from the large amount we were issued with, they seem easy to retrieve. We could go on like this all day!"

244

"You speak for yourself!" said Yuri, realising that the water inside his suit was now up to his waist and still seemed to be rising.

A particularly large eel swept in and was fired upon simultaneously by Jazmine and Mallory. The creature let out a strange noise as it was lit up with electricity, then swam away. As if the collective mind of the eels now seemed to finally realise that their chosen prey were not going to submit so easily, they seemed to adopt a new plan.

"Look, I think this bed of eels is moving closer!" said Yuri, noting that the entire circle of swimming creatures seemed to be reducing their distance, coming ever nearer.

"Bed of eels?" repeated Mallory. "Bed of eels? Are you serious? You can barely string an English sentence together and yet you know the collective noun for eels?"

"What can I say?" said the Russian, firing off another shot while also grabbing a used dart that was floating by. "Yuri is complex, as your language."

"More to the point," said the Professor, "he's right, they are coming in closer and I think they seem to be trying to generate some sort of collective electrical field to use against us!"

As well as moving inwards, the eels also seemed to be now swimming in a tighter formation, lining up close to each other. Small electrical sparks could be seen flickering between them as though they were trying to build up one mighty electrical charge that would be aimed and unleashed towards their prey.

"This doesn't look good!" observed Mallory, as he re-loaded.

"Over there to the left!" cried Jazmine, suddenly pointing into the swarm of eels. "There is one which is slightly bigger than the others and reddish not blue!"

"I see it!" said Mallory, noticing it for the first time.

"By, Jove!" cried the Professor, reloading quickly. "That must be either the Queen or the dominate male! If we can take that one out the others will disperse! Everyone, direct your fire at it!"

Everyone aimed their guns at the red eel and fired. The darts flew forward, and immediately they started to reload, not even waiting to see if they had hit their target. The four darts flew through the water, but everyone failed to strike home, instead hitting the smaller eels which seemed to put themselves in harm's way to protect their leader, resulting in a shower of sparks.

Following the red eel, Mallory and Yuri fired together, but their darts were blocked by a large blue eel that suddenly appeared in front of the red one at the last moment. The large blue eel sparked and fell away, leaving an open gap, which the Professor and Jazmine exploited. The Professor's dart missed, but Jazmine's grazed the creature's body, setting off a small shower of sparks. However, the creature seemed unaffected by the attack.

"Again!" shouted the Professor, seeing the circle of eels contracting further around them. "Just hit the ruddy thing. I think that they are about to let off a massive electrical surge any second."

"Where did it go?" said Jazmine, momentarily losing sight of their target.

"It's there!" cried Mallory. "I think I have a clear shot." He raised his gun and was about to fire, when the red eel seemed to disappear, being pulled away backwards.

Instantly the rest of the eels seemed to break off their formation and start to swim around wildly.

"What happened?" said Mallory. "I didn't fire!"

"Look, there!" cried Jazmine, pointing upwards.

There, coming into view was a strange looking sea creature, tubular in shape, about five foot long and a foot and a half in diameter. The rear of the creature seemed to taper off into a tail, while the front of it seemed to consist of one giant eye. Underneath was a long thin slit which was the mouth, out of which the red eel's tail was hanging limply, before it was sucked inside the creature. Then almost immediately a long thick forked tongue shot out again and wrapped itself round another one of the blue eels, which automatically seemed to light up, presumably activating its self defence mechanism. The singular eye of the strange creature seemed to also light up for a moment, but it held its grip and then the tongue retracted, taking the eel into its mouth, before moments later reappearing again, empty, and ready to grab another victim.

"My goodness!" cried Mallory. "What is that thing?"

"I've no idea," replied the Professor, "but if I didn't know better I would say that it was prehistoric!"

"It certainly ugly and hungry," noted Yuri, as the creature captures another eel.

By now most of the eels had disappeared, only a few confused stragglers remaining. The large singular eye looked right then left, unsure where to strike, before moving in and aiming its tongue at Jazmine, but she, anticipating what was about to happen, managed to dodge out of the way.

"It's trying for a main course!" cried Mallory.

Again the tongue shot out, this time it was aimed for Yuri and the tendril wrapped itself tightly around the Russian's water filled arm, and started to pull him in.

CHAPTER 49

Despite the fact that Yuri was obviously much larger than the eels, and there was the added weight of his water filling up his suit, the sea monster was still able to pull him towards its mouth with relative ease. "I not become your next meal!" cried the Russian, as he lifted his gun and fired at the creature's eye. But just as the projectile was about to hit, the eyelid came down, acting as a shield with the Bakelite dart bouncing off.   Meanwhile a number of other darts, fired by the Professor, Jazmine and Mallory, flew in and hit the creature on its tubular body, making it wriggle with the impact, but other than that having no real effect.

Unable to reload, as the creature had him by the arm, Yuri opted to throw his gun directly at the monster, but the weapon hit the protective eye lid and bounced off harmlessly.

"Use your knife!" called Mallory, as he swum in towards the Russian, getting behind him and grabbing onto his suit. The added weight immediately stopped Yuri from being pulled in any further, and he found the Russian a foot and a half from the creature's mouth and its sharp pin-like teeth. With his free hand Yuri went to his belt, took his knife, and slashed down at the tongue. The sharp edge of the blade hit the tendril and immediately bounced off. Yuri swore. "It like hitting rubber band!"

"Keep going!" cried Mallory, tightening his grip on the Russian's diving suit.

Again Yuri hit down, and again the knife bounced off. So he then opted to place the edge of the blade on the tongue and tried sawing at it. The singular eye seemed to widen and in response the creature tightened its grip further, making Yuri cry out.

"Brace yourselves!" cried the Professor, as he swam in towards the back of the sea monster. In his hands he was holding one of the struggling electric eels, which he had managed to capture. Aiming the head forwards, he thrust it towards the sea-creature, aiming for what looked like a gill. The head went directly into the opening, and the eel immediately let off a defensive electrical charge. There was a large blue flash and a wave of electrical energy shot outwards. The sea-creature let out a shrill cry, released Yuri and then turned and swam off. The Professor, Mallory and Yuri were all pushed backwards from the blast, but were able to quickly regain control of themselves, with the Professor and Mallory speedily making their way back to Yuri to see how he was.

"Are you alright?" asked Mallory.

"I think so," replied the Russian, shaking his head. "I thought I was going to end up meal. Glad I'm out of danger."

"Sadly I don't think you are," said the Professor. "Your suit is still filling up fast."

Water could now be seen in Yuri's domed helmet, just under his chin.

"We have to do something," said Jazmine, swimming in to join them. In her hand she held Yuri's discarded gun, which she passed to him. Silently the Russian took it and returned it to the holster.

"I think all we can do is carry on swimming and hope that there are no more delays and that either we find an air pocket, or that we come to the end of this tunnel," said the Professor, quickly looking down at their air supply gauge. "Well, at least we all have plenty of oxygen left."

"Speaking of which, Yuri, how long can you hold your breath for?" asked Mallory. "I think that is going to be your only option."

Yuri shrugged. "I once got trapped under ice in Bolshaya River. I was under water for maybe six minutes before I managed to get out."

"Well, that's encouraging," said the Professor. "Yuri, you are going to have to do that again. We will be swimming with you and directing you as we go. Follow our instructions, should we give any, to the letter. Do you understand?"

The Russian nodded.

"Right," said the Professor, trying not to sound too worried, "let's go this way." And with that, he started to head off, with Yuri swimming after him, flanked by Mallory and Jazmine.

As they moved through the water, Mallory kept a close eye on Yuri. The Russian was clearly now struggling with the weight of water in his suit, but more worryingly was the fact that the water in the glass dome had risen completely over Yuri's lips and nose. The Russian continued to swim after the Professor, his eyes fixed ahead.

Mallory stole a glance at Jazmine and shook his head. She smiled over to him sympathetically, but also helplessly. Both were aware that it was not just the issue of Yuri not being able to breathe, but the build-up of water pressure inside the reinforced glass dome could crush his skull.

Ahead, the Professor continued to swim, noticeably increasing his pace and occasionally looking back to see how the Russian was doing, and also upwards in the hope of seeing a suitably large air pocket that Yuri could use, but there were none, only tiny recesses that were just likely used, with difficulty, by the Trasgo.

Onward they swam.

The water had now reached Yuri's forehead and he looked over at Mallory and tried to fake a smile, but it was clear that he knew that this was very likely the end for him.

Then suddenly the Professor turned and pointed upwards excitedly; looking in the direction he was indicating they could all see above them a change in the colour of the water, where light was shining down onto them. Instinctively, they all started to swim upwards, aiming towards the lighter patch of water.

The Professor broke the surface first and found himself in an underground chamber. Directly in front of him was a flat stone rock littered pathway which he made for, climbing out before turning round just as Yuri, Mallory and Jazmine appeared. Reaching out he grabbed hold of Yuri and with the help of Mallory and Jazmine they managed to pull the Russian out of the water onto the bank.

"Quick," cried the Professor, "help me get the helmet off him."

Mallory and Jazmine, who had by now also climbed out onto the pathway, immediately started to wrestle with the fastenings of the glass dome, but they would not budge.

"Time to try another tack," said the Professor. The knife he had been given was now in his hand. "Hold still, Yuri,

251

I'm going to have to cut the suit to release the water." With that he thrust the knife forward, but the blade failed to penetrate the material. He tried again, but still the suit remained intact.

Then Mallory left them, reappearing moments later with a rock in his hand. He raised the stone, and then brought it down hard on the glass dome. For a moment it seemed nothing happened, and then a crack appeared, followed by the glass shattering, with the water spilling out and Yuri taking in several deep breaths.

"Are you going to be alright?" asked Mallory.

"Just give me a few moments," Yuri nodded, replying between big gulps of air.

While the Russian was recovering, the Professor, Mallory and Jazmine took off their domed helmets and diving suits, to reveal their own clothes underneath, before retrieving the utility belts which they fastened tightly round their waists.

"I've just had a thought," said Mallory glumly, as he checked the small empty cage was firmly attached to his belt. "Do you think that the Trasgo could have made it past the eels and that other creature? What if it was caught and killed?"

"I did wonder that myself," admitted the Professor. "But considering that it seems that our goblin friend has seemingly made various trips to Upper Karlstad we must assume that it is able to avoid the dangers we faced and is still alive."

After a few minutes rest, Yuri was back to normal and began to take off the diving suit too. "With helmet gone, I won't be able return the way we came," pointed out the Russian, as he picked up his utility belt and empty cage.

"Well I'm hoping that there is another way out of here," said the Professor. "Worst case scenario, we come back here and leave you while we head back to the fortress and collect another helmet that you can use. Are you ready to continue now?"

The Russian nodded.

"Good," said the Professor, looking over to an entrance to another tunnel located on the other side of the chamber, "because it's time we were on our way."

CHAPTER 50

Carefully, the Professor, Jazmine, Mallory and Yuri made their way through the tunnel, which seemed to be lit naturally by a strange green algae that covered the walls. After about half an hour of walking, the passage opened out into a large cavern, about fifty foot wide. The roof was covered with small stalactites, just over a foot in length, the ends of which seemed to be viciously pointed. On the floor below were a number of newly formed stalagmites which could be seen among piles of rock debris. Over the other side of the cavern was the mouth of a small tunnel that would be their exit.

Mallory was about to step forward into the cave, but the Professor grabbed him, pulling him back.

"Not yet Mr Mallory," said the Professor. "I think we have a problem. Jazmine, what do you think?"

Jazmine looked around the cavern, studying the surroundings before slowly nodding. "Yes Father, I think I know what you're driving at."

"What's wrong?" asked Mallory.

"Well," replied Jazmine, "looking at the gaps in the cavern roof and the amount of rubble on the floor, I think that the whole place is unstable. The stalactites are liable to come down on us as we cross."

"You sure?" asked Yuri.

"One way to find out," answered Jazmine, as she picked up a large stone, which she then threw out into the middle of the cave. The rock landed with a crash, sending an echo around the chamber. At first nothing happened, then there was a faint rumble and the stalactite that was directly above where the stone landed started to shake and then fall. The pointed end crashed into the floor and the whole thing shattered into pieces.

"Alright," said Yuri, "that not good, but we can still get cross right?"

The Professor nodded. "Yes, we should be alright, providing we are very careful; so no shouting or sudden moves."

One by one, they all carefully moved out into the chamber. The Professor, taking the lead, slowly navigated a path while the others followed.

"This not so bad," said Yuri, as he carefully stepped over the remains of a broken column.

"Don't jinks things," hissed Mallory.

"Universe does not work like that!" replied the Russian.

"Oh yes it does," said Jazmine. "Look up there!"

Appearing from a hole left by a stalactite that had fallen, was what looked to be a giant hornet; the body of which was the size of a large pear. The oversized insect flew around, examining its new surroundings, until it tried to settle on a stalactite. The weight of the small creature was enough to dislodge it and it started to fall, smashing into the ground.

"That thing's going to be a problem," said Mallory, noting the hornet was now almost flying overhead, and looking as though it was trying to find a new place to land.

"No it won't," said Yuri, as he pulled out his gun and checked that it was loaded. "I can take care of this with one careful shot. It small target but I can get it."

"I'm not sure that's wise," said the Professor. "If you miss you will hit another stalactite for sure."

The Russian shook his head. "Ha! Yuri won't miss!"

"Look," said Mallory, "I really don't think that …."
But it was too late. Yuri had raised his gun and fired. The Bakelite dart flew through the air, but at the last second the hornet, seeing the projectile coming towards it, veered out of the way and the dart smashed into a stalactite which immediately dislodged and fell to the ground. Then from the hole it left, a small swarm of hornets appeared and started to fly around the cavern roof.

"Whoops," said Yuri, looking embarrassed. "Plan good in theory. What now?"

One of the hornets flew straight into a stalactite near them, causing it to drop and shatter.

"Caution to the wind I'm afraid," said the Professor, as he broke into a run. Following his lead, the others started to race for the other side of the cavern as, from above, stalactites began to rain down as the hornets continued to set them off as they crashed into them.

It did not take them long to reach the exit. The Professor went through the gap first, but immediately had to dodge to the left as, from the tunnel he entered, another hornet flew straight towards him. This one was followed by another and then another, with hundreds more not far behind, which forced him, along with the others, back deep into the stalactite cavern, until they found themselves in the centre of the massive swarm.

"I can't see a thing," cried Mallory, as he held his hand up in front of his face. Somewhere to the left a stalactite crashed to the floor. Then another landed somewhere in front of him.

"Where is exit?" cried Yuri who, dodging the hornets that fluttered around him, had found himself totally disorientated.

"This way!" cried Jazmine, trying to push forward through the insects.

"No, not that way!" cried the Professor. "Go left. I mean go right. Blast it I have no idea which is the way out now! Don't let them sting you either. They can carry quite a punch."

"Easier said than done!" cried Mallory, as he held his arm up shielding his face and stepped to the left. As he moved, his foot caught a newly forming stalagmite, which sent him off balance and he fell sideways to the floor. He landed heavily, his head smashing onto a large rock, which knocked him out cold.

"Mallory!" cried Yuri, who dropped to the floor under the wave of hornets and started to crawl over to his friend.

Jazmine and the Professor followed the Russian's lead and ducked down low, where they were able to get their bearings while all around them stalactites continued to fall and shatter on the ground.

"Yuri, how is he?" called the Professor.

"Out for count," replied the Russian, ducking down as he was dive bombed by a particularly large hornet. "He will have big headache when he wakes up."

Just as Yuri finished speaking a stalactite ploughed its way through the sea of insects and landed a few feet to his left.

"Right we need to get ourselves out of here, and fast. Crawl this way!" called the Professor, pointing over to where the exit was. "Yuri, can you take care of Mallory?"

The Russian nodded, and started to carefully move towards the chamber exit, grabbing hold of Mallory as he did so, dragging him along behind.

Eventually, under the swarm of hornets and the constant barrage of falling stalactites, they managed to work their way back across the chamber over to the exit. Then as fast at the hornets appeared; they suddenly began to thin out and disappear into the roof of the cavern where the stalactites had broken off.

"Typical," grunted Yuri, sitting up, "why they not do that before?"

"Never mind, it can't be helped," said the Professor, who was just grateful they were no longer under attack. "How is Mr Mallory doing?"

"Still out cold," replied Yuri. "But pulse is still strong. He will be fine, although I may have bumped head a bit as I dragged him along floor."

"Perhaps that might knock some sense into him," said Jazmine, with a smile.

"Maybe," said the Professor, "but we will have to be careful as we continue. Head injuries can be very …" He broke off in mid-sentence, his head snapping round, a strange sound catching his attention.

Directly over the chamber exit was an impossibly large stalactite, which seemed to be vibrating, then a crack appeared at the end of it and the entire tip broke off and crashed to the floor, sending shards flying into the air. The rumbling continued and the entire stalactite started to move slowly downwards, steadily growing in size and speed.

"Amazing," commented the Professor, "I would say that is actually part of some larger formation that is possibly in a chamber or alcove above us. That is a very rare occurrence."

"Yes Father, maybe," said Jazmine, with a sense of urgency, "but it is also about to block our only way out of here."

"Quick everyone!" cried the Professor, coming to his senses and standing up. "We don't have a moment to lose!"

CHAPTER 51

The Professor, followed by Jazmine, dived through the disappearing gap of the chamber's exit as the stalactite continued to descend. Yuri, who had picked the unconscious Mallory up, had reached the exit a few seconds behind and seeing that there was not enough room for the two of them to go through together, unceremoniously dropped his friend on the floor, before himself diving through.

"Mallory," cried out Jazmine in horror, thinking that he had been abandoned. However, the Russian had no such intention and turned, reaching back into the cavern, under the falling stalactite. He grabbed Mallory by the legs and hauled him through into the tunnel, just as the stalactite smashed down, disintegrating into a massive pile of rubble which blocked the entrance.

"That was close," remarked Yuri casually.

"For second I thought his head was going to get squashed like melon."

At that point Mallory started to wake up.

"Are you alright Mr Mallory?" asked the Professor.

"Um, er I think so," he said, slowly sitting up. "My head hurts, what happened?"

With relief the Professor filled him in on their escape from the stalactite chamber, as Mallory climbed unsteadily to his feet.

"I think you should rest for a while," said Jazmine, but Mallory shook his head, saying that he would be fine and they should press on.

They continued to walk through the tunnel for another half an hour, opting to ignore any of the side tunnels that appeared from time to time along their route, hoping that their quarry had done the same.

"This is getting worrying," said Mallory, after a while. "No sign of the Trasgo or any way out of here. I think we may be lost in here forever!"

"I'm sure everything will turn out fine," said the Professor, who suddenly stopped dead in his tracks and held his hand up to halt everyone else.

"What's wrong?" asked Mallory.

"I don't like the look of this section of floor up ahead of us. It looks different and I think I can feel heat. Stay here everyone." And with that the Professor pressed his back up against the tunnel wall and started to edge his way along, occasionally tapping the ground in front of him. Eventually he stepped back out into the tunnel, turning round to face

259

his friends. "Right, one by one you need to come this way like I did, back to the wall. I am pretty sure that there is a hidden sink hole there."

Jazmine went first, followed by Mallory; both making it to the Professor without any problems. Then it was Yuri's turn. "This easy, but I feel silly," commented the Russian, as he pressed himself closer to the tunnel wall edging himself along. Then, just as he finished speaking, there was a rumble and just in front of him the floor collapsed leaving a perfectly round vertical shaft, at the bottom of which looked to be a pool of lava bubbling away.

"Are you alright?" called the Professor.

"Yes!" replied the Russian looking down. "I think so." He began to move along and as he did so the thin ledge that he was standing on started to crumble. With a yell, Yuri threw himself towards where his friends were standing and ended up landing on the very edge of the sinkhole. For a moment he teetered precariously before managing to step forward onto firmer ground.

"That was close!" said the Russian. "Professor, if you had not spotted change in floor we could have fallen into it!"

The Professor smiled. "Don't thank me, thank the Dean of my University who forced me to teach a Geology class last Christmas. Come on, we better keep going."

They continued onwards for another hour until they came to a steep twenty foot cream covered slope which resembled a waterfall that had been frozen in mid-flow, that seemed to lead up to another tunnel.

"Flowstone," said the Professor, placing his hand on the smooth rock deposits. "It's the runoff from stalactites."

Looking up he could see a number of small stalactites overhead, from which this barrier had been formed.

Yuri shook his head. "I have climbed flowstone before, very tricky. Smooth, wet, with few handholds."

"I'm afraid that we have no choice though," said the Professor, who was still looking upwards. "Our exit appears to be up there."

"I go first," said the Russian. "When I get to top, I can drop rope down and pull you all up one by one."

"How on earth can you climb that?" asked Jazmine.

"Not so much climb," replied the Russian, "more like run and hope. Better stand back, this likely to get nasty."

Following Yuri's advice they all moved away while the Russian prepared himself by limbering up, before he turned to face the flowstone. Taking a deep breath he ran forward, placing his right foot on the mass and then, launched himself upwards. He managed to take two steps and then on the third his foot slipped and he came crashing down, to where he had started, in a heap. He swore in Russian and then picked himself up.

"Are you alright, Yuri?" called Mallory.

"Yes!" he replied. "Foot slip, I try again."

Once again the Russian ran at the flowstone, this time avoiding the spot where he first fell and made two further steps, before stopping, having found a hand hold where he could take a brief rest and to decide his next move. Then after a few moments he headed off again, but promptly slipped, fell, and came crashing back down to the floor.

"That really hurt," said Yuri, who was visibly shaken. "I almost have it!" However, the Russian was sadly mistaken. His third attempt saw him almost reach the top, but the final section was impossibly smooth and resulted in him falling back down again, as did his fourth, fifth and sixth attempts.

"Blast it!" said Yuri, picking himself up again. "I just can't get that final bit."

"Shall I have a go?" offered Mallory.

Yuri shook his head. "No offence, but if I have problems, even with my climbing experience, I think you would not manage. I get it, providing I don't break something on way down!"

Yuri's seventh and eighth attempt also ended in failure. But on the ninth he finally was able to get past the slippery patch of flowstone that was causing the problem; his sheer momentum finally carrying him over. Finding a firm handhold, he managed to pull himself, bruised and battered, into the new section of tunnel with yells of delight from those below. Then Yuri let down the climbing rope and one by one, the Professor, Mallory and Jazmine were able to climb up without incident.

"Can you feel that?" asked Jazmine, looking down the tunnel stretching out in front of them.

"No, what?" replied Mallory.

"I think I can feel a very small breeze."

"You're right," said the Professor, pausing, "and I think that the air has changed too, not so stale. I think that we are nearing the end of the tunnel."

"But no sign of the Trasgo," pointed out Mallory.

"Yes, well that is an important detail," replied the Professor, "but hopefully we will find the little creature as we continue. Come on, is everybody ready?"

They all nodded and then set off again.

After about ten minutes, the tunnel started to narrow, which forced them into single file. Then they found themselves having to crouch down as the roof of the passageway began to get lower. The tunnel continued to shrink until they were forced to crawl along on their hands and knees before eventually having to lay down and pull themselves forward on their elbows.

"Getting cramped," remarked Yuri, who was particularly having problems due to his large frame. "What happen if it gets any smaller?"

"Then we will have no option but to turn back and we will have failed our mission," replied the Professor, worriedly. But, mercifully, after another ten foot the tunnel slowly started to widen out and, turning a tight corner, they were confronted with a gentle slope. At the end of it was a shaft of light which they gratefully headed towards.

One by one they emerged from the tunnel, onto a snow covered mountainside in brilliant sunlight, where they looked around to assess their new surroundings. Far below them, visible through a thin layer of cloud, could be seen the fortress of Upper Karlstad. While above them, perched on a small plateau was a large white building, which looked to be an observatory.

CHAPTER 52

The observatory was hexagonal in shape, and its top consisted of a large dome, constructed from glass and brass coloured metal beams. Visible inside was a large brass telescope.

"Looks like our furry friends seem to have an interest in the stars and beyond," noted Jazmine.

"Not totally surprising considering their advancement in other areas," replied the Professor.

"Shall we investigate?" said Jazmine, eagerly.

The Professor nodded. "Yes, I think we should."

The three of them followed the path that wound its way up the mountainside until they arrived at the building.

"So what now?" asked Mallory. "Do you think that anyone is there?"

"One way to find out," said Jazmine, as she knocked on the door. They waited, but there was no reply.

"Nobody home," said Yuri. He stepped forward to try the door handle, but it was locked. "Looks like if we want inside, we have to break in."

"Blast!" exclaimed the Professor, "and I don't have my lock picks with me."

"If we can't find another obvious way in we'll have to barge the door down," said Yuri, almost hopefully.

"I'm not sure we will have to resort to that," replied Jazmine, eyeing the ornate letter box. Carefully she reached her fingers through the slit and felt around. With a smile she withdrew her hand, and with it a long piece of string. On the end of it was a large brass key which she held up triumphantly.

"How did you know?" asked Mallory, clearly impressed.

She smiled. "Why would they have a letter box? As advanced and organised as these creatures are I think it's highly unlikely they would have regular postal deliveries to such a remote location."

With that she put the key into the lock, turned it, then opened the door and they all stepped inside.

The observatory was split into three levels. The majority of the ground floor resembled a study, but off to one side there was a small kitchen, living room and sleeping area as well as a door that presumably led to the toilet and bathroom. In the middle of the room was a large blackboard. In front of which there was a desk that was covered with books and scrolls; also on the table was a now familiar green crystal skull. The first floor, which was reached via two different decorative spiral staircases at either side of the building, was no more than a metal gantry; four foot wide that circled the perimeter of the building. The wall itself was mostly taken up with bookcases crammed with books, broken at regular intervals with large windows. Over to one side, there was a ladder that went up to another gantry that spanned the base of the glass dome. In the centre of this, on a small plinth, was an oversized reclining viewing chair which was placed directly under the eyepiece of the telescope. The larger main lens was almost pressed up against a section of the dome that looked as though it could be opened, so the telescope could be extended for viewing the night sky.

"Amazing," said the Professor, looking up at the telescope. "The entire dome section seems to be able to rotate so the telescope can gain the required view."

"Father! Come look at this," called Jazmine, excitedly. She had moved over to the blackboard and was studying the writing on it intensely.

The Professor, along with Mallory and Yuri went over to her to see what she had found.

"My goodness!" cried the Professor, casting his eyes over the board. "It seems that the principle study is Mars, and the observations made seem far more advanced compared to what we already know."

"Yes," said Jazmine, "they seem to have made a small, but very detailed, diagram of the 'Canali' or 'Canals' that cross the planet."

"And look at that," said the Professor, pointing to a section circled extensively in a different coloured chalk.

'Ice formations (Natural / From Comets?) High probability of flowing water. Type – Salt? Iron Oxidized? Clear? Other? Able to be used for growing earth crops and sustaining them?'

"Why would they want to grow earth crops on Mars?" asked Yuri.

"For the people who are living there," replied Jazmine. Mallory's eyes widened in surprise. "Do you really think that they have long term plans to travel to and colonize Mars?"

The Professor shrugged. "Quite possible. For a race so far advanced it certainly would be a suitable challenge for them to undertake, and one that they could conceivably achieve."

"Or they could be getting carried away with things," said Yuri, who had spotted and picked up a copy of the recently published 'A Princess of Mars' by Edgar Rice Burroughs from the table.

The Professor smiled. "The line between fiction and science often becomes blurred over time, and it seems that these creatures could accelerate that theory."

"But still," said Mallory unconvinced, "Mars?"

"Well, on that we will have to see, although I doubt that it will be in our lifetime."

"Wait a moment," said Jazmine, a thought suddenly coming to her. "Didn't Izaki say that he didn't agree with Zidal's observations of the fourth planet?"

266

"Yes, that's right," said the Professor, remembering the conversation that had taken place in the archive under The Manor. "Zidal must have been an astronomer, and obviously spent time here. If the Trasgo was here as well, that would explain how he came into contact with it." He paused, looking around. "We need to check to see if our little goblin friend is here. Now, who would like to help me take a closer look at that telescope and uppermost floor?"

"I will," volunteered Mallory.

"Right, come along then. Yuri, you take the first floor and Jazmine you can check out the ground floor. Let us know at once if you find anything." With that he, with Mallory following, went to one of the spiral staircases and started to make their way to the top of the building, while Yuri headed to the second staircase that would take him to the first floor gantry. Jazmine started her search on the ground floor.

It did not take Mallory and the Professor long to reach the gantry that was suspended under the glass dome and very carefully they made their way onto it and across to the plinth where the large brass telescope was located.

"This is certainly an amazing feat of engineering," said the Professor, as he climbed into the oversized viewing chair which appeared to be an adapted Queen Anne Chesterfield leather armchair, the back of which was reclined back slightly to allow comfortable viewing. "Oh very nice," said the Professor, as he put his feet up onto the matching leather footstool in front of him. To his right was what looked like a small control panel. On the top were a number of buttons and levers, which presumably operated the dome. Underneath were shelves on which were a number of books relating to astronomy, as well as a number of note books and pens. No doubt ready to record observations. "Yes," said the Professor, approvingly, "this is an incredible setup and I wager this particular telescope is as powerful as anything we have back at Greenwich." He ran his hands over the buttons and levers on the control panel.

"You are not thinking of trying to operate it are you?" asked Mallory, worriedly.

"The thought had crossed my mind," said the Professor, with a smile, "but I think I had better not. Hopefully we can persuade Netvor to give us a proper guided tour later. Mr Mallory, could you please pass me one of those note books? I would love to see what else has been observed."

Meanwhile Jazmine, who after a while had had enough of searching, had seated herself at the table, by the black board. Casually she started to look at the various bits of paper and scrolls on it, before turning her attention to the green crystal skull. She picked it up and looked it over, before placing it down in front of her, wondering why it was here and not in the creature's sacred space under St Magdalena's church in Upper Karlstad. Then looking at the blackboard she noticed a spelling mistake.
Instinctively, she reached for a piece of chalk that was on the small tray at the bottom of the board and went to correct the error. As she did so she realised that she was being watched. For there, sitting on the top right corner of the blackboard, regarding her with curious eyes, was the small, paint splattered, Trasgo.

CHAPTER 53

For a few moments Jazmine and the Trasgo just stared at each other, before the goblin broke eye contact and started to preen himself.

Jazmine looked to the first floor gantry where Yuri was engrossed in one of the books and then to the dome where her Father and Mallory were inspecting the telescope. For a moment she considered calling out to them, but quickly dismissed the idea in case it scared the Trasgo. The goblin stopped its washing ritual, then silently jumped down onto the table and proceeded to make its way to the far end where it settled with its back towards Jazmine, ignoring her.

Carefully, she reached down to her dart gun and removed it from the holster. Whilst keeping a close eye on the Trasgo, she made sure it was loaded. Then, making sure not to attract the Goblin's attention, she lifted the gun aimed and fired.

The dart flew silently through the air and hit its target; the bookcase on the first floor gantry, a foot away from where Yuri was standing.

Jazmine watched as the Russian turned round and looked down towards her, where he thought the shot was fired. She put her finger to her lips to indicate that he should be quiet then pointed to the Trasgo, at the end of the table.

Yuri's eyes widened and then he looked up to the telescope above him, waving and attracting the attention of the Professor and Mallory, before pointing downwards, so they too became aware they had at last found their quarry.

Very slowly, trying not to make any kind of sound, the three men carefully made their way down and met at the base of the first spiral staircase. Yuri and Mallory had already unhitched the clear Bakelite cages from their belts and had opened the doors in readiness. Then, before they could work out a suitable plan of attack, the Trasgo sat bolt upright and let out an ear piercing howl.

"What's happening?" asked Mallory.

"No idea!" replied the Professor, who was just as confused. "Jazmine? What did you do?"

"Nothing!" she protested, trying to make herself heard over the continuing screams.

The Trasgo jumped to the floor and started to scamper towards the small living area. Yuri, cage in hand, ran after it, but the little goblin made for the bed, diving under it. Yuri was there a moment later and dropped to his knees, looking underneath to see where the creature was. "Ah," said the Russian to the others, who had now joined him, "Imp seems to have been making himself at home. There is nest here and looks as though he has been in residence for some time."

"What's he doing now?" asked the Professor.

"Curling up, looking scared."

"Can you get to him?"

Yuri nodded then, abandoning the cage, reached under the bed to try and retrieve the Trasgo.

"Why would it suddenly start to act so strangely?" asked Jazmine.

"I'm not sure," said the Professor, stroking his beard thoughtfully, "but it is slightly worrying."

"Ah-ha!" cried out Yuri triumphantly, as he held up the creature for everyone to see. "Here he is! Not so brave now are you?"

"Be careful Yuri," said Jazmine. "We don't want to harm it."

"Don't worry," replied the Russian, as he placed both hands under the goblin's arms in a more secure and gentler grip, and then stood up. "He is fine. He is robust little fella."

"He looks terrified," said Jazmine, looking at the Trasgo, who had its ears pinned back and was looking around fretfully.

"Oh don't you worry," said Yuri to the goblin, as though he was talking to a baby. "We just pop you into cage, take you down to Upper Karlstad where they will take a little look at you and then you will be set free!" He turned to the Professor. "They will let him free won't they? I hate to think that he will end up dissected or worse."

"I'm sure they won't let any harm come to the little blood glugging parasite," replied the Professor, with more than a hint of sarcasm in his voice. "Now let's get the little chap into the cage."

Mallory produced the small cage and carefully the still terrified Trasgo was placed inside, and the door firmly bolted.

"There!" said the Professor, "all in all I think that went very well indeed! Now all we have to do is get back to the fortress."

"Back through the tunnel?" asked Mallory.

"No," said the Professor, shaking his head. "I think it will be much easier if we climb down the old fashioned way."

271

Then the Trasgo let out an ear piercing scream.

"Hey, what's wrong?" said Yuri, lifting up the cage to eye level. "You are a scared little fella aren't you?"

The goblin seemed to nod mournfully and howled again.

"Hold on," said Jazmine. "Did you feel that?"

"I'm not sure," said Mallory.

The Trasgo wailed again and the floor started to gently shake.

"What's happening?" said Yuri.

"It's an earth tremor," said the Professor, moving his stance to steady himself. "I think that's why the Trasgo was acting the way he was."

"I don't think it's just a tremor," said Mallory in alarm, as he too had to move to gain firmer footing as the ground shifted underneath him. "It's getting much stronger."

The effects of the tremor could now be seen around the observatory; on the first floor gantry books on the shelves started to move and fall, while on the ground floor pictures on the walls started to shake, and the blackboard started to judder, then move on its stand as items on the table started to fall off of the sides.

"We need to get out of here!" said Mallory.

"No time," cried the Professor. "Duck and cover! That's our best option. Get under the table or the spiral staircase for protection."

But before anyone could act on his information, the entire ground seemed to rise and then promptly fall back down. Then a hairline crack appeared on the stone floor, snaking its way from wall to wall of the building. With the ground still juddering, the crack began to grow and widen.

"Look!" cried Jazmine, "the walls, they are fracturing open too!"

Sure enough, on both sides of the building breaks could be seen appearing at the base of the walls which slowly started to climb upwards. Meanwhile the rift in the floor continued to grow to just over a foot wide with new smaller cracks appearing off of it and spreading outwards.

Then from above there was the sound of glass cracking and, looking up, they could see fractures in the glass dome.

"Under the table now!" roared the Professor.

Realising what was about to happen, everyone made for the still juddering table and dived under it for protection, just as the first few shards of glass started to rain down, some hitting the table top, while others smashed to the floor around them.

"Brace yourselves," cried the Professor, "any second now....!"

Just as he finished speaking there was a groaning and smashing sound from high above, followed a few moments later by a deluge of large fragments of glass crashing down all around them. One massive shard went straight through the table. It missed impaling Jazmine through the head by a matter of inches.

Then, without any warning, everything stopped.

The glass stopped falling and the ground ceased to shake as though someone had flipped a switch into the off position.

An eerie silence filled the observatory, with uncertain looks being exchanged between the Professor, Jazmine, Mallory and Yuri; each not daring to speak or wanting to tempt fate by saying that it was over. Then Yuri passed the Trasgo in its cage to Jazmine, before carefully looking out from under the table and saw that all was now calm.

One by one they climbed out from under their hiding place to survey the wreckage.

The crack in the floor had grown to about three foot wide and the opposite side was noticeably higher by around a foot. The break in the walls had also grown and was now letting in shafts of daylight. All around them there was wreckage and debris of one kind or another, be it books, glass or rubble.

Then from above there was a strange groaning noise. Everyone looked up to see the gantry that was across the base of the dome, which held the telescope, was starting to fall.

CHAPTER 54

On seeing the danger, everyone scattered in different directions. The massive telescope, viewing chair and twisted metal that made up the gantry smashed to the floor, momentarily sending up glass, rubble and other debris high into the air.

The Professor picked himself up off of the floor and looked around. He could see that the huge telescope had fallen across the fissure in the floor, while the viewing chair and stool, both still attached to the small plinth, were now lying among the twisted remains of the gantry. "Is everyone alright?" he called out.

"I think so," replied Mallory, dabbing at his head with a handkerchief, trying to stop the blood running down his face, "well, apart from being hit by some flying glass."

"Where is Yuri?" asked Jazmine, who appeared carrying the terrified Trasgo in its cage.

The Professor and Mallory looked around, but the Russian was nowhere to be seen.

"Well he can't have gone far," said the Professor.

"Wait," said Jazmine, suddenly, "did you hear that?" Everyone stopped and listened.

"Yes, there it is again," answered Mallory. "My goodness, I think it came from the crack in the floor!" Realising where his friend was, Mallory, followed closely by the Professor and Jazmine, made their way to where the sound had come from. Looking down into the fissure, just by the telescope, they could see Yuri, about twenty feet below them. He had his arms and feet braced on either side of the chasm wall.

"Yuri, are you alright?"

The Russian grunted. "I stepped left, when should have stepped right and fall into hole. New experience for me. I usually sure footed even when I drink too much vodka."

"Just stay there," called Jazmine, "we'll drop you down a rope."

"No need, I manage fine. Just good job I manage to stop myself from falling further. I think this hole goes on for some way!" and with that he started to slowly edge his way upwards. Eventually he reached the top of the rift where he was helped onto solid ground by Mallory and Jazmine. "That was harder than I thought," said the Russian, stretching and looking round. "This place looks in real mess."

"Indeed," said the Professor, also casting his eye around. "I'm no Structural Engineer, but I don't think that this building is safe anymore."

"Not just building," added Yuri. "I felt movement in side of rock as I climb up. I think entire plateau and

275

observatory with it about to give way and fall down mountain."

"If that happens Upper Karlstad would be directly in its path," said Jazmine, remembering how that fortress was directly below them.

"But surely they aware of what is happening up here and realise the danger?" queried Yuri.

"I don't think that can be guaranteed upon," answered the Professor, shaking his head. "We need to get down to Upper Karlstad and warn them at once, so they can get everyone to safety."

Suddenly the ground shifted again.

"We need to get there fast," said Mallory. "I don't think that we have a lot of time."

"Then we have big problem," pointed out Yuri. "I experienced climber and I know descent will be tricky for me, let alone you three."

"What if we were to sledge down?" asked Jazmine, suddenly.

"That would be perfect," agreed Yuri. "Only we lack key ingredient of plan – a sledge."

"Oh, I don't think we do," she replied, pointing to the upturned viewing chair and stool. "We could use that."

"It possible," said Yuri, scratching his head. "It sort of right shape and we all fit on it, with squeeze."

The ground shook again.

"Well, with the lack of other options open to us," said the Professor, worriedly, "I think that is our only choice." Realising that the Professor was right, Yuri and Mallory climbed over the wreckage to the fallen viewing chair and between them managed to free it and bring it to an area

ree of debris, where they were able to cast their eyes over
t properly.

Amazingly, despite the fall, the leather chair and foot
tool were still firmly attached to the wooden plinth and
vere undamaged: Although the control panel / book case
hat controlled the telescope and dome had been broken
ff. Most importantly though, was the fact that underneath
he plinth itself were sections of the metal gantry still
ttached, including a small part that stuck out of the very
ront.

"It will do," said Yuri, nodding his head. "We need to
end up metal at front to make it more like sledge."

"But what about steering?" asked Mallory.

"That problem," replied the Russian. "I think only
ption is for me to sit on stool at front with pole. I could
se it like oar and even could act as brake. But I warn you,
ourney won't be pretty!"

"Well I would rather go down that way than as part of an
valanche," said the Professor. "Yuri, you make the
djustments to the 'sledge'. We also need to find a suitable
teering pole for you. Jazmine, how is our little fiend
loing?"

Jazmine held up the cage with the Trasgo inside. "He
eems fine, much calmer now."

"Good, right, let's get going."

It did not take Yuri long to make the adjustments to the
iewing chair platform. Using a chunk of stone from the
roken floor as a hammer he managed to bend up the
emains of the metal gantry on the front of the plinth into a
urve. While he was doing this the Professor and Jazmine
usied themselves trying to salvage the research notes on
Mars, as well as the crystal skull, cramming them into a

cloth shoulder bag that they had found. After a short search Mallory managed to find a large, thick metal pole that could be used for Yuri to steer the sledge.

"How are you doing Yuri?" asked the Professor, as he stuffed a final wad of papers into his bag, before putting it over his shoulder.

"I am ready," replied the Russian, standing back to look at their impromptu mode of transport for the perilous trip. "I sit on front stool. Professor and Jazmine, with goblin on lap, can share seat and there is enough room for Mallory to stand on back of plinth."

Mallory surveyed the sledge and shook his head. "If we don't get ourselves killed on that thing it will be a miracle!"

Then from the walls of the observatory there was a creak and then more debris started to fall.

"Come on," said the Professor. "Time to get out of here."

Between the four of them they manoeuvred the make-shift sledge to the door of the observatory, and carefully through it. Outside they could see the full extent of the mini earthquake on the surrounding area. The fissure that they had seen inside the observatory extended both sides beyond the building's walls and carried on getting steadily wider. Worse still, the entire observatory seemed to be leaning dangerously forward.

"This was much worse than I thought," observed the Professor.

"Then we better move fast," remarked Yuri. "Over there. That slope will be best place to launch from."

Now, resting on the snowy mountainside, they found it easy to move the sledge into the position Yuri had pointed out.

The Professor climbed into the chair and Jazmine, cradling the Bakelite cage in which the Trasgo was being held, sat on his knees. Yuri placed the steering pole on the ledge before positioning himself at the front. Standing to one side, he leant over gripping the footstool with both hands.

Mallory placed himself at the back, standing behind the plinth, gripping onto the back of the chair, ready to push off.

"Everyone ready?" called Yuri.

"Yes," came the unanimous reply.

"Good. Mallory on three. One – Two – Three!"

With that, both he and Mallory started to push and the sledge started to move forward; slowly at first, but then picking up speed as they went down the start of the gentle slope of the mountainside. "Ready Mallory?" called Yuri. "Now!" With that, the Russian quickly seated himself on the stool, and reached down to pick up the steering pole, which he held out in front of him, allowing the front end to dip so it made contact with the snow. At the back, Mallory jumped onto the end of the plinth, gripping onto the back of the chair even tighter than before.

"Hold on tight people!" called Yuri, as the sledge started to move faster under its own speed. "Ride won't be long, but will be bumpy!"

CHAPTER 55

Everyone gripped on tightly, as the sledge continued to travel down the curve of the mountainside, before the ground gave way to a much steeper incline, sending them downwards at an alarming rate. At the front, Yuri used the pole as an oar, placing it left and then right as required, to keep them in a straight line, and when he could, directly out in front of them in an attempt to control their speed.

"This is going better than I thought it would," called out the Russian, as he placed the pole into the snow to correct a slight veer to the right. Then, without warning, the sledge hit a hidden dip and dropped down sharply before continuing onwards. At the front Yuri, who was leaning slightly to the left, almost fell off of the stool, but using the metal pole managed to right himself while Jazmine and the Professor, safe in the viewing chair, remained in place. However, Mallory at the back of the sledge was dislodged, his feet slipping off of the plinth totally and ending up being dragged along behind, gripping onto the back of the chair for dear life, and yelling out that he was in trouble. In response Yuri rammed the steering pole into the snow in front of him to try to slow their descent. Frantically Mallory tried to regain his footing and get back onto the plinth, but at the speed they were travelling, and the fact that they were bouncing over the snow, he was finding it impossible to do so. Then with horror, he realised that his grip on the back of the chair was starting to slip.

"Hold on Mr Mallory!" called the Professor, as Jazmine shuffled forward allowing him to turn round and kneel on the chair. As he was doing so Mallory's hold gave way totally and he started to fall.

"No you don't!" cried the Professor, reaching down and grabbing onto Mallory's left arm.

"Yuri! Stop the sledge!" called Jazmine.

"Easier said than done!" responded the Russian, who was wrestling with the braking pole. By now the Professor had reached down with his other hand and managed to grab hold of Mallory's shirt and was desperately trying to pull him back onto the sledge. Then the sledge hit a bumpy patch of snow, the resulting jolt was the leverage that the Professor needed, allowing him to pull Mallory upright. Taking the opportunity, Mallory grabbed the back of the chair and at the same time managed to get both feet back on the end of the plinth.

"Really not the time to get out and walk," said the Professor with a smile, as he climbed back down into his seat.

"No, indeed," replied Mallory, who realised that if he had have fallen and had been left behind, there would be no way for him to reach Upper Karlstad before the mountainside fell, and he would surely have been killed.

The sledge continued onwards, gaining more and more speed. By now they could clearly see the Fortress village of Upper Karlstad below them, but also directly in front of them, they spotted a problem in the shape of a natural ramp formed out of the snow that there was no way of avoiding.

"Brace yourselves!" roared Yuri. "Big jump ahead!"

The sledge thundered towards the slope, bouncing slightly as it hit the base, before continuing up it and over the edge.

For a moment they were airborne, flying about four feet high in the air, but then gravity took hold of the heavier back end of the sledge and pulled it to the ground, with the

281

rear of the plinth hitting the compacted snow first, followed moments later by the front end slamming down hard. The impact, along with a slight drop in the ground they happened to come across at the same time, added to their forward momentum, resulting in the sledge tipping forwards with the rear end rising up high into the air.

Yuri reacted instantly by slamming the steering pole into the snow to stop them toppling over totally. The force he exerted caused the metal rod to crack and then break in half, becoming useless. For a few more seconds they continued forward, perilously balanced and in danger of tipping over totally, but then the back end of the sledge came crashing down landing on the ground with a bump.

"My goodness," cried the Professor, "I thought we had had it then!"

"Still time Professor," replied Yuri, throwing the remains of his metal pole away. "Our steering and break is lost!"

"Blast it," cried the Professor. He was about to give the order for everyone to abandon the sledge, when it suddenly started to bounce as it hit a patch of uneven snow that was more like ice. The sledge kept in a straight line, but then hit a large mound sticking out of the ground making the right side of the sledge tip upwards. Amazingly it continued along for a few moments, balanced on the left hand edge of the plinth. Then, hitting a rock, the whole thing turned and started to roll, tipping out its occupants, who started to tumble down the mountain side. As they were falling, the sledge, which came crashing after them, broke up, the stool and the chair breaking away from the plinth and, along with numerous other bits of debris, came crashing after them. At one point the stool hit Yuri as he ell, making him yell, while the heavy leather chair maintained a constant path close to Jazmine.

Onward they all tumbled until, about fifty feet away from the high wall that surrounded Upper Karlstad, the ground suddenly started to flatten out and they hit a deep snow bank, which they sank into, stopping them suddenly. The snow also stopped the broken fragments of the sledge, which mercifully embedded them without hitting anyone.

"Is everyone alright?" called the Professor, pulling himself out of the snow.

"I think so," replied Mallory, standing up.

"Where is Yuri?" queried Jazmine, looking around. Amazingly, throughout the fall, she had managed to keep hold of the Trasgo's cage. Inside, the goblin was alright but looking slightly ill and the base of the cage was covered in a blue vomit, making it clear that the creature did not travel well.

"I can't see him anywhere," said the Professor, looking round.

"Yuri!" shouted Mallory.

"Be quiet you idiot," hissed Jazmine. "Do you want to cause an avalanche?"

"Sorry," whispered Mallory, looking embarrassed.

"Look! There!" said the Professor, pointing to a set of boots sticking up out of the snow, twitching slightly.

"Quick!" cried Jazmine. "Get him out of there!"

The three ran to where Yuri was buried. Mallory went straight to his friend's feet, grabbing hold of them and started to pull, but the Russian was buried too deep and did not move.

"Start digging!" ordered the Professor, throwing himself down and starting to rake at the snow with his hands.

283

Mallory did the same, while Jazmine momentarily paused to put down the Trasgo cage and pick up a piece of broken wood to use as a shovel and also started to dig. From beneath the snow they could hear muffled shouts and could detect movement.

"Faster!" cried the Professor. In response Mallory and Jazmine quickened their pace, until there was a large pile of snow around them, and more of Yuri's body could be seen. Then Mallory again grabbed hold of the Russian and started to pull. This time Yuri started to move and, with the Professor and Jazmine helping, he was dragged free of his icy grave, coughing and spluttering.

"Are you alright?" asked the Professor.

The Russian nodded, climbing to his feet. "I think so. Although me nearly drowning or suffocating seems to becoming habit!"

Seeing he would be alright, the Professor smiled. "Come on, we don't have a moment to lose!"

Quickly Jazmine retrieved the Trasgo, and the small party headed the short distance towards the wall that surrounded Upper Karlstad, arriving at a big wooden door set into the brickwork.

The Professor banged on the door furiously. "Let us in! Open up!"

"It's no good," said Jazmine. "I don't think there is anyone there. We will have to work our way round to the main gate we originally came in through."

But just then there was a sound of a bolt being drawn back and the wooden door opened, and they were greeted by one of the creatures that called Upper Karlstad home.

CHAPTER 56

The creature stared at the small party in surprise, and from the small cage Jazmine was clutching, the Trasgo, on seeing a possible source of food, started to gnash its teeth excitedly.

"We need to see Netvor, at once," said the Professor, as he pushed his way past the creature and into Upper Karlstad. Looking down into the village he could see that the walled pond with the clock where they had started the search for the Trasgo was now boarded up.

"Um er, I'm not totally sure where he is," the creature said, stepping back as he allowed Mallory and the others to also enter the fortress.

"Well you need to find him!" continued the Professor, urgently. "You are all in danger and this place needs to be evacuated at once!"

"What?" replied the puzzled creature.

"There is an avalanche coming," explained Jazmine.

A look of alarm spread across the creature's face and then without a word he disappeared off. The Professor, with everyone else following, headed down into the village, past the boarded up pond until eventually stopping outside St Magdalena's church. All about them, creatures and people could be seen carrying on with their lives as normal, unaware that their secluded world was facing destruction.

"I hate to think of this place being destroyed," said Jazmine, looking around.

"Well, we have no idea how bad things will get," said the Professor. "The fortress walls look sturdy enough, but we can't guarantee they will protect the village totally. Now where is Netvor?"

After what seemed an age Netvor appeared, and with him were not only Douglas but also Fritz, who, noting their surprise at his presence there, quickly explained that the cable car between Lower and Upper Karlstad was now repaired and fully working. Quickly the Professor outlined what had happened during their trip into the cave system, how they captured the Trasgo in the observatory, and most importantly of all, about the earthquake and the impending danger the fortress and those who dwelt there faced

"Are you sure?" asked Netvor, trying to take in the news.

"I don't doubt it," replied the Professor firmly. "We need to get everyone out of here at once."

"Everyone? But where would we go?" asked Netvor, thinking of the entire population that lived in the village.

"There is only one option as far as I can see," said Fritz. "Lower Karlstad."

"But how? We can't all just turn up there. We would be seen," said Netvor.

"Not if we put everyone in The Golden Rose," replied Fritz, thoughtfully. "We can move the guests that are currently there into The Post and other hotels in the town."

"Well, I suppose that will be possible," replied Netvor, still not sounding convinced. "But what if we have to stay there long term? Remember our number is over seventy five."

"We can worry about that later," answered Fritz. "Right now, getting everyone to safety is the main priority."

"Alright then, what's going on here?" interrupted a grumpy voice. They turned to see Izaki moving as fast as he could towards them on his cane. "Ah!" he cried in delight on seeing the battered Bakelite cage and its contents. "You caught the Trasgo, well done! You have been gone a while so I presumed that you had died! Just as well, the condition of Rakasa and Padaras has got worse. I was going to suggest they were to be shot to put them out of their misery."

"I'm afraid that we have bigger issues to worry about now," said Fritz, who went on to quickly explain the danger they now faced, while Izaki took the Trasgo's cage from Jazmine and started to examine the goblin up close.

"Well," said Izaki thoughtfully, "that does create a few problems, especially regarding Rakasa and Padaras. They can't be evacuated, due to the possibility of them turning violent. They will have to stay in their current location under The Manor, along with the guards assigned to them. I'll need to stay also, as I'm the one working on the cure. We will be perfectly safe underground. No matter what happens above."

"What of my treatments?" asked Douglas, suddenly remembering his own predicament. "I will need regular access to the crystallisation chamber, otherwise I will die."

Izaki grunted. "That won't be a problem. There is a tunnel linking The Manor to the undercroft of the church, so I suppose you will have to stay with me too. There is also another tunnel that leads from the undercroft out to the mountainside and our standing stones. That means we won't end up totally trapped underground, should things end up really bad."

"You have standing stones?" said the Professor, his professional interest tweaked.

Izaki smiled. "Well, what did you think we did with the crystallised bodies of our deceased after we removed the heads and placed them in the chapel?"

"I hadn't given it a lot of thought actually," replied the Professor, in all truthfulness.

"Well I can show you them later, assuming that they survive. Now Netvor...."

Smash!

Izaki's words were cut short.

Everyone turned round.

Just above the door where they had re-entered Upper Karlstad, a large rock had ripped through the top of the wall sending bricks and debris showering down. The rock itself landed on the ground and shattered, sending fragments flying. Looking directly upwards over the breach in the wall towards the mountain, they could see movement in the snow high above them. Around them the residents of Upper Karlstad, who happened to be in the town square, started to chat nervously and some started to move away.

"We are too late," cried Netvor.

"I don't think so," said Izaki. "That looks like the warm up act before the main event. We still have a bit of time, but not much."

Another boulder smashed into the wall and landed near the remains of the first. This was followed by a shower of debris, some of which was recognisable as wreckage from the observatory.

"Right," said Izaki, holding up the cage with the Trasgo in it. I'd better get to The Manor with my new friend here, while I can start to get to work on a possible cure. Douglas, you know how to sound our general alarm?"

288

"Yes, it's the siren in the church's bell tower isn't it?"

Izaki nodded. "Yes, that's right, keep it going for four minutes, which would be enough to warn everyone. Then go directly down into the undercroft and make your way to The Manor and meet me in my archive."

"Won't the sound of the siren hasten the avalanche?" asked Jazmine, fearing that the creature had made an oversight.

"Not this one," Izaki replied, as he started to head off towards The Manor. "It works at a higher level that only my kind can hear. It won't cause us any trouble."

Taking Izaki's lead, Douglas headed off in the opposite direction to the church, opening the door and disappearing inside.

"I'll throw open the South Gate and then go to the cable car to warn them what's happening," said Fritz, heading off quickly. "I can also use their telephone to let Lower Karlstad know what's going on."

"Thank you," said Netvor with relief. "Ah, there goes the siren."

Of course, the Professor and the others could not hear anything, but looking round, the creatures that were in the town square could be seen stopping, and doors of buildings opened with other creatures venturing out to find out what was wrong.

"To the South Gate!" called Netvor, as he waved to catch everyone's attention. "Quickly! Everyone to the South Gate at once! We have to evacuate immediately! Make sure the young and elderly are looked after, as well as the humans! Please hurry, but don't panic!"

The response was instant. The creatures did exactly what they were instructed to do, with no question or fuss, and within a short time the evacuation was finished apart from Netvor, the Professor and the others who gathered together just outside the doors of St Magdalena's.

By now the movement of snow they had seen, which had turned into a small avalanche, had reached the fortress wall, with large rocks bouncing over it and smashing down into the square and onto surrounding buildings. There was a crash and the door in the fortress wall, which the Professor and the others had entered through a few minutes before, burst open and snow poured in. More snow spewed over the breaches from where the boulders had smashed through and then the entire wall seemed to momentarily ripple before cracking and then collapsing totally, allowing a vast river of snow to pour into Upper Karlstad.

CHAPTER 57

Seeing the approaching danger, Netvor, the Professor and the others moved further into the village, away from the church, as the surge advanced. Within a few moments the snow and the debris it carried with it reached the walled up pond. There was an ominous cracking sound and the wooden boards splintered and broke, and the temporary structure seemed to topple and was totally engulfed as the torrent of snow continued forward into the village square, before coming to a halt just past the front door of St Magdalena's.

"I hope Douglas will be alright," said Jazmine, seeing the large bank of snow that was pressed up against the church door.

"He will be fine," assured Netvor. "The siren has stopped, meaning that he is now getting himself to safety, and I suggest we do the same as there is no more that we can do here now."

As he finished speaking, strange shafts of light illuminated his face momentarily. Everyone looked up to see the cause of this strange phenomenon, to see a large, battered, brass object tumbling down the mountain towards them, rolling on its edge at frightening speed, and behind that was what looked like a big brass tube; both of these objects were being followed by a massive snow bank.

"By the Protector! What on earth are those things?" asked Netvor.

"Unless I am very much mistaken," replied the Professor gravely, "I think that is the dome of the observatory and the telescope itself behind it."

"My goodness, yes," said Netvor, taking another look, "I do believe you are right."

The dome continued to roll down the mountainside, gaining more and more speed as it went. It was about thirty feet away from the fortress wall when, without warning, it bounced twice and then soared high into the air, presumably through hitting some unseen object.

"Oh no, that not good," said Yuri, mentally working out the structure's trajectory. "I think it going to land on church."

Everyone stared at the dome as it started to descend, having easily cleared what was left of the fortress's outer wall and houses, before it smashed edge down, onto the roof of the church just behind the façade. For a brief moment it looked as though the roof would hold, and the brass dome would bounce off and continue onwards, but with a crack, the top of the church partially collapsed and the mass of metal lodged itself in the hole it had made, balancing precariously. Then, after a few moments, the façade of the church seemed to move slightly and then start to sway back and forth, before starting to slowly fall away from the rest of the building and smash to the ground, throwing up debris and a small cloud of snow. With the façade of the church gone, there was nothing to keep the dome of the observatory in place, and that too tumbled forward landing with a crash onto the broken masonry and bricks that once were the front of the church, bending and buckling under its own weight.

By now the telescope, which was travelling end over end, had reached the fortress wall, which it sailed over and continued flipping until passing the drift of snow from the avalanche and smashing down onto the much shallower snow on the town square, where, with a massive thump, it landed on its side and then started to roll towards the Professor and the others at alarming speed.

With no time to get themselves clear, only one option remained; to jump over the spinning cylinder, or be hit and severely injured.

Tackling the danger head on the Professor, Jazmine and Mallory ran forward to hurdle the telescope, clearing it with ease and landing safely as it went past. However, as Netvor was moving into position to ready himself for the jump, his foot slipped sending him off balance. Yuri, who was just by him, realised what was happening and lunged towards the creature grabbing him, then launched upwards.

The telescope rolled harmlessly underneath them and Yuri and Netvor landed in a heap on the floor, unhurt.

"That was close," said Yuri, helping Netvor to his feet.

"Yes, but the danger is far from over," said the Professor, looking round to see the massive wave of snow reaching the fortress wall, smashing into it. The left hand side of the wall seemed to hold, but the middle section, which already had the breach in, allowed masses of snow through, adding to the drift that was already there. However, on the far right, behind the Manor, the avalanche had a devastating effect, crashing through the fortress wall, allowing tonnes of snow to smash into the back of the large building.

The entire Manor was lifted off of its foundations and was pushed forward about two feet, before the entire structure disintegrated into piles of rubble which, with the force of the avalanche still behind it, continued slowly onwards, across the large snow covered lawn, towards the airship which was in front of the house. The airship itself, the front of which was pointing towards the now mostly destroyed church, consisted of a gondola, constructed from brass and glass, which could house two people comfortably, including the pilot. Attached to the back was a small engine, out of which was a small four bladed propeller. On top of the gondola were a series of metal struts which connected with the large ridged cigar shaped canopy, at the very back of which were fins and a rudder.

"No!" cried out Netvor in alarm. "My airship!"

"That's alright," said the Professor sympathetically. "If it is destroyed it can be rebuilt."

"No, you don't understand," spluttered Netvor desperately. "The airship is filled with my new gas compound, the elements of which are highly flammable. The whole thing could explode. If it does, the blast would be more than enough to reduce the entire fortress to a pile of rubble."

"Oh my goodness!" cried the Professor, clearly shocked.

"You mean you have big bomb sitting on your front lawn all this time?" asked Yuri.

Netvor shrugged. "Until now, it was never really an issue."

"I'm presuming that Izaki had no idea about this?" inquired the Professor, remembering the ancient creature's negative comments about the airship.

Netvor shook his head. "Of course not! Can you imagine what he would have to say about it?"

All eyes returned to the terrace where the mountain of rubble had now reached the gondola. At first the entire ship was pushed along, before it then started to tip over and crash down on its side, where it continued to be shoved along until reaching the rim of the terrace.
The canopy was propelled over the edge and the ship overbalanced resulting in it barrel rolling in mid-air. The base of the gondola smashed down onto the top of the building below, which disintegrated, leaving the airship resting upright in a massive pile of rubble, but by some miracle fully intact. At that precise moment the mass of debris that once was the Manor reached the lip of the terrace, where it stopped. For a moment there was silence, everyone stared at the airship and the scene of devastation that surrounded it.

Eventually it was Netvor that spoke. "Thank the Protector! I thought that we were done for. Oh why did I take such a foolish risk?"

"Wait!" said the Professor. "I don't think that we are out of the woods yet, do you hear that?"

Everyone listened.

From the terrace there was a strange hissing sound then, before anyone could say anything, in the wreckage where the airship was resting, flames suddenly appeared surrounding the ship. After a few moments there was a loud bang, which sent flaming rubble and debris flying up into the air, much of which ended up hitting the large canopy which then caught alight.

"The canopy," said the Professor quickly. "Can it resist the flames?"

Netvor nodded. "For a while at least. I coated the outer skin with a special protective coating. It won't hold forever though."

"How long?" asked the Professor.

"I would say about ten minutes, if we're lucky."

"Is there any way that we can put the flames out?" asked Mallory.

Netvor shook his head. "We did have fire-fighting equipment based at the Manor, but of course now it's beyond us…" His voice trailed off as he looked up at the destroyed building. "Oh what have I done? I have as good as destroyed the fortress!"

CHAPTER 58

For a few moments, everyone stared at the airship before Yuri broke the silence. "Netvor, you say that airship full of gas?"

The creature nodded.

"Then simple! You are overlooking obvious. We fly airship out of here, sent it on way and it explodes away from fortress out of harm's way."

"I don't think it's going to be that easy, I'm afraid," replied Netvor. "My new gas compound has not been properly tested."

"Well, we have to at least try," said Yuri, as he set off towards the burning airship, before any more could be said or anyone could try to stop him.

"I'll have to go with him," said Netvor, also heading off. "He'll never be able to work out the controls on his own."

"We'll come too," said the Professor, starting to follow, with Mallory and Jazmine a step behind.

"I'm afraid that won't be possible," said Netvor, stopping them. "This is a one, two person job at the most. Besides, the less of us there are the more chance there is of getting it airborne and clear of the fortress."

"Alright," said the Professor, grudgingly. "Good luck!"

Netvor nodded silently, turned and raced after Yuri, running across the cobbled square and up the stone stairway to the terrace where he eventually joined the Russian who had stopped to survey the scene. "This is worse than I thought!" said the creature, looking at the destroyed building and crashed airship.

Yuri nodded. "First problem; how we get into craft? Door blocked." He then pointed to a large pile of wreckage that was obstructing the main door to the ship.

"There is a hatch on the top of the gondola," replied Netvor. "But with the flames all around it, I'm not sure how we can get to it without setting ourselves alight."

"Ha!" laughed Yuri. "You obviously have never played at 'Snow Angels!' Follow my lead!"

With that he lay down on his back in the snow and started to move his arms and legs up and down, before rolling onto his front and doing the same, leaving on the ground what would look like, when viewed from above, an outline of a winged angel. The Russian then started to grab handfuls of snow and smeared himself with it. Realising what Yuri was doing, Netvor did the same, and after a few moments both were soaking wet with clumps of snow clinging to their clothes and fur.

"There," said Yuri finally, standing back up as he wiped two handfuls of snow over his face to finish things off, "that should help. You ready? We run through fire and climb onto roof."

Netvor got to his feet and nodded, and then together they ran forward over the rubble and through the flames towards the gondola. Yuri got there first and reached up, grabbing the edge of the roof, and started to pull himself up. Grunting as he did so, through the physical effort and the fact that the meagre protection of the snow was already starting to wear off. Once he had clambered onto the roof, he turned round to help Netvor up, who was visibly struggling.

"You alright?" asked the Russian, seeing the pained look on the creature's face.

Netvor nodded. "Slightly singed, but otherwise fine."

Yuri smiled, and with that he opened the hatch on the gondola's roof and then dropped down inside, with Netvor following moments later, slamming the door shut behind him.

The inside of the Gondola consisted of a small control panel at the bow that was covered with brass dials, switches, and levers. At the stern of the ship was a red leather sofa, in front of which was a small chess table that had a drinks bar located underneath.

"Very nice," remarked Yuri looking around. "By the way, I have question. If airship filled with air, how come it not float up already? It wasn't even tied to the ground."

"Ah," said Netvor, proudly going over to the controls where he started to press a number of buttons and levers. "That was one of my innovations. The bed of the canopy is divided into two compartments containing separate gasses. I carefully release these gasses into the top section of the canopy, like this." As he spoke, he made a show of pressing certain buttons on the control panel and from above a strange hissing sound could be heard. "And when they mix, it creates a new gas which lifts the entire ship into the air."

"Very clever," said Yuri, "but what happens when you want to come down again?"

"Simple, I vent the gas from the main canopy."

"Good, how long it take before we start to rise up?"

"Assuming that the gas does its job," with a hint of doubt in his voice, "not long at all. It has over five times the potency of helium."

"And make your voice go funny too?" said Yuri, thinking of the fun he had with a canister of helium that had been left unattended at the Marshall & Snelgrove Department Store.

Netvor nodded, with a childish smile on his face, before suddenly looking serious.

"What's wrong?" asked Yuri.

"The engine," said Netvor, as he pushed and pulled on a brass lever. "I cannot get it started! We need it so it can move us away from the fortress." He continued to struggle with the controls, and in response the engine made a spluttering sound then promptly died.

"This not good. Let me try," said Yuri, stepping forward, practically pushing Netvor out of the way. "In Russia we have ways of dealing with such things."

"Please be careful," said Netvor. "The controls are delicate and need a gentle touch."

"No problem!" said Yuri, as he slammed his fist down hard on the console while at the same time pulling the starting lever backwards. For a second the various bulbs that were on the control panel flashed and then the engine sprang into life. Turning to look through the rear window, the propeller could be seen spinning furiously. Netvor gave a sigh of relief. "Now all we have to do is wait until the gasses hopefully do their job, and we are away."

"Great!" replied Yuri. "Then we power ship forward and fortress saved!"

"I'm afraid it's not as simple as that," replied Netvor.

"You starting to sound like Professor," grunted the Russian. "What is problem?"

"We have to turn the ship around and go east over the fortress wall to an unpopulated area where it can explode safely. If we go West, as we are pointing, or South, we will end up over Karlstad or the surrounding towns and of course we can't go North because of the mountains."

"Makes sense," replied Yuri.

"Oh, there is another thing," said Netvor, nervously. "We will need to stay in the ship until we are clear of the east wall; just in case any problems occur that we need to deal with, but as soon as we are over it we can bail out and land safely in a snow bank."

Yuri nodded in agreement, and as he did so the gondola gently started to shake underneath them.

"It's working," cried Netvor, with delight. "The combined gasses are working!" Then very slowly the airship started to rise up out of the rubble and leave the ground. As soon as they were airborne Netvor grabbed hold of a handle, and started to rotate it. From behind came the sound of the rudder moving and the airship started to turn anticlockwise. Then, halfway through the manoeuvre, the whole control panel lit up and the ship stopped dead as the engine and the rest of the controls failed.

"Netvor, what happened?"

"I'm not sure," replied the creature, as he tried, and failed, to restart the ship.

Then from nowhere, a sudden gust of wind hit the side of the canopy which started to slowly propel them sideways and also slightly downwards towards St Magdalena's church.

"Netvor!"

"I know, I know," cried the creature. "Nothing is responding! We are at the mercy of the wind!"

"If we keep on like this, we are going to hit Church's bell tower," observed Yuri.

"We can't let that happen!" said Netvor. "The ship has already taken too much damage from when it fell off of the terrace; another knock would spell disaster."

"Then do something," said Yuri, looking out of the window to see that the ship was now over the village square and continuing on relentlessly towards the church.

CHAPTER 59

Netvor quickly dropped to his knees and opened a door under the main control panel to reveal a mass of wires, cogs and gears.

"Can you see what's wrong?" asked Yuri.

"Yes," replied Netvor, almost at once, "one of the glass electrical valves has shattered, but the filament is still intact and it's sending out electrical surges. I need to remove it. I'm not sure how without the glass surround to hold onto."

"What about if you just destroy filament?" asked Yuri, reaching to his belt for the dart gun.

"That would work," replied Netvor, "but the dart might rebound and cause more damage to the internal workings."

Yuri again looked out of the window to see they were now over the front of the church. "Sorry, time is running out. This seems our only option." With that, he looked inside the panel and, once he located the damaged filament, placed the nozzle of the gun up against it and fired.

The Bakelite dart smashed into the filament destroying it instantly, and then continued on, lodging itself harmlessly in the back of the machinery. Seeing that the sparking had stopped, Netvor stood up and started to press buttons and dials on the control panel and after a few moments the engine came back to life. He then applied full power to the engine and the entire ship moved forward, with the rudder of the airship just missing the bell tower by a couple of feet. Breathing a sigh of relief, he pulled hard on the steering lever and the ship began to turn round in a tight circle, until it was pointing in the right direction. Happy with the new heading, he slammed the steering lever forward and the ship headed off straight ahead. However, due to their new position and reduced height, they were on a collision course with the fortress's east wall.

"That was close," said Yuri, putting the gun back in his holster, "but we need to gain height."

"I know," replied Netvor worriedly. "I've released more gas into the upper chamber, but it's not working. We just don't seem to be getting enough lift. We can't risk hitting the wall. I don't think the ship could take it!"

"Then we need to lighten the load," said Yuri, turning round. The Russian then moved to the chess table and picked it up, with the chess pieces and the drinks bottles underneath dropping to the floor.

"What are you doing?" asked Netvor.

"Getting rid of extra weight," replied the Russian, as he turned and then thrust the table at the nearest window, smashing the large pane before throwing the table itself through.

"I don't think that's going to help much," said Netvor.

"Agreed, but getting rid of large leather sofa will. Quick, give Yuri a hand!"

Netvor left the controls of the ship and went over to the Russian where, between the two of them, they managed to lift up the heavy sofa and manoeuvre it to the smashed window. With some difficulty, they pushed it through the opening. As the sofa plummeted down, the airship instantly began to rise higher, but levelled out just short of clearing the fortress wall.

The ship continued onwards with Netvor, who had moved back to the controls, shaking his head. "It's not working! We are going to clip the wall!"

"Maybe not," said Yuri, thoughtfully. "I have plan as to how we can lose little more weight."

"Well whatever it is, make it quick, we are almost there!" said Netvor, noting that they were less than fifteen feet away from disaster.

"Don't worry, I will!" said Yuri, as he stepped forward and grabbed Netvor by the fur and then propelled him towards the broken window.

"Yuri! What are you doing?"

"Sorry Netvor, we need more height, so need to lighten load more and this only way. Happy landings!"

With that, Yuri hoisted the now struggling creature into the air and through the window, and watched him tumble downwards. His fall was broken by the large waggon full of straw, just inside the east wall of the fortress, which Yuri had carefully aimed him towards.

With Netvor gone, the airship immediately started to rise upwards and Yuri, who had quickly returned to the controls, noted that the gondola would now clear the top of the fortress wall with less than a foot to spare.

The ship continued forwards and the Russian held his breath, not daring to move in case in doing so would cause the airship to drop. Then looking out of the side window he could clearly see that the gondola was now passing over the thick wall of the fortress.

Letting out a sigh of relief Yuri inadvertently leant on the control panel and immediately from above, there came a hissing sound as gas from the top of the canopy was vented out. Instantly the airship dropped, landing with a thud on top of the wide fortress wall where it ended up perfectly balanced but grounded. In a reflex reaction Yuri stepped back, taking his hands off of the controls, which instantly stopped the venting of gas and announced, "Wasn't me!" but then realised that there was no one there to hear his defence. Moving back to the controls he looked down at the array of buttons and dials, realising that he would have to somehow get the ship airborne again, but was not sure what to do. Bracing himself for the worst, Yuri tentatively started to press buttons and dials to try to repeat the steps he had seen Netvor make earlier; to start the processes of sending gas into the main canopy and praying as he did so, that he did not accidently switch off the engine or, worse still, vent out any more of the gas.

Then from behind him he heard a spluttering noise and turning round he could see the engine was giving off a small black plume of smoke, as well as small licks of flame. The Russian reacted instantly, making for the fallen bottles from the drinks cabinet and inspecting them quickly, discarding any alcoholic ones until he picked up a bottle of tonic water, which he started to shake vigorously as he headed towards the back of the gondola. Opening the rear window, he smashed the bottle open on the edge of the frame and as the contents started to spurt out he aimed it onto the engine. Instantly there was a hissing sound and the flames were extinguished.

Breathing a sigh of relief Yuri returned to the control panel and continued to press buttons and turn dials to try to get the airship to rise.

Then from above came the sound he had heard earlier of the two gasses being sent into the main canopy chamber, and after a few moments the entire ship seemed to rock back and forth before it very slowly started to lift. As soon as the gondola had separated from the top of the wall, the engine started to push the airship forward and over the edge of the fortress.

Once Yuri was certain the ship was completely clear, he checked the controls were locked in place and then moved to the broken window where he climbed through, opting to lower himself slightly before letting himself drop down to safety. He fell thirty feet, landing flat on his back, in, as Netvor predicted, a bank of snow on the side of the mountain.

Moments later, he found himself surrounded by Netvor, the Professor, Mallory and Jazmine, who had made their way out of the South Gate and round to try and find where the Russian had ended up.

"Are you alright?" asked Mallory, as he helped Yuri to his feet.

The Russian nodded. "I think so. What happened to the airship?"

"Moving away nicely," replied the Professor.

Turning, they could see in the distance the ship still heading further and further away from the fortress, rising slightly as it got caught on thermal updrafts. The entire top of the canopy, as well as its sides, were now alight with bursts of flame shooting from it into the air. Then without any warning, the airship exploded in a massive ball of bright yellow and orange flames, fifty foot wide, which lit up the sky as well as making the ground shake.

"Thank you, Thank you," said Netvor, gratefully turning to the Professor and the others. "Between you, you have saved many lives, and Upper Karlstad, from being totally destroyed."

"You are very welcome," said Yuri, cheerfully. "That was thirsty work. I don't suppose you have any bottles of Funkelwiesen lying around handy?"

With that everyone burst into laughter.

CHAPTER 60

For the next few weeks the Professor, Mallory Jazmine, and Yuri stayed in the Golden Rose Hotel and divided their time equally between Upper and Lower Karlstad.

The Professor and Jazmine ended up spending long periods in Izaki's archive, which survived the fall of The Manor undamaged, studying the history of the creatures, their technological advances and the notes they retrieved from the observatory regarding the planet Mars.

From the Trasgo, a sample of blood was taken for Izaki to create a cure for Rakasa and Padaras. Then, when both showed clear signs of recovery, a vaccine was manufactured that was given to all of the creatures of Upper Karlstad, just in case a similar event ever occurred again. As for the Trasgo itself, one night it was taken and released into the wild, far away from creatures it regarded as food.

Mallory and Yuri put their time into helping with the repairs that were needed to Upper Karlstad. Building work had started straight away, with extra attention paid to the fortress wall that was breached, making it much higher and stronger than before. Plans for a new observatory, bigger and better than the one before were also drawn up and a new site for it chosen. Izaki aimed to have it completed by the Summer of the following year, so he could continue with Zidal's studies of Mars.

306

Work also started on Jazmine's idea of a cylinder that Douglas could carry around with him, which would supply him with a regular dose of the crystals that repaired his lungs. The concept worked well and although he would be tied to Karlstad for the rest of his life, by placing replacement canisters at strategic points around the fortress and main town, he would be able to live a relatively normal life. Word that he was alive and reasonably well was sent to Jane in London and she immediately made the trip to be reunited with her husband. It was soon decided that their house in London was to be sold and a property for the two of them would be provided in Upper Karlstad. Douglas also contacted the Vienna National Gallery, explaining that he was now a resident in the country and would be available for work. The Gallery jumped at the opportunity to employ him as an advisor, even though it was made clear that, due to his 'illness' he would not be able to spend any time in Vienna itself. Arrangements were soon made by the gallery for documents and paintings to be brought to him to work on. One of the first tasks Douglas set himself was to purchase the painting that had originally led him to Karlstad, just in case anyone else followed the same trail. As it was not a significant artwork, this was easily done and it was given to Fritz, who hung it in his office at the Golden Rose.

In the first week of August The Professor, Jazmine, Mallory and Yuri finally packed up their bags ready to return to London, and a small farewell party met them on the rear forecourt of the Golden Rose ready to see them off.

Netvor helped Mallory pack the last of their luggage onto the back of the now fully repaired Brachial, a task made all the more difficult by the numerous bottles of Funkelwiesen that Yuri insisted on taking home with him.

The Russian was so enamoured with this non-alcoholic health drink that he found he no longer needed or wanted his previous tipple of vodka. Although he acknowledged he had just replaced one addiction with another, it was agreed that Funkelwiesen would do him a lot less harm, and he was even given the recipe so he could make his own.

"I must say," said Jazmine, stepping back to cast her eye over the Brachial. "It's very kind of you to let me loose in your car again."

"It's no problem," said Fritz, who had come along to see them off, "just as long as you don't plan on making any mountain detours! If you could just park her in the station car park, we can pick her up later."

"You will come back and visit us won't you?" said Douglas, who was wearing his breathing cylinder.

"Yes," added Jane, "you must come back and see us. You are always most welcome."

"Oh yes," agreed the Professor, with a smile. "You can be sure of that. I can see us spending a lot of time here over the coming years."

"Good," said Fritz, with a smile, "and I will hope you will consider yourself honouree members of our community."

"And," said Izaki, with a serious tone in his voice, "do you remember the promise you made?"

"To keep the secrets of Karlstad safe?" said the Professor. "Oh you can be sure of that! Although poor Dr Fredrickson at the Natural History Museum is going to be most put out when I tell him we found nothing!"

"I was thinking more of our agreed game of postal Karlstad chess," replied Izaki, with a smile, "but yes, for the moment anyway, it is imperative that you keep what you have seen here a secret."

The Professor nodded. "I fully understand, but I hope you will remember *my* promise. If you decide that any of your technologies should be released into the public domain, we will be more than happy to facilitate it."

Netvor nodded. "I am sure when the time is right we will take you up on that."

Then from the rear of the hotel there came a cry and, turning, they could see Heidi appearing through the door, running up towards them clutching four thin parcels wrapped in brown paper under her arm. By her side, in her motorised chair, speeding along, was Greta.

"Phew," gasped Heidi, arriving to them. "I thought that I was going to miss you! Here, these are for you, a farewell present. The Professor, Jazmine, Mallory and Yuri were then each given one of the parcels which they opened immediately to reveal a painting, each depicting a different scene of Karlstad.

"Ha! I recognise this," said Yuri, with a smile.

"I thought you might," replied Heidi, "they are paintings from the artist you chose to pick a fight with to allow Mallory to get into the burnt out surgery."

"I really do appreciate the gift," said Yuri, looking the picture over; particularly the bottom right corner where the artist's signature was clearly printed, "but I still think that this A. Hitler chap is just an average artist."

Fritz shrugged. "I know, we only bought them in the end to calm him down. He made quite a fuss with his ranting and raving after his encounter with you. We were more

309

than happy when he caught the train to Munich, I can tell you. In all honesty I found him a very strange and even sinister little man."

"Father? Father, are you all right?" asked Jazmine, suddenly noticing the distant look on the Professor's face.

"Um yes, sorry, that name, 'A Hitler.' When Yuri spoke it I just had a sudden feeling of sheer horror and dread; almost like some sort of premonition." He shrugged, trying to ignore the strange feeling. "Ah, well, never mind, I'm sure it's nothing. Right, we had better get ourselves going, otherwise we will miss our train."

"Have you got time for a quick picture?" asked Greta, eagerly producing a small camera. "I have an invention I would like to try out."

Everyone nodded. Then from the side of her motorised bath chair she produced what resembled a long wooden oar and placed the camera on the end. "I call it a 'Self Photography Paddle'. It allows you to take pictures of yourself if there is no one else about, and is great for group photos."

Everyone exchanged a quick glance, not totally convinced about the concept.

"Quick, gather round me," she cried, as she struggled to lift the paddle in the air. In response, everyone crowded around her bath chair and she took the picture.

"You see Izaki," Greta said smiling, "your kind are not the only ones who are good at inventing things!"

Izaki smiled at her politely. "Yes, just don't be too disappointed if it doesn't catch on my dear! I'm not sure I see a real call for it."

With the final goodbyes said, Jazmine took her place at the wheel of the Brachial and her Father, Mallory and Yuri climbed into the vehicle taking their seats. Then with a roar of the engine, they headed off down the dirt track that would take them to the Karlstad train station where they would leave the town, its technology and the creatures that provided it behind.

The George Roebuck Chronicles

The Dark Star Diamond

This first adventure sees explorer and adventurer George Roebuck, with the aid of the mysterious Josephine Danvers, trying to recover the stolen 'Dark Star Diamond'. The diamond is the source of the Roebuck's family fortune and is also responsible for the 'Second Industrial Revolution,' which has transformed the world of the mid 1800's.

Technologies that were only written about in fiction are now abundant and thriving in a world of cogs, gears and steam.

Planned releases in the series –

The Dark Star Diamond (2017)

The Army of the Resurrected

The Anteros Murders

The Emmaus Grail

The Hellfire Club